TEMPTED BY THE ROGUISH LORD

Mary Brendan

MILLS & BOON

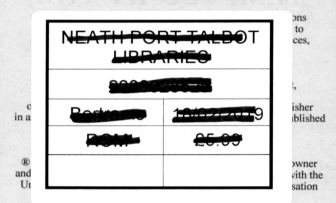

Portmead   18/07/2019

ROM   £5.00

First Published in Great Britain 2019
by Mills & Boon, an imprint of HarperCollins*Publishers*
1 London Bridge Street, London, SE1 9GF

© 2019 Mary Brendan

ISBN: 978-0-263-26893-5

MIX
Paper from
responsible sources
FSC® C007454

This book is produced from independently certified FSC™ paper
to ensure responsible forest management.
For more information visit www.harpercollins.co.uk/green.

Printed and bound in Spain
by CPI, Barcelona

Chapter One

Circa 1816

'Please put down the gun, Papa! This gentleman has not harmed me, but done me a great service.' Miss Emma Waverley strove to keep her voice lowered. From a corner of an eye she'd noticed their neighbour's curtain twitch in an upstairs window.

'Done you a *service!*' the elderly fellow roared. 'That's what he told you, is it!' He descended another step towards the pavement. By fully stretching out his thin arm, he brought the duelling pistol to within an inch of an elegant waistcoat. 'These infernal rakes have no shame in the matter.' He shook the weapon to reinforce his intention to pull the trigger. 'I can tell he is a villain just by looking at him.' A pair of rheumy eyes took in the stranger's slight air of inebriation and dishevelled attire. Even these drawbacks couldn't disguise the fact he was abominably handsome… and rich. Such expensive tailoring would be cared for by a valet. As for the equipage parked at the kerb, only the wealthiest young bucks took to the road in one of those racy contraptions.

If the individual under threat feared he might soon expire from a bullet, he gave no sign of it. The Earl of Houndsmere had upon his dark features a wearisome expression.

'Should this business be conducted inside, perhaps?' he suggested drily and jerked his head to indicate their audience.

Across the road two kneeling servants had halted their yawning and scrubbing to turn on their steps and gawp at the spectacle of an ancient, garbed in flowing nightgown and tasselled cap, pointing a gun at his daughter's supposed seducer. Soon the emerging dawn would give way to the glorious spring morning promised by the blush on the horizon. This busy square would begin to throng with people and carriages. How they'd appreciate starting their day viewing this tableau.

'Please, Papa, give me the gun.' Emma extended a determined hand to take the weapon, but her father stubbornly drew it back towards his chest with a warning growl.

'I'll not! First I'll hear his good reason for

bringing you back at this hour in the morning. I imagined you to be safe in your bed.' Mr Waverley gazed fiercely at his daughter. 'You're really in trouble now, miss, I hope you realise it.'

Emma did know that...more than her father yet understood. Worrying as it was, her conscience wouldn't allow her to shift the blame to hide her culpability. She swept a glance at her saviour from under her lashes, wincing beneath the sardonic glitter in his blue-black eyes. But there was no recrimination. He didn't regret having stopped to help her. They'd barely spoken to one another, yet she'd wager he wasn't a man given to questioning his own behaviour. He'd not looked sorry when he'd battered two men for her either.

With a muttered oath, the younger man sprang up two steps and, gripping the gun muzzle, wrested the weapon out of a set of bony fingers. Its owner looked affronted to have been so easily divested of it.

The immediate danger past, Emma dashed forward to grip her father's arm and usher him out of sight of prying eyes.

Left alone on the pavement, the Earl planted a broad bronzed hand on the rusty railings and examined his torn knuckles. An irate old man shaking an empty duelling pistol at him was a novel experience, although he was no stranger to having a loaded gun pointed at his head by a jealous rival. He was sorely tempted to simply continue on home to find his bed. But with a sigh he took the steps two at a time, keen to get it over with. He entered a dim hallway and closed the door behind him. As all was quiet he stayed where he was, hoping she might have placated her father without his assistance. He wanted to get some sleep, not get drawn into defending his unwise heroics.

Despite the fact he was suffering the effects of over-indulgence, his breeding had dictated he act properly and accompany the chit indoors to confirm that she was still as innocent as she said she was. How innocent that actually was, was up for debate. The Earl also had his suspicions as to why a genteel young woman would be out alone at such an hour. A black-haired, tawny-eyed beauty, past the first flush of youth, might have a history of slyly seeing her beau. It was possible her father wasn't as shocked as he was making out at catching her returning to the house at an ungodly hour. But if the wily old cove believed he could act the outraged parent and turn this to his spinster daughter's advantage he'd find he was much mistaken. The Earl of Houndsmere had been on the receiving end of many an engineered plot to get him to meet a debutante at the altar. All had failed.

This one looked to have made her come out some time ago. Possibly at around the time his father had died and Lance had resigned his army position to take his birthright. His sister had nagged him into visiting Almack's balls a couple of times during that Season, hoping he'd find a wife. He didn't recall seeing his damsel in distress there. And he would have remembered her. He might even have made history by booking a dance instead of spending the evening with like-minded friends, champagne in one hand and Hunter in the other, as they waited for a reasonable time to elapse, allowing them to slip away and seek the company of less decorous ladies. A nostalgic smile tipped up a corner of his mouth as he dwelled on those distant days…

Emma appeared on the threshold of the parlour to see her reluctant hero looking amused about something. Well, she was glad somebody could smile about it, she thought tetchily. He'd noticed her so she beckoned him, then untied her hat, letting loose an abundance of ebony locks.

'Please join us in here, sir.' Emma was attempting to apologise for everything with her tone of voice and the expression in her large honey-coloured eyes. The look she received in return both alarmed and annoyed her. He seemed to have some sarcastic comment to make, but was holding it in. Well, she'd not asked him to act knight errant although she had to admit she'd been glad he had. Left to her own devices she might have ended up ravished or murdered, possibly both. She knew that her father believed this stranger had lecherous intentions towards her, but in truth he'd not manhandled her at all. Other than to toss her up into his phaeton to start their hair-raising journey home, they'd not touched again until he'd helped her down outside.

'You can start by introducing yourself, sirrah!' Impatiently, Bernard Waverley had appeared in the parlour doorway beside his daughter.

'Come and sit down, Papa,' Emma hastily said, embarrassed by her father's attitude. 'You, too, if you will, sir.' Again, she glanced at the stranger. He appeared to be in two minds whether to comply, or to leave. She couldn't blame him for wanting to go about his business.

'Lance Harley at your service, sir.' An indolent bow followed the introduction. He approached Mr Waverley, depositing the pistol on a table as he passed it.

'I know that name.' Mr Waverley ignored the fellow's outstretched hand and commenced frowning. 'Why is that? Have you caused me trouble before, Harley?'

'I'm sure he has not, Papa. You should thank Mr Harley. He has been a boon.' Emma swiftly took up the story before her father could level more accusations. 'This gentleman was good enough to stop and rescue me from some footpads and bring me home.' Her father probably recalled the stranger's name because the two men frequented the same club. Although with decades separating them in age it was unlikely they shared the same friends. Not that her father had many of those left. 'I am very sorry for worrying you, Papa, but thankfully no great harm done.'

'No great harm done?' her father thundered. He pulled off his nightcap, revealing tufts of greying hair, and began marching to and fro across the threadbare rug. 'We'll see about that once the tabbies have had time to do their work. You might be past your prime, but you're still young enough to draw a man's lust and a woman's spite.'

Emma flushed to the roots of her silky black hair. Usually such a remark from her father— quite pertinent as it was—wouldn't have bothered her. Yet she found having her advanced years bandied about in the presence of this gentleman was mortifying, though she strove not to show it.

Mr Waverley seemed oblivious to his daughter's discomfiture. 'So you were nearly robbed and of more than just your purse, I'll warrant.' Agitatedly, he turned to their Good Samaritan.

'No doubt you're waiting for my thanks and my coin to keep you quiet about her behaviour. Well, be that as it may, you won't get any of it. I'll not reward you for getting involved in her prank.'

At that point Emma swallowed her chagrin for long enough to direct an exceedingly apologetic look the gentleman's way. It was met by a pair of cynically amused sapphire eyes. He might just as well have said he had no need of her father's paltry-sounding reward. Her attention was dragged back to her father as he punitively shook her arm.

'What in damnation did you think you were about, creeping out of the house behind my back?' Bernard looked as though he might raise his hand to his daughter, and Harley stepped closer, as though to intervene on her behalf.

'We can discuss it all later, in private, Papa.' Emma gave her father a cautioning look that made him press together his crinkled lips. The Waverley family were used to keeping secrets and this certainly fell into that category. 'Mr Harley might like some tea before leaving.' She issued her barbed hospitality, hoping he'd just go and imagining he wanted to do exactly that. He was probably offended by her father's conduct and hers, too, although he certainly wasn't showing it.

Harley met her expectations, gesturing that no

such trouble was necessary on his account. His hand travelled on to his mouth, discreetly suppressing a yawn. He'd been vigorously engaged for most of the night, largely pleasurably, until he'd heard this minx scream while struggling to keep hold of her reticule. After that he'd expended what remained of his energy in a bareknuckle scrap. A corner of his mouth twitched. She'd been putting up a good fight before he stepped in to take over; he'd seen her land a couple of blows on the felons.

'Will you return me the courtesy and introduce yourselves?' He was alert enough to be curious as to who she was.

'You've been alone with my daughter and not even bothered to enquire after her name?' Mr Waverley looked aghast.

'I might not know her name yet, but tell it to me now and I'll not forget it, that I promise.' Houndsmere's penetrating blue gaze settled on Emma, capturing her eyes for a moment before she broke his hold. He wasn't just being polite, Lance realised. He would remember her, although he couldn't understand how she was getting beneath his skin so quickly when they'd barely spoken or touched.

It seemed that her father was feeling too indignant to introduce them so she blurted, 'My name is Emma Waverley and my father is Ber-

nard Waverley.' She noted at once the gleam of
interest raising Harley's weighty, black-lashed
eyelids. He didn't appear nearly so bored by pro-
ceedings as a moment ago. But at least there was
no contemptuous curl to his lip as had often been
the case with others on learning their identities.
Even the local shopkeepers still talked about
them behind their backs, yet the scandal that
had bankrupted her father was many years old.

Now Houndsmere knew who he was dealing
with he was more inclined to believe she'd been
in the mean streets of London not by folly, but
by design. He'd not asked her business there, but
he had asked her name and enquired where she
lived. She'd only answered part of his question,
directing him to Primrose Square in Marylebone. Then, once she'd dutifully thanked him,
she'd kept her face averted for the remainder of
the journey. There had been gossip years ago
about a Bernard Waverley being sent to the Fleet.
Lance recalled some salacious jokes in the gentlemen's clubs about a fellow being so mired
in debt that he had nothing left to sell but his
daughter. He now knew who she was and wished
that he'd taken more notice of it at the time. But
he rarely bothered with tattle doing the rounds.

Mr Waverley was obviously still on his uppers
and wouldn't want last night's events worsening
his family's lot. There were spiteful cats aplenty

who had nothing better to do than shred the reputations of young ladies so their own offspring could race ahead in the popularity stakes. Her father had been right about that.

From her modest cloak and bonnet the Earl had imagined she was a high-ranking servant, in the area visiting humble relatives, when he'd first come upon her. Her breeding had become apparent after they'd exchanged a few words. He'd assumed she'd had a tryst with a feckless swain lacking the decency to escort her home. There were an abundance of cheap lodging houses crowding the vicinity where impoverished clerks and apprentices lived. But perhaps he'd got the wrong end of the stick and she'd been with somebody prepared to pay for her company.

The East End of London was home to commerce of every description. Bawdy houses and gambling hells rubbed shoulders with office buildings bearing brass nameplates of the educated fellows trading from within. After dark, gentlemen sought diversion in the neighbourhood. He was one of them, although he housed his mistress in a superior street to that in which he'd spotted her. It wouldn't be the first time that a genteel woman, fallen on hard times, used whatever assets she possessed to stay afloat. And without a doubt Emma Waverley had something worth selling. For all his outrage, it was possible her father was aware of what she got up to, because he had survived bankruptcy courtesy of it.

Emma was aware of the subtle change in him. She'd encountered that shrewdness before in the faces of gentlemen ruminating on her unenviable situation of shabby gentility and fast-approaching old maidhood.

'I see no reason to detain you further, sir,' she said crisply. 'My sincere thanks for your assistance, but it is still uncommonly early and my father should get back to his bed.'

He was being dismissed and that made the Earl of Houndsmere's smile deepen. Only his mother and sister had ever sent him away when he upset them.

He picked up the pistol from the table. 'If you intend to threaten somebody again with an unloaded gun, avoid pointing it into the light. A military man will know you're bluffing.' He returned the weapon to its owner.

Mr Waverley's cheeks became puce. He wasn't used to being corrected in his own home, in front of his child. He turned to her. 'You have some explaining to do, miss, and I would hear it directly.' He stomped to the door, gun in hand. 'If what you've said is true, you do owe him a debt of gratitude.' He jabbed the gun in emphasis. 'I see no reason to stand on ceremony now you have already been private with him. Oh, see the fellow out, then I will expect you in my study.' The door was banged shut.

Emma was aware that it wasn't only her father who wanted to know what she'd been up to. For all his air of ennui Mr Harley was also curious about her risking her life and reputation in a slum in the early hours of the morning. She did owe him more than her thanks and her apology. But that was all he would get. She couldn't tell the whole truth to anybody she didn't trust. And she didn't trust anybody other than her father with this news. He would be shocked to the core when she told him why she had gone to a squalid lodging house at dead of night.

'I believe you will do me the courtesy of keeping this episode to yourself, sir.' Her edict emerged rather more forcefully than she'd intended.

A dangerous spark lit his night-blue eyes. She imagined nobody told him what to do. Worryingly, he looked as though he'd shaken off his weariness and was paying great attention.

'And I believe you will do me the courtesy of telling me why I should,' came his drawled response.

She swung to face him. 'Common decency springs to mind, Mr Harley.'

'Common decency appeared to be sadly lacking in your behaviour earlier, Miss Waverley. What were you doing in that dive?'

'I might ask you the same thing,' she shot back. 'I'm sorry…that was very impertinent. It's none of my concern why you were in a neighbourhood populated by low life.'

His mouth twitched at that backhander. 'I wasn't in that neighbourhood. I happened to pass close by when I heard you scream and drove into it. Do you go there regularly?'

She sent him a fiery-eyed look. If he believed her to be a harlot who'd got out of her depth, then let him say as much.

'Are you going to answer me?'

'I'll tell you this, sir, and no more. I was not in the neighbourhood on business, but to meet somebody.'

'I believe it amounts to the same thing, my dear.'

'A relative,' she snapped, hating him for his lazy sarcasm.

'Distasteful…but not unheard of, so I understand,' he returned in the same mordant tone.

'My brother,' she burst out. Horrified at what she'd divulged, she pivoted away from him, blood draining from her cheeks. She had allowed him to goad her and fallen into his trap.

'Your brother?' he repeated after a brief silence.

She said nothing and inspected the dust on the tabletop with her fingertips while her mind whirred and she tried to think of a way to distract him until she could show him out, hopefully to then forget all about what she'd just let slip.

'I won't pretend complete ignorance of your family's misfortune, Miss Waverley. Surely your brother is dead and has been for quite a time.' His voice sounded clipped, unemotional. He'd just recalled more of the family's misfortune when she'd mentioned her brother. Waverley Junior had duelled over a woman, then fled abroad after killing his adversary. It was the sort of misfortune that would have drawn sympathy from peers who accepted that there but for the grace of God went they. Lance had himself participated in more than half a dozen such dawn meetings; thankfully, none had ended in a fatality.

'I never discuss our family's private affairs, Mr Harley. I'm sure you understand. Thank you for all the assistance you gave to me, but I must insist you leave. My father is waiting for me.'

'I wouldn't want to outstay my welcome,' he said drily. 'May I call another time to speak to you?' He came closer as though to prompt her agreement.

'Why?' Emma's gaze raked his face and she instinctively took a pace backwards. She wasn't happy to continue this conversation now or in the future. 'I'm sorry if I sound ungrateful, but I see no reason for us to renew our acquaintance.'

She had eyes in her head and could tell that they were poles apart. He had plenty of money, whereas her father had none. And Mr Harley would know that, simply from having entered a house that was in a state of disrepair. She'd never before felt ashamed of the faded wallpaper and threadbare armchairs, but now she did. Even without those clues he had made it plain he remembered the scandal that had decimated their family. Emma and her father had remained in their home courtesy of others' financial support. Those people had dwindled and now only one remained. The very one that Emma had hoped would be first to abandon them. She knew that if she continued to refuse Joshua Gresham's terms, they would have no option but to pack up and leave this house.

The Earl propped a hand on the mantelshelf, a polished top boot on the battered fender. Emma found her eyes drawn to his crusted knuckles. He had been injured on her behalf. Now that she was closer to him she could glimpse the graze on his unshaven jaw, too, slivers of raw flesh beneath dense stubble. He seemed unaffected by the wounds got from defending her. Perhaps he was used to participating in brawls in seedy parts of London in the early hours. As she slipped another glance up at his concave cheek and thin, almost cruel, lips, she could believe that to be true. And now they were again just inches apart, with no breeze between them, she could sense the warmth of his body and the scent of dissolute living. It reminded her of her twin brother: a sweet reek of alcohol, overlaid with to-bacco smoke and a woman's perfume. Robin had been drinking whisky when she'd been with him about an hour ago, yet he hadn't held so strong a whiff of liquor. She hadn't asked her brother why he smelled of violets. She knew. Robin had been keeping company with the petticoat set from his late teens. He had been a reprobate the whole of his adult life, but she sensed this man's habits could be worse than her twin's. She blushed and stepped away as he turned his head and caught her studying him.

He smiled. 'Do I disturb you, Miss Waver-ley?'

'Not at all,' she retorted, although her colour had heightened.

'You disturb me.'

'What?' Emma said under her breath.

'I want to know why you were out risking all manner of peril when, as your father rightly said, you should have been in bed.'

Emma felt a sting of heat in her cheeks. His

eyes had taken on a rather sultry gleam when he'd said that.

'I have not quizzed you over your nocturnal habits, sir; please accord me a similar courtesy.'

He smiled. 'Well, let me volunteer some information, then, in the hope you'll do likewise. I was visiting a friend.'

'As was I.' She boldly met the dare in his vivid eyes.

'His name?'

'Is none of your concern. Her name?' Emma challenged, wondering why when she was tired, emotional and way out of her depth, she was engaging in this game with him. She'd wanted this stranger gone just moments ago, and now…he didn't seem a stranger.

'I forget…' he said and smiled because it was almost the truth. The only woman on his mind now was the one he was with. Miss Emma Waverley had captured his attention and sobered him up faster than a dousing with a bucket of water.

Emma had guessed he'd been with a lady friend so wasn't sure why hearing his half-admission niggled at her. She heard her father's study door slam shut and it brought her to her senses. The last thing she wanted was her papa returning here to drag her away for a scolding. Briskly, she stationed herself by the parlour door as though in readiness to close it after him. 'You brought me home safely and I'm grateful. But now I must say good day to you, sir.'

He pushed himself off the oak mantel and gave her a sardonic bow before strolling into the hall. She heard him shut the street door quietly and stood with her heart racing beneath her bodice, unsure why she was regretful rather than relieved to see him go. She darted to the window and from behind the curtain watched him flick the reins over the fine-looking chestnut horse that had patiently awaited his master's return. He seemed the sort of man to have obedience, even from his animals.

She craned her neck until she lost sight of the phaeton, then lowered her countenance into her open palms. At that moment she hated her twin brother for entangling her in his woes. But as he was wont to remind her, the problems he had were of her causing and she owed him all the help she could give.

Turning from the window, she sighed. She had an awful task ahead of her in breaking the news to her father that the son he adored and believed had perished was actually alive and living in a hovel. But the most wounding thing for Emma was in knowing that she must take the greatest share of the blame for the mess her family was in. She had hugged Robin before they parted at the top of the rickety stairway of his lodging house. On reaching the hallway she had turned back to give a final wave, but he had already disappeared inside his room. She had felt guilty leaving him in a vile place that possessed nothing in the way of comfort and stank of mould and boiled cabbage. Blinded by tears, she'd emerged into the street without her wits about her. She'd taken a wrong turn and brought herself into the territory of the two robbers. Now she must pray that this new calamity was contained and quickly dealt with and that no gossip arose from what had just happened. But one thing *was* certain: there were more, difficult times ahead for the Waverleys.

Chapter Two

'Are you *quite* sure it is him, Emma?'

At first, Mr Waverley had gawped at his daughter as though she were talking in double Dutch. At the second attempt, he'd managed to garble out a pertinent question.

'Yes, Papa. It is Robin.' Emma wasn't surprised by her father's stunned reaction to the news that his son and heir wasn't buried in France in a pauper's grave after all. The same son who had recklessly caused a disaster so great that his father had bankrupted himself trying to extricate the boy from it would be welcomed back as a prince, not a pariah. Emma couldn't help but feel a prickle of unease as she saw the burgeoning joy lifting her father's features.

Her hedonist of a twin brother was back, expecting assistance from them, and their father would do his utmost to give it, whatever the cost to himself and his other child.

Her thoughts returned to the man she'd ejected from the parlour under an hour ago. If only she could remove him from her head as easily and fully concentrate on this family crisis. But the memory of a pair of startlingly blue eyes and long-fingered hands torn about the knuckles constantly interfered with her attempt to investigate how Robin's return would affect them. If it were to come to light he was again on English soil, he would be arrested and the scandal would have new life breathed into it. A trial...a prison sentence...a death sentence...all were possibilities facing her brother. And much as Robin had infuriated her at times with his behaviour she'd always loved her twin dearly.

'Oh, you are a good girl to bring me such wonderful tidings.' Her father slumped down into the seat behind his desk, overcome. At the first mention of his son's name he had forgotten about punishing his daughter and had listened intently to what she had to say. 'How does he seem? Is he still the handsome boy I remember?' Tears began trickling on to his freckled cheeks. 'He is well? Tell me he is well with no ill effects.' Bernard lifted his swimming eyes to his daughter's pale, heart-shaped countenance.

'He seems healthy, Papa. Perhaps a little thin.'

'What did he say of me?' Having recovered some composure, Mr Waverley eased himself up from behind his desk, keen to learn more. 'He must come here after dark and we shall make plans to put things right so he can come home for good. He must be so eager to see his old papa.'

'Of course he would like to see you,' Emma fibbed when her father looked impatient for her reassurance. But she couldn't tell the truth and break his heart.

Her brother had forbidden her to speak about their clandestine meetings to anybody, even their father. But her run-in with the footpads had changed all that. Had she managed to return home undetected, slipping in through the side door in the same way as she had left the house, then she might have been able to carry on the subterfuge a little longer. But her father's bedroom faced the street and he was a light sleeper. He'd heard a vehicle draw up outside and had come down to investigate. Wraith-like in his nightshirt, he'd appeared on the step as she was being helped down. Quite understandably, he had been outraged to witness such a scene.

With hindsight, Emma wished she'd sensibly told her escort to stop at the corner. But from the start of their journey, when Mr Harley had lifted her as though she were feather-light and plonked her on the seat, she'd had difficulty thinking straight. He'd driven through the quiet streets like a daredevil. She had been dazed from the shock of being attacked, the journey passing in a breathless whirl. It had taken all her effort to stay upright as the vehicle careered around corners with her clinging to her hat with one hand and the upholstery with the other. She'd imagined he'd wanted to be rid of her with all due haste so he could then get about his own business.

Her father had a beatific smile on his face as he gazed into space. Then his frown took over. Emma guessed he was mulling over how to clear Robin's name. But her poor papa was deluding himself that his prodigal son could re-enter society. A fugitive from justice would struggle to pick up the life he'd had. Neither did Robin seem to want to. All he required from his family was as much unconditional help as he could wheedle.

She had been on her way to the library a few days ago when her twin had sidled up to her, almost giving her a heart attack when she'd identified his features beneath the hat brim he'd pulled low. Taking her elbow, he had steered her towards a piece of heathland dotted with trees where once, as children, they'd spent happy hours playing. But there had been no laughter in this reunion. There had been so much she had wanted to know: how had he got back into the country? Where was he living? How was he supporting himself? But Robin had been more concerned with asking favours. He needed some

money and his clothes and his books, and if they
were still in his old room would she please sneak
them to him under cover of darkness? Indeed,
they were still in the house. Her father would
never disturb any of Robin's things and his bed-
chamber had been kept as a shrine.

Before they'd parted, Robin had briefly told
her he wished to finish his law studies and get
employment. He was already using a false name
and, although he'd been reluctant to disclose it
to her, she had insisted on knowing it. Charlie
Perkins was not a very camouflaging alias. Her
father would immediately recognise it as Perkins
had been his wife's maiden name and Charles
had been her father. But for all Robin's talk of
having missed his family, he'd made it clear he
didn't want any interference from the people he'd
left behind. Now he was Charlie, he'd said, and
they must help him set up afresh.

Emma glanced at her father, smiling happily
to himself as he anticipated a wonderful reunion. She should tell him that Robin was determined on having a new life, not his old one back.
But she couldn't. It would only make him the
more determined to go and find his son. Emma
guessed her twin was cohabiting with a woman
because she'd spied stockings hanging over a
chair in a bedroom. But Robin wouldn't answer
questions and had slammed shut the adjoining
door, cutting off Emma's view of the clothing.

'I'm tired and want to retire now, Papa.' Emma knew it would be wise to remove herself from her father's presence before he found more awkward questions to ask.

'Yes, off you go, my dear, and rest for a few hours.' Mr Waverley shushed her away. 'I think I shall see about some breakfast, though I'm so excited I doubt I shall eat a morsel.' He sat down and drew forward pen and paper. 'I will make some notes of strategies to help our dear boy. First, a good lawyer will be needed. A top man, not a cheap charlatan.'

Emma closed the study door and set off along the hall with a lingering sigh. Top lawyers demanded top fees and the only way her father would lay his hands on more funds was to go back to the usurers to borrow them. Yet already they were being dunned. Just last week her father had let two burly men into the house to take some furniture to keep a creditor at bay. He owed Joshua Gresham the most. But that lecher wouldn't be fobbed off with sticks of furniture. He wanted something else in settlement.

She'd not had a wink of sleep and felt utterly exhausted. But she wouldn't be able to rest with her head crammed with anxieties. The most persistent of which was that her knight in shining armour had gone off without giving his word to keep his lip buttoned. How stupid of her to mention her brother to him! As she closed her bed-chamber door, she played over in her mind their conversation and felt a modicum of relief. She'd not said she'd *seen* Robin, only that she'd had a meeting to attend. She could hint at having heard a rumour that her brother had been spotted in London. Of course, that hardly explained why she'd go out searching for him at dead of night.

Her father had received an anonymous letter a year ago informing him that his son had died of consumption in France. The note had been written in a woman's hand, although the person hadn't disclosed any more than they were 'a good friend' of the deceased's. Emma now believed it had been sent by a French mistress of Robin's, on his instruction, so he could plot his eventual return to his homeland. Obviously, he hadn't trusted his family enough to know the whole truth. And still he didn't, it seemed!

Emma closed the bedroom curtains against the early sunbeams striping the walls with golden light. She undressed quickly, putting on her nightgown, then tidied away her clothes before climbing into bed and pulling the covers to her chin. She lay gazing up at the ceiling, then closed her eyes, willing herself to drop off for a few hours at least. But three men occupied her mind: her father, her brother and Lance Harley. Of the trio, a dark visage with mocking sapphire eyes and a cruel mouth took the longest time to banish, but eventually she did fall into a dreamless slumber.

The Earl of Houndsmere's manservant was under no illusion as to what his employer got up to when out carousing until dawn. Thus he found nothing unusual in coming upon the scoundrel dunking his battered right hand in a basin of water. Watching him, though, he was hoping the damage was limited to his lordship's person. It would break the heart of any valet worth his salt to gaze upon an exquisite superfine tailcoat ripped about the seams. Yet were it so, the garment would be tossed to him to dispose of rather than to repair and his lordship's Italian tailor would rub together his greedy palms. Reeves edged closer, attempting to ease a muscular arm out of a sleeve so he could spirit away the jacket to inspect it. He was bluntly told to desist. A few moments later the Earl of Houndsmere was stretched out on top of his four-poster, fully dressed. Reeves muttered something about sacrilege, but managed not to slam the door of the huge bedchamber as he disappeared to leave his lordship to nap.

Lance pillowed his scalp on his hands and frowned thoughtfully at the tasselled canopy overhead. He was annoyed with himself for being unable to put Emma Waverley from his mind. He liked a pretty woman as much as the next man, but there were plenty to brood upon who liked him in return and were expecting him to do something about that. Perfect manners aside, she'd been cool to him, despite his derring-do, and he didn't think she was acting coy to pique his interest. He doubted she'd have been any more impressed by him had he introduced himself by his title. He wasn't sure why he hadn't…other than to save her father's feelings. The man lived in a shoddy house and might have become yet more defensive on discovering a nobleman was within his humble abode. The poor fellow did have worries aplenty: a son who might or might not be dead, a daughter given to making midnight visits to slums and pockets quite obviously to let.

But Mr Waverley was fortunate in that his beauteous daughter was protective of him. Lance believed she was also protecting her brother. If so, he must have faked his own death to avoid pursuit after killing his opponent. It wasn't an unusual trick for a duellist to flee abroad, then send home a tale of his demise before rising phoenix-like years later after the fuss had died down.

Lance regretted charging right up to her door like an idiot and getting her into trouble, yet…he was glad he'd gone inside the house and had the chance to talk to her. From the moment they'd been left alone together and he'd got a proper look into her glorious golden eyes he had seen a sadness that no amount of defiance could disguise. Something was very wrong in her life. Intrepid little thing that she was, she'd nevertheless possessed an endearing vulnerability that had moved him and had made him pry not simply from curiosity, but to understand if there was a way in which he might help. He wasn't given to sentimentality or to solving puzzles, but he knew this one would eat away at him if he didn't look further into it. Besides, dwelling on Emma Waverley and her intriguing family would make a change from pondering on his own kin making of themselves a blasted nuisance. If it weren't for his sister Ruth nagging him to sort things out, he would have long ago turned his back on his stepmother and her tiresome daughter in the same way his father had.

He sat up and shrugged out of his coat. Although he still felt enervated, he knew he wouldn't sleep. The day stretched in front of him and he needed something to occupy the time that didn't involve him joining Ruth at her afternoon salon. The prospect of drinking tea and listening to her friends wheedling for him to attend their debutantes' balls was enough to send him off early to his club with the intention of remaining there until nightfall.

'What in God's name are you doing up at this hour?'

Lance addressed the newcomer, but continued taking off his crumpled clothes as his friend sauntered into his bedchamber and slunk down on the window seat.

'I'm not up... I haven't retired yet.' Jack Valance dragged some fingers through his fair hair. 'And neither have you by the look of it.' He yawned, watching the Earl ripping off his boots and lobbing them into a corner. 'Any chance of some coffee? Or a kip in your bed if you've finished with it?' Jack stretched out his legs in front of him, then crossed his arms and rested his head back against the wall as though to snooze.

'Ask Reeves for coffee.' Lance jerked his head to indicate the anteroom where his valet would be skulking.

'Fancy a trip to Newmarket races later?' Jack asked, opening one red-rimmed eye to watch his friend's reaction to his suggestion.

'Can't. Got things to do.'

'What?' Jack perked up, hoping to hear about something interesting that he could get involved in.

'Family matters.' Lance dampened down his friend's grin.

'I don't know why you bother with that chit.' Jack sighed. 'The girl will end up in Bridewell if she don't settle down.' Jack knew that his friend's stepsister was a minx. The Countess had been a courtesan before becoming the old Earl's second wife. Now the daughter appeared to be taking up where the mother had left off. Lance had already hushed up one scandal after the girl was spotted without a chaperon, visiting relatives on her mother's side who lived by the docks.

Jack ordered the coffee by poking his head round the anteroom door to speak to Reeves. He found the window seat again with a sigh. 'I'm in Queer Street since I put twenty guineas on a mare. The damnable filly cantered in second from last at Epsom.'

Reeves backed into the room, bearing a tray holding cups and a silver coffee pot. After the valet deposited it on a table, Lance handed him his creased jacket with an apologetic smile. He'd noticed his servant's mournful gaze kept returning to it.

'Do you need some salve for those knuckles, sir?' Reeves was eyeing the Earl's grazes.

Lance idly flexed his fingers, having forgotten about the wounds, if not the woman who'd caused him to get them. 'They're only scratches.'

'Had a scrap last night, did you?' Jack approached to investigate the damage with a raised eyebrow.

'Nothing worth mentioning,' Lance said and commenced lathering his skin with a shaving brush.

Jack knew when he was being shut out. They were close friends, but the Earl had a private side and Jack knew better than to pry into it.

Having poured the coffee and distributed the cups, Reeves perambulated the room, foraging beneath chairs and cabinets for shoes and boots for polishing while the gentlemen continued their discourse. He halted with an armful of supple leather to say, 'You should allow me to do that for you, my lord.' Reeves was frowning at the sight of his master shaving himself.

Lance half-smiled. 'You're probably the only man I would allow to hold a blade to my throat, Reeves.' He drew steel up a column of tanned throat to a square, bristly jaw, then dipped the soap-edged razor into warm water. He'd been in the army for six years and had grown used to doing things for himself…even cooking over an open fire. Dragging a servant along on campaign to mollycoddle you was to his mind an unnecessary vanity when all any soldier needed was a surgeon and a priest on standby. Lance heard a gruff laugh and his eyes strayed to his friend's reflection.

Jack had been observing an entertaining spectacle of a street urchin pickpocketing for some minutes. He'd been giving his friend a running commentary as the scene unfolded. Jack gave another guffaw before dabbing his eyes with a handkerchief. 'Just what I needed to wake me up,' he said, turning to Lance.

'Escaped, did he?'

'The little toe-rag did at that,' Jack concurred with an amount of admiration.

Lance continued shaving with one hand, his other extended meaningfully.

Jack groaned and plunged a hand in a pocket. He dropped a coin into his friend's damp palm.

'Shall I bring a breakfast tray, my lord?' Reeves offered over a starchy black shoulder. 'Or will you go to the dining room for a proper sit-down?' His master was wont to breakfast quite insubstantially. A pot of tea and a plate of toast was not a meal fit for an earl in Reeves's estimation.

'Toast and tea will suffice,' Lance said, and Jack rubbed his hands together in anticipation of a quick snack.

Lance was deftly folding a sepia-silk cravat as he strolled to the window and looked out over Grosvenor Square. Smart vehicles thronged the street, people strolled and a few liveried servants could be seen weaving busily between the gentry. Mentally, he sorted through his business affairs. There were several matters to finalise before he journeyed later to Hertfordshire to find out what in damnation his stepsister had been up to this time. If he were to bring her home he first needed an idea of where to find her. He hadn't spotted Augusta in town for weeks and neither had he heard gossip about her, which was unusual. She was staying in town with a chaperon chosen by her mother. Obviously the woman was unable to discipline Augusta well enough to keep her out of trouble.

Within a short while Lance's mind had wandered back to Marylebone and an image of an exquisite raven-haired woman. Before he left town he knew he'd be compelled to call on Miss Waverley again. He wasn't particularly vain, but for some reason he needed to show her he wasn't a drunken ruffian…well, not very often, anyway. And he knew she was no fallen woman, although he'd hinted as much to her and seen her bristle angrily. But what in damnation had she been thinking of, going to a rookery at night, even to meet her fugitive brother? He felt a genuine concern for what might have happened to her had he not gone to Cheapside to visit Jenny last night. And he had been in two minds about it.

Although she'd been his mistress for less than a year he was already contemplating pensioning her off. He never accounted to a mistress for his whereabouts or his behaviour and Jenny had lately been expecting he might do both. Lance knew an opera singer was angling for his attention and he'd given Maria enough reason to expect he might approach her. Now he couldn't recall what about the soprano had attracted him.

The more he tried to forget Emma Waverley, the more his thoughts returned to finding an excuse to pay a call at Primrose Square. He could go back to ask after her welfare following her mishap. Another meeting between them would be unwelcome to her, she'd made that clear, so the reception he'd get was uncertain. But he liked a challenge and was desperate enough to be in the same room with her again to take a few barbs.

'White's or Watier's?' Lance asked over a shoulder. 'We could have a game of Faro before I set off. You might win your losses back.'

'Fat chance of that if you're in on it.' Jack snorted grumpily. 'Watier's…the food's better,' he opted, having given the matter a second of consideration. 'Besides, yesterday there was some talk at the Faro table about a duel on Wimbledon Common. Didn't recognise the names of those involved, but I'm curious to know who was victorious.'

Lance gazed down on to a sunlit street scene,

hands thrust into his pockets. 'On the matter of duels, d'you recall anything about a fellow called Waverley fleeing abroad after a scandal?'

'That's going back some years,' Jack said in surprise. 'This duel was over a woman, but nobody deserves to end up in the dung like Robin Waverley. Damnable pity for him.'

'Refresh my memory,' Lance said. 'I can't bring it all to mind.'

'Why d'you want to know?' Jack crossed his arms over his chest, looking inquisitive.

'If I ever need to act as your second, I'd like to know what I'm getting into.' Lance shrugged into a charcoal-grey tailcoat his valet had laid out.

'Same as last time you acted as my second… or I acted as yours,' came the dry reply. 'I know you ain't forgotten as it was barely a month ago I met Bellingham.'

'That was over a Covent Garden nun. Was Robin Waverley's sister involved in his trouble? I don't recall the details.'

'I believe she was. She eloped with Simon Gresham. At the time nobody knew why she'd do that when Gresham could have approached her father for his consent. Still, they wanted to do it on the sly and her brother discovered the reason for it and pursued them. He brought her back and called Gresham out.'

'How old was she then?' Lance was listening intently.

'About eighteen, I think.'

'Simon Gresham wasn't acceptable to her father, perhaps?'

'I should say he wasn't!' Jack snorted. 'If they'd reached Gretna and done the deed he'd have made of himself a bigamist.' Jack poured himself the dregs from the coffee pot. 'That's what Robin Waverley found out: Simon Gresham already had a wife.'

Chapter Three

'You look rather tired, my dear.'

'I stayed up reading until quite late,' Emma replied coolly, meeting the watchful eyes of the man standing opposite her. She knew he was expecting her to invite him to sit down. But she wanted him gone, not making himself comfortable. 'My father will not be home for some hours. He has gone out on business. You should return another time, sir.'

Joshua Gresham refused to take the hint to leave. He shifted his feet even wider apart, crossed his arms over his bulky torso and treated her to another of his false smiles. 'But I am here to see you, as I imagine you well know.' He glanced at the small servant hovering in the doorway of the parlour. 'Will you send her away?'

The maid's expression didn't change and neither did she move. Mrs O'Reilly remained where she was, glaring into space. But Emma knew that the woman was biting her tongue in the same way she was herself. In her Irish brogue, and behind his back, Cathleen O'Reilly had called Mr Gresham *a nasty fat feller* on previous occasions that he'd visited.

Customarily he'd turn up unannounced on the pretence of visiting her father. But she wouldn't put it past him to have watched and waited for Bernard to leave the house today before knocking on the door to trap her alone. She was well aware that she was the one he really wanted to torment.

'I am expecting my friend to call on me this afternoon. We are going shopping.'

'Then we have a chance to talk before she arrives,' he purred.

'As you wish.' The effort of being civil to this loathsome individual made Emma's stomach squirm. She avoided Cathleen's eyes. The maid was muttering beneath her breath and Emma knew the woman was itching to be told to show him out. But there were things that even her father wasn't aware of that had gone on between his daughter and this man.

She'd not pretended to have an appointment, but her friend wasn't due to call until four and the clock on the mantel had only just chimed three.

Joshua Gresham propped an elbow against the chimneypiece, cocking his head to peer at her. His stance reminded Emma of another gentleman who had recently been in this room. But Joshua, shorter in stature and thicker of frame, had none of Mr Harley's fine physical attributes. Neither did he have that man's character. Oddly, as she compared the two of them, she realised that she had found Mr Harley quite charming… a fact that she imagined might make him give her one of his ironic smiles, did he but know it.

Emma went to the window and gazed along the street, hoping her friend might come early and save her enduring Gresham's company. For all his sham politeness he was a nasty piece of work and his brother had been little better. It had been a terrible error of judgement on her part to get involved with Simon, let alone fall in love with him. She had put her faith and trust in a lying wretch and thereby destroyed her family.

Yet, even knowing Simon had tricked her couldn't prevent a residue of wistfulness welling up inside. The man she'd wanted to marry had been the same one who had driven them all into debt and disgrace, losing his life in the doing of it. Her brother and her father had declared it was his own fault and no less than the scoundrel deserved. But Emma had shut herself in her room and howled for days when she found out that the man she'd believed she would grow old with had died. She pushed memories of Simon from her mind as his elder brother spoke to her.

'I have been patient, my dear, but must insist on having my answer from you.' Joshua had crept up behind her and was curving over her shoulder as though he might touch her face with his lips.

Emma swerved away as the sour smell of his person infiltrated her nostrils. Joshua Gresham and Lance Harley had both brought the whiff of licentious living inside the house. But her rescuer hadn't turned her stomach. A hint of sandalwood soap had emanated from Mr Harley as well as the night-time aromas gathered from hours of revelry.

'I would remind you that you had your answer many months ago. I have nothing else to say about it, sir.' Emma was relieved that she'd managed to sound polite when what she really wanted to do was curse him as a devil.

He returned to pose against the mantel and a set of stubby fingers commenced drumming out a tattoo on the oak shelf. 'You are intending to hold fast to that decision, are you, and put your father in jeopardy in his twilight years?'

'I would also remind you that I have asked you before not to blackmail me.' Outwardly, Emma retained her icy aplomb. Inside, she was anything but calm. Joshua's detested proposition had been issued after it became apparent that her father would struggle to repay him his money. Her tormentor had been biding his time, believing eventually his threats of retribution would make her submit. She could tell he was done with waiting. His eyes were on her bosom and his tongue was slithering about his lips like an excited worm.

'I have it within my power to finish the Waverleys once and for all,' he growled. 'Don't think me bluffing!' He strode up to her so fast that Emma put a chair between them, fearing he might here and now attempt to assault her as he had before. But on that occasion she hadn't been in her own home!

When the knock came at the door, Emma managed to keep her gasp of relief barely audible. Her friend had fortuitously turned up early.

'I told you I was expecting company. I must insist you leave as I am going out shopping.' Emma hurried into the hallway, and when Mrs O'Reilly, who was a little hard of hearing, didn't immediately appear to answer the knock she did so herself, impatient to let Dawn in and vile Mr Gresham out.

'My apologies for turning up unannounced...'

Emma's lips parted in astonishment. Quickly, she pressed them together and closed the door. A heart-stopping second later she realised she had not only been unbelievably bad mannered, but most unwise. She jerked open the door. He was still there as though he'd expected her to reconsider once her reflex to put a barricade between them had been overtaken by common sense.

'May I come in?' the Earl of Houndsmere asked with barely a hint of amusement lurking in his voice.

'Yes… I'm sorry, sir… I… I…' There wasn't a plausible reason for her rudeness that she could quickly think of so deemed it best to stay quiet rather than stutter nonsense like a fool.

He seemed to understand in any case, judging from his half-smile. Having the door shut in his face didn't appear to have bothered him.

But Emma was bothered; instead of being annoyed that he'd returned when she'd told him not to, a sweet, joyous feeling was unfurling within. She banished it. Explained it away. It was simply that of the two men presently bedevilling her peace of mind, Mr Harley was easily the nicer to deal with.

Or he had been so far.

She knew nothing about him and he could yet turn out to be an equal threat to her family. She'd not forgotten mentioning her brother to him. That foolish slip was again pricking at her conscience, but she gave thanks for the fact that at least Joshua couldn't molest her in another man's company.

'So this is your companion, is it?' Unbeknown to her, Gresham had come out of the parlour. A moment later he got a proper look at the gentleman and his disbelief caused him to gawp for some silent seconds. 'Houndsmere?' he eventually burst out in a tone that mingled awe and disbelief.

Joshua Gresham was on the fringe of society, not the exalted inner circle this fellow occupied. Nevertheless he knew him by sight, as most people did who coveted being permitted entry into his glamorous world. 'I'm surprised to see you here, my lord.' He executed a stiff bow.

'I'm afraid you have me at a disadvantage. I can't remember your name,' Lance returned, looking at the florid-faced fellow and then at Emma.

Her tawny eyes had widened on him in surprise before narrowing in suspicion. So he'd concealed his true identity. She couldn't be sure who her Good Samaritan really was.

'Joshua Gresham, at your service, my lord.' The introduction was barked out and he jerked another bow, smarting at the inference he was beneath the Earl's notice.

'And your business here, Gresham?'

'Mr Gresham has come to see my father,'

Emma interjected quickly when it seemed that Joshua might explode in indignation at being cross-examined. 'Now he knows Mr Waverley is not at home, he is about to leave. I believe you are here for the same reason, so will bid you good day also, sir,' Emma said.

Lance didn't look at her or acknowledge his dismissal in any way. He merely opened the door and pushed it wide with a finger flick so that the other man could pass on to the step.

Joshua snapped a curt nod from one to the other of them, then strode from the house.

Emma had believed she'd contained her relief in seeing the back of him, but she must have been mistaken.

'Has he been troubling you?' Lance asked.

Emma's wary gaze darted to him, then lingered. It was hard to believe that this startlingly handsome and elegantly attired gentleman was the rumpled rogue who had driven her home in the early hours of the morning at breakneck speed. But indeed it was he. His long chestnut hair was no longer tousled, but neatly styled. The hard blue eyes and cruel mouth were complemented by a clean-shaven jaw and a fresh set of expensive clothes.

She parried his question with one of her own. 'Shall I tell my father you called, sir?' Her heart felt as though it were beating furiously enough to burst through her bodice as she moved to the exit. She waited, as she had earlier that day, to see him out of the house. This time he was not so easily despatched.

Lance moved her aside, then shut the door and leaned back against the timber panels. 'There's no need to mention my visit if you don't want to.'

'I will not, then, as I'm not actually sure who you are,' she said acidly.

That prompted another smile from him, but he didn't rectify matters. 'I'm here to see you, Miss Waverley, as I think you already know. You look well… That reassures me that you suffered no lasting damage after your ordeal last night.'

That took the wind out of her sails. Had he really come simply to check on her welfare? 'I am very well, thank you, sir,' she said carefully.

'Good…' Under the guise of his concern he took the opportunity to study her from top to toe. She was small and slender yet curvaceous enough to make his hands itch to run from her tiny waist over the swell of her hips. Her heart-shaped face was slowly gathering colour along its sharp cheekbones as she became aware of his scrutiny. Her chin was tilted, her soft pink lips pressed together. She might look fragile as a china doll, yet there was a spark in her feline eyes and steel in her tone when she spoke.

'You know my name, and you are in my

house. I think it only fair you properly introduce yourself, sir.' She walked away a few steps to break their entangled gazes. Her hand was raised to rub the place where his hold had scorched her forearm. She abruptly placed those fingers back at her side. She wasn't going to let him fluster her by look or touch.

'My name is Lance Harley, though some people just call me Houndsmere.'

'Or they call you *my lord.*' She swung about to face him, delicate eyebrows arched enquiringly.

'I'm an earl so I can claim the privilege if I wish. I don't expect you to use my title, Miss Waverley.'

'Thank you,' Emma said with muted sarcasm. 'I shall not then. Now formalities are over with I will let my father know you called. I'm sorry, but you have to go, sir, as I am expecting my friend soon.'

'I won't take up too much of your time. I also have an appointment to keep. Is Joshua Gresham related to Simon Gresham?'

Again, their eyes clashed in the dim hallway and Emma moistened her lips with a slip of her tongue. He wasn't one for beating about the bush, then. 'Yes...they were brothers,' she said and tilted her chin. 'Have you been checking up on me?'

'Yes...'

'Why?'

'I'm curious about you.'

'Why?' Emma demanded with more feeling. She was alarmed as well as baffled by his persistence. Peers of the realm didn't bother themselves with spinsters sullied by scandal. She'd noticed Joshua Gresham's deference to Houndsmere. The moment he'd understood that the Earl expected him to go, he'd complied with that unspoken command. But both men were privy to shameful secrets about her behaviour. And aristocrat or no, Lance Harley might not be above using what he knew against her in the same way as Simon's brother intended to do. Perhaps in that they were equally base.

'What did Gresham want?'

'I think that is none of your business, sir,' Emma spluttered.

'I could ask him. I'd sooner you told me.' He paced away from her and every slow measured step echoed on the hallway flags like a drumbeat.

'I've no intention of satisfying your inquisitiveness, sir,' she said stiltedly.

'That's a pity…my need for an answer is in no way altered by your refusal to do so.'

Emma made a small exasperated noise. How dare he treat her like this! A stranger she'd known not yet one full day! The arrogance of the man!

But Joshua might tell him all he wanted to know and disparage her in the doing of it. He would brag about his intentions towards her, especially to a superior who'd seemed to strike admiration into him.

Gentlemen who were married still kept mistresses. Simon had told her that when the whole sordid story of his duplicity had come out and he'd tried to justify what he'd done. He would have gone through a sham marriage for her sake, he'd said, as though that were enough to appease her outrage at his appalling betrayal. Joshua had proposed to her after Simon died, saying his conscience wouldn't allow him to see her spurned and ruined. She had turned him down immediately and made it clear she would never again want to hear him martyr himself by repeating his offer. And he hadn't. He'd married Simon's widow and some years later had offered Emma a position as his doxy. Joshua had since proved many times that his claims to want to help the Waverleys were spurious. She understood now that he had always desired her, even when Simon had been alive, and her continual rejection had made him bitter and vengeful.

The silence in the hallway throbbed with tension. Slowly, Emma came to the conclusion that *my lord* was expecting her obedience as well as Joshua's. Well, loathsome Mr Gresham might have bowed and scraped to Houndsmere, as he'd called him, but she'd never do the same.

She jerked open the door and said stiffly, 'If you wish to speak to Mr Gresham that is your own affair, sir.'

'Are you his affair?'

'He would like to make me so,' she hissed and banged shut the door in a temper. Why had she given in and let him goad her into telling him that? She tilted back her head, exasperated with herself.

Lance felt his hands balling at his sides. So he'd been right in thinking that Gresham had been here with lechery on his mind. He'd seen the possessive way the fellow had looked at her. 'I could quite easily make him leave you alone. He would never come here again if I told him not to.'

'No!' Emma swiftly approached him. 'You must never do that.' In her agitation she had come too close and her hand had raised as though to shake an immaculately sleeved arm in emphasis.

'Why not?'

She gestured hopelessness, but avoided the two blue eyes that were boring into her. She could properly see the damage to his jaw now that it was no longer covered in stubble. A wound he'd got protecting her. She realised they ought to go somewhere more private to finish this conversation. She trusted Mrs O'Reilly not to gossip, but even so discretion was called for and he'd not leave until he had an answer of some sort. She gestured at the parlour, then rapidly entered the room confident he'd follow without waiting for more of an invitation.

He closed the door, stationing himself against it with his hands plunged into his pockets. He watched her as she paced back and forth across the rug, her countenance bearing an expression of fierce concentration. He imagined she was trying to decide whether to dissemble or blurt out the truth.

'My father owes lots of people money,' Emma informed him very quietly. She'd concluded that she was divulging nothing that couldn't easily be found out from any fellow at any gentlemen's club. 'Papa's main creditor is Mr Gresham. If you meddle, he will call in the debt from spite and take this house. He has the deeds as security and has threatened to make us homeless, and he will.' She lifted proud amber eyes to clash on his steady blue stare. 'Now are you satisfied? I have admitted we are beggarly, but you already knew that, didn't you? You just wanted to hear me say as much.' She walked closer to him, gazed at him accusingly. 'What I can't understand is why an earl would bother with any of it. Unless of course you and Mr Gresham are of a kind and both see an opportunity to be had in being privy to my misdemeanours.' She detected a slight reaction to her accusation; an increased slant to his mouth and a spark of something far back in his eyes. Perhaps he deemed risible her hint that he found her desirable.

'Every person with a memory long enough is privy to your misdemeanours, my dear.' She'd touched a raw nerve with that accusation. He wasn't sure himself how pure were his motives.

'They might think they know it all,' she said bitterly. It was an unguarded comment that she immediately regretted and tried to cover up. 'Nobody other than you and my kin know what happened last night. I would be obliged to have your word that you will not speak of it.'

'Your kin?'

'My father,' she murmured, inwardly wincing at yet another slip.

'Why are you pretending I don't know that your brother is alive and that you visited him? What does Gresham know that gives him a hold over you? Has he found out your brother didn't perish in France?'

She turned from him, biting her lip in frustration. Lance Harley might have saved her life last night, but he was now proving to be a devilish danger.

'I take it this mess springs from your brother defending your honour years ago. Is he feeling worried enough about developments with Gresham to risk breaking cover to protect you?'

'The mess was my doing and I can look after myself.'

'Are you sure about that?' Before she could answer he demanded, 'Did you know that Simon Gresham was married when you eloped with him?'

'Of course not!' Emma sounded outraged.

'I doubt your brother meant to kill him, just teach him a lesson. I expect his heroics have stranded him in no man's land. And that's a bad place to be.'

'I'm afraid, sir, I don't know what you mean...' She tried to escape, but he again closed five hard fingers about her forearm, keeping her still.

'I think you do. You know your brother is lying low, alive to his family but dead to others... especially Joshua Gresham and his vengeance, I imagine. You sought your brother to ask for his protection again. But if he's supposed to be buried in France, how can he intervene on your behalf, Miss Waverley?'

'Well, you're wrong there!' Emma sounded triumphant. 'I did *not* ask him to help me!' She swung her face up to his so violently that loose tendrils of ebony hair swung to cling to her flushed cheeks. This time she swallowed what was on the tip of her tongue. Blurting out that the boot was on the other foot would be foolish in the extreme.

'What made you risk everything to meet your brother last night?' His eyes dropped to her soft lips as she licked moisture to them.

'I have no more to say on the matter. We are barely acquainted and I find your interference in our private business vulgar and most unwelcome.' Boldly, she locked her gaze with his.

'You're in trouble, my dear, and could do with making friends, not enemies. I imagine your father will see the sense in that even if you do not.'

He was right about that! Once Bernard Waverley knew his daughter's saviour was a powerful man he'd jump at the chance of furthering their acquaintance. Her father was quite shameless in his constant quest to borrow funds from people. Even before the scandal sent them to rock bottom, he would invest in high-risk schemes, then seem bewildered when his expectations of becoming rich floundered. It wasn't surprising that his son had followed in his footsteps and rarely had two ha'pennies to rub together. But her father had always had good intentions, chasing a dream of financial security and demolishing what little they had along the way. Robin had squandered all his money through his addiction to the high life.

But she was right, too…about something else. Lance Harley hadn't just returned to be inquisitive. He desired her; she'd seen the heat in his eyes, felt the fingers on her skin soften into a caress. She jerked her arm from his clutch. He'd be her friend, would he? At a price…

'If you feel incapable of telling me the truth, Miss Waverley,' he said, strolling away from her, 'I'll not waste any more of my time or yours.'

Before he could open the door she felt compelled to have the last word. Why should he demand her trust? He might be high-born, but high principles didn't automatically follow. If only half of the tales that had reached her ears about the aristocracy were true, alley cats had better morals.

'I have told you the truth, sir. I am expecting my friend Dawn Sanders very shortly. So I'll bid you good day.'

He gave an ironic bow. 'Tell your father I called to see him and will return another time.'

'Why?' she gestured in exasperation. 'Why come back? What do you want with my father?' She marched towards him. 'Are you going to tell him about Joshua Gresham's interest in me and cause him yet more worry and heartache?'

'Gresham is easily dealt with.'

'And my brother?'

'Is another matter entirely.'

She knew it would be better if they parted company harmoniously. Then once he'd left the house he might reflect on it all as just a quaint foible…something not really worthy of his time or attention. But if she piqued him into doggedness she'd find she had a tiger by the tail and Joshua would seem a lapdog in comparison. Emma quickly pulled open the door and went into the hallway. Mrs O'Reilly was polishing the console table. She stopped and gaped, mid-swipe, at the gentleman emerging from the parlour. Her comical expression needed no explanation: it certainly wasn't the fellow she'd been expecting to see her mistress showing out.

'Good day to you, sir.'

'And to you, Miss Waverley,' he replied. A nod preceded him swiftly descending the stone steps and springing aboard a crested travelling coach.

The footman found his place at the back of the grand conveyance and it set off at quite a speed. Emma noticed rather a lot of curtains twitching in the houses opposite. Some neighbours even appeared to have business that had taken them out on to their front steps. She closed the door, leaning back against the panels, hoping that none of those people had been up early enough to see him bring her home at the crack of dawn or tongues really would be wagging.

Chapter Four

'You seem a bit down in the dumps, Em. What's up?'

'Oh, sorry, I didn't mean to be a sourpuss.' Emma had been dwelling on her mounting problems as she and Dawn Sanders promenaded. They were intending to look at the window displays of the new French modiste who'd lately set up in business on Regent Street. 'Nothing is wrong really.' A bright smile lifted the frown from her face as she linked arms with her companion. She was actually enjoying herself; the two young women had been close since schooldays and were comfortable enough with one another to be able to discuss things that they couldn't mention to anybody else. Even so, Emma daren't confide in Dawn about recent events. A genuine concern that she *could* air was niggling at her, though. 'I'm worried that

Papa wasn't back before I left. The physician has warned him to rest his bad leg or it will worsen.' Her father had said he'd only be out an hour or two, but hadn't returned. With such vital goings-on rumbling in the background she'd been brooding on what might have delayed him.

Last autumn he'd stumbled while pruning the garden and an ulcer had developed on his shin. The pain of it often made him wobbly on his feet. Emma prayed he'd not tired himself out and taken a tumble while searching the East End for Robin. He had gone off earlier, buoyant about a reunion with his son. But he had warned his daughter to be constantly on her guard: stealth was called for, he'd said, until a good lawyer was consulted on the best way to bring her brother back into the bosom of his family. Emma had been made to promise—unnecessarily—that she wouldn't breathe a word about any of it.

'Mr Waverley called on my father just after midday and they went off together to their club.' Dawn reassured her friend with a pat on the arm. 'Your papa looked in fine fettle. They're probably too mellow with brandy by now to notice their aches and pains.' She grimaced. 'Papa's arthritis rarely keeps him at home. I wish it would,' she added darkly. 'Then he might not have met that woman.'

Emma knew her friend was referring to the

widow to whom Mr Sanders was betrothed. Dawn didn't get along with her prospective step-mother and had told Emma—only half-joking—that she'd marry any gentleman who asked her just so that she wouldn't have to live beneath the same roof as Julia Booth after the wedding at Michaelmas.

'Oh, drat!' Emma groaned. Up ahead was somebody she definitely didn't want to bump in to. Joshua's wife didn't like her, as was perfectly understandable, considering the woman had first been married to Simon. It wasn't only the scandal surrounding Simon's death that had made Veronica bitter towards her. The woman had found out that Joshua had proposed to Emma Waverley, and been turned down, before he'd settled on her as a substitute. Emma wondered how much more resentful Veronica would feel if she ever found out Joshua was still lusting after his first choice.

'Let's browse the counters in here.' Dawn had seen the direction of her friend's consternated gaze and steered them towards a small haber-dasher's. Emma had told her she'd been propositioned by Joshua Gresham many months ago. 'Has that disgusting lecher been bothering you again?' she whispered.

'He visited earlier,' Emma informed her, gladly entering the shop with Dawn. 'Unfortunately Papa had already gone out, but I managed to quickly get rid of him.'

Or rather the Earl of Houndsmere had, ran through her mind. But she couldn't tell Dawn about that gentleman without also going into how they'd met. And her night-time trip to see Robin had to remain a secret, even from her best friend.

At a safe distance, it all seemed like the sort of thrilling adventure that happened to intrepid heroines in novels. Being rescued from robbers by a handsome earl, then dashing through dark streets in a racing phaeton with him at the reins, didn't really happen to shabby-genteel spinsters. But it had happened to her. Alas, with her family's well-being tangled up in it the gloss had been tarnished.

It was no romantic fantasy. The Earl of Houndsmere could present as real a threat to them as did Joshua Gresham.

Gossip about their eminent visitor would soon be circulating after he'd turned up in the middle of the afternoon, creating a stir among the neighbours. People would assume that he was one of her father's creditors, although why he would personally chase his debt when he could afford to send duns would be more of a puzzle to those determined to get to the bottom of it.

'Bother!' Emma had seen Joshua's wife and her companion follow them into the shop.

'I'll wager that's no coincidence. She's pursuing us and is out to cause a bad atmosphere,' Dawn warned.

'Well, she'll get no help from me in the doing of it!' Emma said in a pithy whisper. It wouldn't be the first time the woman had attempted to humiliate her. Veronica Gresham had nothing to crow about and there had been times when Emma had felt tempted to tell the woman about her vile husband just to wipe the smirk from her face. But she would not…could not…while a lingering guilt over Simon's death remained with her. And it would until the day she died, she imagined, even though she had been an innocent dupe in all of it. But so had Veronica been fooled by Simon.

'Miss Waverley…' Veronica called with sly amity. 'Don't run off just as I'm about to say hello.

'Heavens above, but she is determined!' Dawn hissed, giving Emma an encouraging smile.

The older woman stopped by the same counter and turned to a mousy-looking lady at her side. 'This is poor Miss Waverley, her debut far behind her and still on the shelf. Her father has begged my husband to loan him money to get her wed, but still nobody wants her, it seems. I wonder why that might be?'

Emma was too shocked to react for a second then she clipped out, 'Thank you for your concern, but Miss Waverley is quite content with her lot. Good day.' Though white-faced with fury, she dipped her head before moving on with Dawn. 'The cheek of the witch!' she fumed when they were outside. 'To do something so ill after years have passed.'

'Awful, wicked woman! It is little wonder Simon was unhappy. Who would want to be shackled to her?' Dawn wrinkled her nose in disgust.

Emma murmured agreement. Simon had told her that he'd been forced into a marriage by his family and that he didn't love his wife and never would. But he wouldn't have told her anything at all if Robin hadn't confronted them at a tavern, halfway to Gretna, and beat the truth out of him. She realised that they might have lived together as man and wife for months before she finally discovered that her husband wasn't her husband at all because he already had a wife living in Yorkshire.

'Perhaps Veronica has guessed Joshua has designs on you and is feeling more hateful than usual,' Dawn said.

'I'll never be her rival for that swine. Actu-

ally, they are a perfect match.' Emma realised
that it was understandable, if unforgivable, that
Simon had sought happiness elsewhere.

'Come back to our house and have tea,' Dawn
urged.

Emma felt frustrated that their outing had
been ruined, but relieved that she'd managed to
hold her temper when provoked. It was a pleas-
antly mild spring day and she'd gladly got out
of the house for a while. Although she couldn't
afford to buy even a length of ribbon it had been
nice to mingle in the crowds of shoppers and
absorb the atmosphere. But she was ready to go
home, too.

'Oh, there's a hackney.' Emma made to hail
it, then dropped her hand back to her side, letting the vehicle sail past.

'Never mind, another will be along soon,'
Dawn said, bobbing about to locate one.

Emma barely heard her friend's comment;
she'd spotted somebody and her heartbeat had
accelerated alarmingly at the sight of him. On
the opposite pavement, dawdling by a lamp post,
was her brother. He appeared to be engrossed
in fiddling with a tinderbox to light the pipe
clamped in his teeth. She wasn't fooled by that.
He was aware of her and was intermittently
flashing eye signals at her from beneath the
peak of his cap.

An icy sensation trickled down her spine. It was no coincidence that Robin was here. He'd sought her out because he wanted to speak urgently to her.

Regent Street was crowded with people and it was easy enough to lose oneself in the noisy throng. Nevertheless, Emma wished he'd not taken a chance coming to a place where he might bump into old acquaintances. Grimy of countenance and dressed in a labourer's clothing, there was nothing to hint at the dandy her twin had once been. A coarsely woven jacket engulfed him almost down to his knees and a wide-brimmed cap concealed his features. A coal cart was parked nearby and now he was confident she'd seen him he stepped quickly to it, sheltering behind the mountain of black sacks. Emma wondered if he really was employed as a coalman or had just donned a disguise. And what a disguise it was! Even a bankrupted gentleman's son might do better for himself.

'There's one!' Emma waved and the cab drew up at the kerb. 'Don't fret over that horrible woman,' she said kindly when they were settled on the seat. She had noticed that Dawn looked rather depressed following the unpleasant episode in the shop.

'I won't let such as *her* bother me,' Dawn said

dismissively. 'Come and have some tea with me and we can end our day nicely.'

'I'm afraid I'm going to be a spoilsport. I've got a headache now so won't be much fun.' Emma's temples *had* started throbbing, but she blamed her brother for it rather than Mrs Gresham. She took a peek over a shoulder, guessing the coal cart might be following them. It was. Whatever Robin had on his mind she'd sooner know about it straight away. She was glad he'd located her in Regent Street rather than risk dawdling close to their house in case their father had spotted him.

'I saw you go off with a man last night. Who was he?'

'What?' Emma bristled at her brother's curt interrogation. 'Have you risked breaking cover just to ask me that?'

'I told you to come alone last night,' he scolded. 'I thought I could trust you, Em. Who was he? Did you tell him about me? Does he know where I lodge?'

'Well, if you were close enough to have seen him you must know that two robbers set about me.' Emma gave her brother a blameful glare. 'Why did you not come to my rescue, then I might not have needed a stranger's assistance.'

'He was a stranger?' Robin sounded relieved. 'You don't know him, then, Em?'

'Well, I do know him now,' Emma said flatly. 'I had no alternative but to make his acquaintance after he saw off those two villains and delivered me safely home.'

Emma watched her brother restlessly pacing to and fro over the grass. Instinctively, she had known that he would wait for her to join him where they'd talked before. As a girl she had been allowed to go to the local heath in her twin brother's care to play with bat and ball. Unbeknown to her father—who would have banned further trips had he known—she'd climb the trees with Robin and on one occasion had torn her elbows falling off a low branch. The greensward, dotted with oaks, was isolated enough to allow them to talk unobserved, but not so remote than she might arouse suspicion walking to and from it on her own. A few scamps were at play, darting in and out of the woods, whooping and hollering. The boys were too young to bother to pay attention to the odd sight of a lady deep in conversation with a rough-looking fellow.

'You told me you were studying law.' The speaking look that travelled over Robin from top to toe needed no explanation.

'I am studying at night, but I have to earn a living as well. Lawyers ask their apprentices for references. I have none to give and must in time set up my own business as Charles Perkins. My boss, Milligan, doesn't want to know more from Charlie than whether he finished his rounds and got payment for all of the sacks he delivered.' He spoke sourly of his alter ego, but hadn't been sidetracked from having an answer to what really interested him. 'Who was your Good Samaritan? That high flyer looked as though it cost a pretty penny.'

His sister didn't answer immediately and he guessed she was still indignant that he'd not rescued her. 'After we parted last night I came after you because I should have owned up to something important,' he started to explain. 'I would have knocked those ruffians down for you, Em, but I was too late to be of help.' He'd been glad of that, having been loath to bring himself to the attention of a passing parish constable by brawling. 'I caught a glimpse of your rescuer's face and...' He tailed off into silence.

'And?' Emma prompted. 'Who did you believe him to be?'

'The Earl of Houndsmere, but then I thought I must be seeing things.' Robin sounded bashful.

'Well, you weren't. It was him,' Emma said shortly.

Robin took a step back, then another, looking dazed. 'Are you sure?'

'Yes, of course, although I only found out he was an earl this afternoon.'

Robin gripped her shoulders, giving her a little shake. 'You didn't tell him you'd seen me, did you?'

'Why…he doesn't know you, does he?' That question was met by silence so she demanded, 'Did you come into contact with him years ago?'

Robin vigorously shook his head. 'I know him by sight, but I've never spoken to him before in my life. But he's not a man to cross, Em.' He dropped his face to his palms. 'Hell's teeth! Why did it have to be *him*?'

Emma roughly dragged his hands from his face to study his tortured expression. Increased uneasiness was curdling her stomach. There was something she didn't know about and perhaps whatever it was had made Houndsmere persistently question her earlier.

'You'd better tell me everything, Robin. The Earl delivered me home and our father saw him. I had to explain my absence to Papa. He knows you are alive and in England. He is naturally overjoyed and wants to see you.'

'You didn't relate all of it in front of Houndsmere?' Robin had turned ashen.

'Of course not. But he did me a good turn and now believes he has the right to question why I risked being out late at night. He's shown more interest than is normal for a man in his position.'

'God in heaven! He knows! I'm done for! I've returned to England just for him to kill me.'

'Don't be so melodramatic!' Emma sounded cross, although her twin's reaction had greatly alarmed her. 'Why would an earl be interested in you if you've never even met?'

'Because I've been living with his stepsister as man and wife,' Robin croaked out.

Dumbfounded, Emma stared at her brother, then sank down to sit on the grass. He immediately kneeled beside her.

'Augusta told me she was a shopkeeper's daughter. I'd never have got involved with her if I'd known she'd also got connections in the aristocracy. Such people are too powerful for me to tangle with.' He swung his head in despair. 'Her mother was a milliner and the old Earl's mistress. He went on to marry her and they lived at Houndsmere Hall in Hertfordshire. Augusta truly is the Earl's stepsister. It's not a fantasy she has concocted.'

Emma pushed back her bonnet to hang on its strings, then raked her fingers through her dusky hair. 'This can't be true! Are we so beset by bad luck that such a bizarre coincidence can really be?' she wailed.

'It seems so,' Robin replied bleakly. 'Her step-

brother will search for her to take her home. I
wouldn't be surprised if he puts her in a convent.
She has run away so often that he threatened
to severely punish her next time. God knows
what he'll do to me. I didn't seduce her...if anything, she chased after me. But if he finds us
together that'll count for nought. There'll be an
uproar. I'll be exposed, Em. What then? I think
I'd sooner Houndsmere put me out of my misery with a clean bullet than risk a noose round
my neck.'

'Don't talk rot!' Emma cried. 'Would you
break our father's heart all over again?'

Robin appeared not to have heard that emotional plea. He leapt up, enlightenment straining
his features. 'Houndsmere is closing in on us. He
was out searching for her last night when he happened upon you. Did he state his business there?'

'Lance Harley isn't the sort of man to explain himself,' Emma replied tartly. 'He was
not searching for you, I'm sure of it,' she reassured. 'He had been drinking although he wasn't
drunk. He seemed to be on his way home after
a night of revelry.'

Robin looked a mite relieved as he prowled
about on the turf. 'Augusta said she believed the
same. He has a *chère amie* living in the district.
He must have visited her.'

Emma couldn't understand why hearing her

brother confirm something the Earl himself had half-admitted should niggle at her. Lance Harley was nothing to her and neither was the woman who left a hint of rose perfume clinging to his clothes. She put him from her mind, noticing that a couple were strolling their way. 'You should go now, Robin, before we arouse suspicion.'

Robin hastily turned his back to the onlookers.

'Will you give me a message to pass to Papa?' Emma got to her feet, brushing down her skirts. 'I know he will ask me if I've seen you. He is so happy to know you are back. Please don't do anything to hurt him again.'

'I imagine our father knows I need some money if you have told him how I am living.'

'He has bankrupted himself once for you, Robin. He mustn't get deeper into debt or he will end up in the Fleet again.'

Robin looked disappointed. 'What about you? Why haven't you married? A brother-in-law might have been of help to me.'

'A dowry might have been of help to me,' Emma returned shortly. 'Gentlemen who fancy a wife who is poor, ruined and past her prime are few and far between.'

Robin had the grace to blush. 'Well, don't blame me for everything. It's not my fault your portion has been spent. You started all the trouble in any case.'

'I pleaded with you not to call Simon out!' Emma felt hurt by her brother's attitude, but knew it wasn't the time or place for bickering and apportioning blame. What was done was done and, if not forgotten, was best left alone. 'I have to go now. Papa will be wondering where I am.' After a few steps she turned back to him. 'You said you came after me last night because you had something important to tell me. What was it? To say you had a woman in your life?'

He strode closer. 'Partly it was about Augusta. Also I had changed my mind about you not telling our father. I cannot stay in that hovel. Augusta is increasing. She is constantly crying and saying we must move somewhere nice.' He paused to make a hopeless gesture. 'I do love her, you know, and don't want to see her suffer. We should marry or the child will be born a bastard. Our father will want to assist me in finding a decent home, for his first grandchild's sake.'

Dismayed by that news, Emma swallowed her questions and quickly took her leave of her brother as the strolling couple looked their way. 'I will do what I can and get word to you at your lodgings,' she rattled off.

'Worse and worse…' she groaned to herself as she hurried on towards home. But something else had occurred to her. Augusta hadn't shown herself last night, but must have been close by to send Robin after her. Now Emma knew who her brother's woman was she felt a rather vulgar desire to meet Augusta and get to know a bit about Lance Harley's family, just as he seemed keen to know all about hers.

Chapter Five

'Get dressed and meet me downstairs. I'll wait no more than ten minutes before I head back to London.'

The Earl of Houndsmere had spoken dispassionately while surveying rumpled bedding and entangled limbs. The chamber occupied space in a tavern that was situated far too close to his Hertfordshire estates for his comfort. The blonde had received the brunt of his flint-eyed contempt. She extricated herself from the covers and her lover and levered herself up on an elbow.

'Who do you think you are, ordering me about? I'm your father's widow and you can show me respect, Houndsmere.'

'It'll be a cold day in hell before I do,' Lance drawled.

He was lounging against a door through which he had moments before inconspicuously entered the room. The woman gulped an indignant breath, but of shame at having been so discovered she displayed not a jot.

'Once again I have been greatly inconvenienced by you and your daughter. If you wish my help in finding the tiresome chit, make haste and meet me downstairs. I'll listen to whatever tale you have to tell, but know this: I have far more important things to attend to than searching out hostelries where you might be found fornicating.' His eyes wandered on, prompting her beau to swing his legs over the side of the bed. Swiftly, the youth snatched at his breeches discarded on the floor and jumped into them. 'Who's this? The latest recruit to my stables?'

The young man turned florid.

'Introduce yourself?' the Earl suggested, thinking he had seen him somewhere before.

'Peter Rathbone,' came the barked reply.

'God almighty…' Lance said in genuine surprise. Now he recognised his neighbour's son. The last time he'd clapped eyes on him the boy had been attending Eton and his voice hadn't properly broken.

'How old is he? Eighteen?'

'I'm twenty,' the fellow interjected, his blush deepening.

'Be that as it may, I'd be obliged if you'd take

yourself off now and, if you wish to stay healthy, keep your distance from her in future.'

'He may visit me whenever he wishes, wherever he wishes,' Sonia spat furiously. 'The Dower House is mine and you have no say in it.'

'I believe I do and you should take the time to read the documents you were given after your husband died. I can raze it to the ground if I wish and eject you back into the gutter whence you came. I tell this milksop to stay away from you for his own good unless he welcomes a dose of pox before he turns twenty-one.'

Peter Rathbone hastily grabbed at his coat and within a few moments the man's escape was audible as he clattered down the stairs. Her young lover's desertion caused the woman's scarlet mouth to form a tight knot. In frustration, she swiped an empty brandy bottle from the side table and hurled it. Lance easily evaded the missile and stepped away from the glass shards.

She jumped naked from the bed and flew at him, fingers curled into talons that were aimed at his face. 'How dare you tell him I've got the pox!'

Lance easily held her off and, spinning her about, shoved her back towards the mattress where she sprawled on her belly. 'Well, if you haven't caught it yet, I imagine it's only a matter of time. He's only a year older than your daughter. For common decency, leave the lad alone.' *Common decency* wasn't a phrase he'd usually use and he was immediately reminded of the woman who'd recently said it to him. Dark-haired and quietly beautiful, she was as far removed from this painted-face jade as was imaginable. Laughably, this woman would be far more welcome in society than would Emma Waverley.

Sonia peeped over her shoulder at him, wiggling firm buttocks and purring, 'You may pull that insolent face, but you wanted me once…oh, how you wanted me…so many ways, Lance…' Her gyrating became more provocative.

'That was a long time ago, when I was as pitiable as that fool who's just left.'

'I'm only a few years older than you, so don't make out I'm an ageing hag. We were a good match, Lance. I gave you everything you wanted and made you happy.' She whipped over on to her back and, resting back on her elbows, openly displayed what she'd given him to his lazy gaze.

'You never made me happy. That wasn't it at all,' he said with arrant self-disgust.

She crooked a finger, beckoning him as her knees dropped further apart. 'I made you horny then. I bet I still can…'

'Well, put your money down and I'll take it. I couldn't raise a smile for you, sweet. Now get dressed and meet me downstairs or you can search for Augusta yourself. And next time you want a tryst with a cicisbeo, travel out of Hertfordshire to bed him and pick on someone who isn't one of my neighbours. I'm done with listening to gossip about you at the village inns.'

She bounced on to her knees, glaring at him. 'And I'm sick of listening to talk about which scheming little strumpet has caught your eye.'

Lance turned on his heel and went out. He'd allow she had a point there. The opera singer had started a rumour that she'd hooked him. Just a week ago he'd have allowed her to be right. But for some reason his lust for Maria had cooled. And neither had he felt any inclination to visit Jenny again. As for the woman he'd just left…the thought of bedding her made him feel sick and not just because she'd been his father's wife. But he wasn't without fault. He'd once allowed himself to be taken in by her flattery and lies, and that had set in motion consequences of which he would always feel guilty and ashamed.

Below in the back parlour he was served cognac by an obsequious landlord who diplomatically avoided looking directly at his lordship. The man could feel the rage emanating from his grand patron although the Earl's demeanour was cold as ice. The woman upstairs was a regular and it wasn't always the same fellow. Although she had been in with young Rathbone several times and they always took the same chamber and a bottle of port and one of brandy upstairs with them. The mystery was why the Countess didn't entertain her lovers more discreetly on home ground. He concluded the cat had some twisted sense of decorum and was loath to foul her own doorstep.

Lance took a chair by the window and gazed out into the sunlit afternoon. Much as he tried to concentrate on the business in hand, his mind wandered back yet again to London and Miss Emma Waverley. He couldn't remember any woman having such a grip on his thoughts. Telling himself the mystery of her brother's resurrection was what really absorbed him wouldn't work. She was the draw… He was already trying to think of a reason to go back and see her again. He wanted her to let him help solve whatever problems the Waverleys had, but knew if he asked her to trust him her golden eyes would fire with suspicion. A wry smile tugged at a corner of his mouth. And who could blame her for being cautious? Was he going to deny that he wanted her so much he was starting to ache and think he was suffering some sort of brain sickness? He'd only been in her company twice, yet the last time he'd been obsessed in such a way he'd been a green boy of eighteen and under the spell of the woman upstairs. But he was no callow youth now as Sonia had just reminded him. And Emma Waverley was no ingénue. And when he got back to London he'd need to do something about approaching her and regaining his peace of mind.

He watched Peter Rathbone tipping coins into the palm of the ostler who'd brought round his carriage. Soon the vehicle was swaying away, and Lance observed the gangly youth's departure with a frown. He liked the Rathbones and hoped Peter wouldn't persist in seeing Sonia or he might be disinherited. His parents wouldn't suffer the humiliation of being saddled with a daughter-in-law, almost twice their son's age, who might be a countess yet acted like nothing of the sort. He recognised himself in the boy: he'd been about the same age when Sonia had sunk her claws into him.

Within nine months of starting his affair with Sonia Peak, Lance had seen through her deceit and recognised his own shameful gullibility. It had taught him a much-needed lesson about allowing his loins to overrule his intelligence where women were concerned.

He'd discovered she was not a gentleman's daughter who had been ruined by a cruel seducer, then abandoned by her family to make her own way. She was the offspring of a stevedore and she and her older sisters had been working at dockside taverns since they'd turned fifteen. Having done well from whoring, by the time she was eighteen she owned a part-share in a millinery. And that was where Lance had met her a few years later. He'd been shopping with the woman who'd then been his mistress. Full of spunk and youthful conceit, he'd been susceptible to the pretty blonde shop girl's ardent pursuit and faux devotion. Much as his father had been years later. But Sonia's greatest deceit had been over her daughter. The child had been kept hidden away with her parents while Sonia schemed to trick the Earl of Houndsmere's heir to elope with her.

When he'd told her it was over her fury and spite had erupted. One thing Lance hadn't anticipated was that, as a last resort to get him to marry her, she'd travel to Hertfordshire with her daughter, claiming the child to be his. If it had been true, he would have sired Augusta when still at school. Sonia gave up spouting her lies when she'd no further use for them. Within a short time of petitioning Lance's father for assistance she had trapped easier prey. The widowed Earl, lonely and vulnerable, had made her his mistress despite Lance warning his father about her true character. But William Harley was beguiled by his young lover's sweet attentiveness as he described her fawning over him. By the time the silly fool had discovered her sweet attentiveness wasn't exclusively lavished on him it was too late. He'd married her. Within a year of the Earl's second marriage his bride had given up the sham, flaunting lovers, spending wastefully and breaking her husband's heart. William's humiliation at having been taken in by her poisonous charm made him an embittered man in his final years. Thankfully, Lance had been reconciled with his father before that man's demise. But William went to his grave despising his second wife. He'd made sure that Sonia would get very little from the Houndsmere coffers. She was cunning but uneducated and had believed her position in the Dower House secure. Yet every acre of land and every property on the Houndsmere estates belonged to the Earl to do with as he saw fit.

Lance got up and strolled to the window. He checked his watch. He'd given her enough time to show up and hadn't been bluffing about setting straight back on the road for London. He swallowed what was left in his glass and was turning to leave when she sashayed into the room with a sulky look better befitting her teenage daughter.

Sonia helped herself to brandy straight from

the bottle, gulping at it quickly before wiping her mouth on the back of her hand.

'Well?' Lance sounded impatient. 'What have you to tell me?'

'Augusta ran off to visit her grandparents in Wapping. I went there to bring her back, but she's disappeared without saying where she was off to. I believe she's still in the eastern quarter, but I haven't the cash to pay investigators to find her.' A blameful look followed that complaint. 'I have so little money I can barely afford to eat,' she added theatrically.

'Stop gambling away your allowance, then,' he returned with a significant glance at her ample figure. She looked as though she ate rather too much. 'I received a letter from Harry Wentworth enclosing your IOU for twenty pounds.'

'Did you pay it?' Sonia asked eagerly.

'I did not. I returned it to him.'

'Tight-fist,' she muttered. 'You have to bring Augusta back, Houndsmere, and find a rich gentleman to marry her before she ruins herself.'

Lance burst out in genuine laughter. 'Heaven help me…you're not even joking, are you?'

Sonia had the grace to look abashed at that. 'If you provide her with a large enough dowry, some impoverished nob will take her just so they can boast that they're your brother-in-law.'

'I'll not foist her on to any man and make

him suffer like my father did when he married you.' He strolled to and fro, glancing out into the courtyard. 'If she's in Wapping, perhaps it's best to leave her there where she feels at home.' He gave her a glance. 'I'm surprised you haven't drifted back where you belong.'

'I belong with you at Houndsmere Hall,' she replied petulantly. 'Like it or not, I'm an aristocrat now and I'll fight to keep what I've earned.'

'And earn it you did. Would you could earn respect so easily. You've made of yourself a laughing stock in the neighbourhood. Take care to be more discreet in future or I will remove you from my property and house you somewhere distant. I've an empty hunting lodge that would suit.'

Sonia glared at him. 'You wouldn't dare.'

'I think you know I would,' he answered flatly. 'If I find your daughter is servicing seamen down by the Thames, don't expect me to fight for her honour. And I won't lie to some unsuspecting fool about her making him a virtuous bride.'

'But you will look for her, Lance? I do worry about her.'

'Do you know how ludicrous that sounds? If you're worried about your daughter, madam, give up your whoring and gambling and spend some time in her company, disciplining her on how to behave.' He knew he was wasting his breath. Sonia was incapable of disciplining herself, let alone her child. 'I will investigate her whereabouts and if I find her I'll bring her home...for the last time. After this episode I wash my hands of you both,' Lance said. And he meant it. But it suited him to go back to the East End and take a look around. He might turn up Robin Waverley's hidey hole.

'Will you take me home, please, Lance?' Sonia asked slyly. 'I'm stranded here now Peter's run off with his tail between his legs.'

'I'll ask the landlord to loan you a gig. I know you can drive as I've seen you. Take the reins yourself rather than commandeer a stable lad you know you can seduce.' He threw that over a shoulder as he went out of the door.

'I shan't drive myself! I'm a countess!'

'Then act like one,' Lance said cuttingly and went off to find the landlord.

Once he'd paid the shot he went into the courtyard and directed his driver to head for Mayfair. Stretching his legs out in front of him, he settled back against the luxurious squabs and closed his eyes.

He'd already forgotten about his stepmother. A goddess with dusky hair and tigerish eyes was once more filling his mind. He gave up the fight, allowing Emma Waverley's image to dance behind his eyelids while he searched for excuses to return to Primrose Square to see her again. He genuinely wanted to improve her lot in life, but the urge to visit was not solely altruistic and therein lay the root of his problem. He desired her, wanted to make love to her and, what's more, she knew it.

Chapter Six

Lance Harley wasn't the only man frequently brooding on Emma Waverley's lovely countenance and lush figure in a manner that would have made her turn crimson had she known about it. Joshua Gresham had her in his lustful thoughts, too.

The incongruous sight of the eminent Earl of Houndsmere entering Bernard Waverley's shabby hallway was something else he couldn't forget. The whole *ton* now knew that a few days ago Houndsmere's carriage had been stationed in Primrose Square before he set off for his country retreat. The consensus of opinion was that Waverley had secured a fresh injection of cash. The puzzle was why somebody like Houndsmere would bother to make his acquaintance or to help him.

As the Earl was out of town he couldn't shed

any light on it even had his lordship felt inclined to break his rule never to discuss his business. Bernard was also keeping tight-lipped, although he hadn't denied Houndsmere's recent visit. Oddly, he hadn't boasted of it either as people had expected him to do.

Joshua had attempted to engage him in conversation earlier, but the older man had been evasive and had scuttled off. Joshua wasn't giving up yet on having some answers, though. He lounged back in his wingchair, sipping port. The game of cards he'd been observing from his comfy spot in his club was coming to an end. As usual the solitary sovereign left to Waverley wasn't returned to his pocket, it was flipped to join all the others he'd staked in an attempt to win the pot. To no avail, as it turned out. The young buck sitting opposite triumphantly threw down his cards face up; his other hand dredged the table of a small fortune, pulling it close to his chest.

Seizing his opportunity, Joshua pushed himself out of his armchair. His quarry was looking vulnerable, sitting alone at the table as the gamesters disbanded to seek other diversion.

The moment Bernard noticed who was in the process of pulling up a chair he attempted to rise from his to escape. Joshua tugged on his sleeve, making him sit back down.

'I'm not chasing my money, Waverley, although I am conscious that my interest payment is long overdue,' he added craftily.

Bernard sighed in relief at the reprieve. He didn't like or trust Joshua Gresham, but had to allow that the man had shown patience. Other creditors had embarrassed him by commandeering his furniture in front of the neighbours.

'I could forward you another small amount if it would help.' Joshua sounded full of concern.

Bernard brightened.

'But I expect your new friend has taken care of that side of things for you.' Joshua slyly withdrew the offer.

'My new friend?' Bernard echoed, looking mystified.

'Why, everybody knows that Houndsmere has called on you, Waverley. You probably have no further need of my paltry assistance with such as he backing you.'

'No...he...it is not that. He has offered me no financial help.' Bernard shot to his feet. 'I must get on my way... I have an appointment.' He pushed through the throng, being paid little heed. His friend, Roland Sanders, detached from the crowd and accompanied him outside.

'I saw Gresham stalking you. After his money, is he?' Roland sounded sympathetic as they strolled along the street towards home. Usually, the friends remained at their club until dinner time, but Bernard didn't want to risk further interrogation. He knew that Gresham wasn't the only fellow keen to discover how he had got the Earl on his side. The galling thing was, he hadn't. Houndsmere hadn't visited for a good reason. Rather than being able to crow about having made the acquaintance of an aristocrat, he must try to cover it up.

'Joshua's asking questions about Houndsmere.' Bernard glanced over a shoulder as though believing he might be pursued. 'I know I sound like an ingrate, but I wish that fellow hadn't brought my daughter home.' He tutted in exasperation. 'Trouble will ensue if Houndsmere takes too much interest in our affairs.'

'Why would he do that?' Roland sounded bewildered.

Bernard shrugged. 'I just feel he will. Emma told me he called again a few days ago…simply from courtesy to see that she'd suffered no ill effects from being set upon.' He shook his head glumly. 'I think there is more to it. He suspects something and is keen to get to the bottom of it. He sits on the magistrate's bench, you know.' Inwardly, he shuddered at the idea of a man of the law scenting a fugitive close by. 'He must never discover that Emma got into trouble that night on her brother's account. Houndsmere could put a noose round Robin's neck.'

'You wouldn't want Gresham getting wind of your boy's return either. I recall Emma turned down his marriage proposal.' Roland paused. 'He acts amiable, but I'm not sure he is to be trusted.'

'Gresham *is* to be trusted to want a profit!' Bernard trumpeted, rubbing together thumb and finger. 'He charges more interest than the veriest usurer. Little wonder he pretends to be my friend and lets me keep his money for so long. I am making the confounded skinflint rich.' Bernard tapped his nose. 'I haven't forgotten that bad blood exists between us.'

'I wish I was in a position to help you, then you'd not need to turn to him,' Roland said.

Bernard patted his friend on the shoulder in appreciation of the sentiment. Roland had chosen to propose to a rich widow to keep the wolf from his own door. It had occurred to Bernard to follow his friend's lead and find himself a lady with a healthy bank balance. Unfortunately, with a scandal dragging him down and no invitations to socialise adorning the mantelpiece, meeting a kindly soul who might overlook his faults was nigh on impossible. Besides, he knew he'd never feel again the love he'd had for the mother of his twins. Sarah had lost her life bringing those two cherubs into the world. At her graveside her tearful husband had vowed to do his utmost to be a good parent and a man she would have been proud of. In the years since he'd berated himself for having failed to live up to that boast. Both of his children had lost their way without their mother's guidance. Neither had he been a credit to her memory, gambling too much and making hasty, ill-thought-out decisions. One of which was even now pricking at his conscience.

'You are a good fellow, Roland. But you will keep all of this business with Robin under your hat, won't you? I swore my daughter to secrecy on it and shouldn't really have blabbed…but how could I keep to myself such wonderful tidings? Impossible!'

'You haven't blabbed!' Roland sounded a tad miffed. 'You have confided in me…your trusted friend.'

Bernard issued a mollifying smile. 'Indeed. And if you can come up with a solution to how I might engage a top lawyer to act for my boy who will take payment in shirt buttons instead of coin, I'll be pleased to hear of it.'

'Put me thinking cap on,' Roland answered drolly.

'You know, when Emma told me she'd discovered that her rescuer was an earl I believed her to be pulling my leg at first.'

'Understandable,' Roland rumbled. 'Hardly the sort of neighbourhood you'd expect a peer of the realm to haunt.'

'Unless you knew a bit about the rogue,' Bernard returned darkly. 'Emma tells me he was ever the gentleman with her, though. So I've no complaints.'

'He is too well served by the petticoat set to have a flirtation to spare, I imagine.' Roland's observation elicited a sniff of indignation. 'Your Emma's a beauty, but pleasingly modest, too, despite what she's endured,' he hastened on. 'Rakes like Harley aren't attracted to virtuous ladies until they're ready to set up a nursery.' Before he dug himself into a deeper hole he changed tack. 'I recall there was quite a to-do when the old Earl married for the second time. The scheming hussy was one of his son's cast-offs! The Houndsmeres have long been a scandalous lot. Descended from privateers, so I believe.'

Bernard knew his friend meant no ill by implying Emma was outside the Earl's sphere of interest. He knew it himself and as her father it actually gave him a certain amount of peace of mind. Houndsmere wouldn't be denied anything he wanted. Bernard knew he wasn't up to taking on such a powerful adversary. He hadn't even been able to best the fellow when Harley had been unarmed and he had been in possession of a gun to point at his handsome head.

'Last week I took Mrs Booth to the opera and Houndsmere was there with his chums.' Roland was enjoying having a gossip. 'Quite a stir he caused during the interval when the soprano left the stage and joined him in his box. My fiancée was mightily entertained in observing all the green eyes turning their way.'

'Fine figure of a man,' Bernard allowed. 'Though Emma seems immune to him, thank heavens. She was as relieved as me to see the back of the fellow.'

'Our girls are as pretty and pleasing as any of those out this year,' Roland proudly announced. 'But it's a deuce of a job settling daughters once they're the wrong side of twenty-four and their portions are gone. I shall set aside a sum from my fiancée's dowry for Dawn. I'd like to see her with a husband and family before she gets too much older.'

'I'm happy to have my Emma at home,' Bernard replied, feeling guilty that he had no rich widow to fall back on. 'I wouldn't want her married for convenience. She deserves another chance at happiness. It wasn't her fault she gave her heart unwisely and was cheated of her best years by a scoundrel—' Bernard was brought to a halt by a nudge in the ribs.

'I say…ain't that the Earl's carriage?' Roland jerked a nod to a crested travelling coach pulled by a set of matched greys. It was proceeding at quite a crack along the street. 'He wasn't out of town long, then.'

Bernard forgot about his aching leg and put on a spurt. If Houndsmere was heading towards Primrose Square, he wanted to be home to greet him this time and find out what the fellow was after.

'The Earl hasn't called, Papa. What made you think he might have been here?'

'Oh, nothing…' Mr Waverley clasped his hands behind his back and ambled to the window to gaze out as though believing Houndsmere might yet put in an appearance.

Emma could sense his uneasiness and that put her on edge. Had her father discovered that a member of Houndsmere's family was entangled in their lives to an alarming degree? Worse still, had the Earl discovered that his stepsister and her brother were lovers? A shiver undulated along her limbs at the thought of how justifiably livid Lance Harley was sure to be. Augusta might have sprung from lowly stock—a milliner's daughter, she recalled Robin had said— but the girl would have been expected to make a good match once the late Earl of Houndsmere became her stepfather.

She wished now she'd told her papa straight away about her meeting with Robin earlier in the week. But she hadn't wanted to speak about it without first giving it careful thought. Robin was desperate for assistance and Emma wouldn't put it past him to exaggerate his plight to secure the money he wanted. She believed he'd fallen in love with Augusta, but as for the expected child...had he dreamt that up to pluck at her father's heartstrings? Hers, too. She loved the idea of being an aunt. But if the couple went ahead and married in secret, what then? The marriage might be annulled and the child whipped away somewhere and never allowed to know its wicked father's family. Rich and powerful people were adept at dissolving *mésalliances* and hushing up scandals.

'I expect the Earl has grown bored with us.' Bernard turned from the window, sighing. 'A relief to know it, of course,' he said, but with little conviction. 'I wish I could forget all about the man, Emma. But I cannot stop dwelling on how sweet life could be if circumstances were different and we could foster an acquaintance with him.'

How well Lance Harley knew her father!

'You're in trouble, my dear, and could do with

making friends, not enemies. I imagine your father will see the sense in that even if you do not.'

His words came back to mock her. Indeed, her father would adore having a social connection to the Earl. But Houndsmere didn't know the whole story. When he did…as he surely would… he might grind the Waverleys beneath his shoe in restoring his stepsister's reputation.

Emma knew there was a way of destroying her father's dream of a *sweet life* as he'd called his yen for a friendship with Lance Harley. And do it she must, for confessing to another meeting with Robin was long overdue. Her father would desire keeping a great distance from Houndsmere once he knew the nature of this new calamity.

'There is something I must tell you, Papa. When I was out shopping with Dawn in Regent Street I saw—'

A sudden bang on the door interrupted her.

Bernard immediately hobbled to the window, anticipation lifting his brow. He hoped to spy a smart conveyance fit for an aristocrat parked at the kerb. He was disappointed. A plain hackney cab was just heading off.

A moment later Emma's friend was shown into the parlour by Cathleen O'Reilly.

'Shall I be making a pot of tea, Miss Waverley?' the servant asked.

'Thank you, Mrs O'Reilly.' Emma clasped her friend's hands, happy to see her again so soon after their excursion earlier in the week. 'This is a lovely surprise, but a bit late in the day for a shopping trip.'

'Is all well with your papa, my dear? I only quit his company about an hour since.' Bernard also realised it was an odd visit at this time of the day.

'He is very well, thank you, sir.' Dawn smiled broadly.

'I'll leave you two young ladies to your chat. Oh, what had you to tell me, Emma, about bumping into somebody on Regent Street?'

'We can speak of it later, Papa,' Emma quickly replied.

'Have I turned up at an inopportune moment?' Dawn pulled an apologetic face as the door was closed behind Mr Waverley. 'You were going to tell him about Veronica Gresham being a cat, weren't you?'

'Indeed I was not! I wouldn't worry Papa on *her* account.' Emma drew her friend towards the sofa, keen to change the subject. 'Now, sit down and tell me what's happened. I can see you've something on your mind that won't wait.'

'I have.' Dawn sounded excited. She opened her reticule and drew forth a parchment. 'I've something to show you and I want you to tell me I'm not dreaming and we really have a fine opportunity to go out somewhere nice.'

'We?' Emma took the gilt-edged card and scanned the elegant script that invited Dawn and a friend to take tea at Mrs Sweet's in Belgravia.

'Mrs Sweet? I'm not sure I know of her. Of course, if you'd like me to come I will,' Emma said bravely. She wanted to show support, but her mind had already flown to the practicalities. Her clothes were shabby. She hadn't had a new gown in ages. There had been no point in going to the expense when she was never invited anywhere. 'Would you not rather go with Mrs Booth, though?'

'Julia would certainly like to accompany me, she's made that plain,' Dawn said. 'She's taken credit for me having received an invitation at all, hinting she's elevating us by marrying Papa.' Dawn rolled her eyes in disgust. 'I want *you* to come with me.' She squeezed her friend's fingers. 'It is a perfect opportunity for you to slip back into society.'

Emma wistfully wished it could be that easy. She often dwelled on her salad days of parties and balls, gaiety and laughter, often with Dawn by her side. Then fate turned against the Waverleys. Now she feared that her unwelcome presence at a gathering could blight Dawn's acceptance, too, making them both feel miserable. 'It could reflect badly on you if I go.'

'You're my best friend and will always be so,' Dawn replied stoutly. 'If Mrs Sweet didn't already know that, then she should have taken more care with her guest list. We might have a nice time, Em. And if we don't, then we can take our leave early. I'm not bothered if I never get another invitation out of it.'

Emma gave her friend an affectionate hug for her loyalty. 'Do you know Mrs Sweet? Is she nice?' she asked, her voice husky with pleasure.

'Mrs Booth admits she has never been introduced to her, but has heard that the woman is pleasant and popular. Julia claims to be top notch, but actually her circle is mediocre. I'm certain she knows little of Mrs Sweet…other than she is an aristocrat's daughter who married beneath her, for love.'

'Well, she sounds very nice in that case,' Emma said.

'That is settled then.' Dawn gained her feet before her friend could change her mind. 'Now I must go. Papa wants to dine early as he and Julia are going to the theatre. He has said he will drive us himself in his gig to the party. I believe he is as excited as I am about this.'

Having waved to her friend, Emma closed the door, wondering how her father would take the news. With all this business with Robin swirling about them the unexpected chance to make new friends had come at completely the wrong time.

'Shall I be drinking this meself, then, miss?' Cathleen asked with a pointed rattle of crockery.

Emma smiled apologetically and took the tea tray from the woman. 'Thank you, Mrs O'Reilly. My friend could not stop after all, but I shall have some tea and I expect Mr Waverley might like a cup, too.'

Cathleen went off with a sniff and Emma headed towards her father's study. She doubted that a nice cup of tea would make more palatable the news she'd yet to break to him. Neither would knowing that his daughter had been invited to socialise for the first time in years.

As she'd suspected, the news about her invitation seemed to barely register with her father once she'd confessed to her last meeting with Robin.

Bernard stomped to and fro, then flung himself down in his chair and rested his head in his hands. For a moment it had seemed he might weep his voice became so croaky. Emma sped around the desk to embrace his quivering shoulders.

'There is no need for despair, Papa. You said earlier in the week that the Earl is out of town so there is yet time to try to talk sense into Robin. He must send Augusta home.'

'Houndsmere is back. I saw his carriage go past...at a rackety pace, too, as though he indeed had something urgent to do.'

Emma felt her stomach somersault at that information. Had he been racing to find his stepsister?

'I must quickly find a way to get some money to help Robin. A move to the countryside is what he needs. A place where nobody will know him. Oh, why couldn't he have just kept company with a doxy as he usually does?'

Emma knew her father was utterly distracted to have come out with something like that in front of her! And still he seemed preoccupied.

'Joshua Gresham hinted he might forward more cash. But will it be enough to set things straight?'

'Not him, please, Papa,' Emma interrupted. 'You know he is two-faced.'

'I do know and, in truth, neither do I trust him.' Bernard got wearily to his feet. 'But beggars can't be choosers, my dear.' He frowned. 'Should we just tell the Earl what we know?' he ventured. 'He is a magistrate, but might concentrate on saving his stepsister's reputation and think my son beneath his notice.'

'I fear it is too great a risk, Papa...' Emma

paused, noting that her father's limp was more pronounced since she'd upset him with this news. 'You must rest now; we can talk of it again at dinner. Perhaps in the meantime an idea might come to us.' She tried to sound optimistic before quitting the room. She hadn't mentioned the child. She had intended to, but just knowing about Augusta had immediately overset her father. He was a man of the world and could work out for himself the possible consequences of his son cohabiting with a woman.

For the first time she felt a surge of real anger towards Robin for having turned up out of the blue, bringing troubles aplenty with him.

Chapter Seven

'Welcome home, my lord.' The Earl of Hounds-mere's butler took his master's coat, draping the costly garment over his arm with a flourish. 'Your morning post has been put in your study. This letter has just arrived. A maid delivered it.'

Wilkins proffered a silver salver he'd picked up from the hall table. Lance pocketed the note, having identified Jenny's tiny script on the parchment. Sealed within would be a complaint about his absence, he imagined, or a request for cash because she'd run through her allowance. Either that or she'd got wind that wagers were being put on an opera singer deposing her. Whatever it was, it was of little consequence; he'd already asked his lawyer to deal with her severance pay. Aware that Wilkins was waiting to be dismissed, he gave a nod and the elderly fellow immediately withdrew.

Lance proceeded to the stairs, intending to change out of his dusty clothes and then visit his sister and brother-in-law. He might have an irritating stepfamily, but he was very fond of his elder sister and her husband and children. Besides, he wanted to check on forthcoming social events.

He entered his chamber to find Jack Valance stretched out on the counterpane of his bed.

'Hell's teeth, Jack,' Lance said, veering between exasperation and amusement, but his pace towards the huge clothes press didn't falter. He flung open the doors and pulled out a pristine lawn shirt. 'Haven't you got a home to go to?'

'I believe not,' Jack declared dramatically. 'My landlady's thrown me out. Can I move in here until my father forwards me something and I can pay the old harridan her rent?'

'No,' Lance said.

Valance came upright in an athletic forward roll. 'Can you loan me ten pounds, then? I need to pay some bills that won't wait.'

Delving a hand into a pocket, Lance pulled out some notes that were dropped on to the bed.

'Much obliged.' Jack grinned. 'My sweet Becky will be obliged to you, too. The little minx has been complaining that her room in Barrow Lane is cold and damp and she won't receive me until I pay her fuel bill. I've been promising to fill her scuttle to warm her up.'

'Is that a euphemism?' Lance shrugged out of his tailcoat so Reeves, hovering at his elbow, could take it.

From the side of his mouth, Reeves muttered, 'I tried shifting him by telling him you'd not be back for days, but he wouldn't have it, my lord.'

Lance knew that his valet wouldn't have tried too hard to rid himself of the interloper because he liked him. Reeves might adopt a po-faced disapproval of Jack's bawdy tales, but he often forgot himself and chortled at them when believing himself unobserved.

The dresser bore a few depleted decanters and a tray filled with a variety of used crockery and cutlery, evidence of the hospitality Jack had enjoyed in his host's absence.

'Have you been eating me out of house and home, Valance?' Lance asked, unbuttoning his shirt.

'Only took a bit of bread and cheese and a sup of porter, m'lud.' Jack tugged his forelock and winked at Reeves when that man snorted at such a blatant lie.

Lance didn't begrudge his friend a crumb of the roast meats, pies and pickles he could see remnants of. He could be generous to those he was fond of or felt indebted to and Jack fitted the bill on both counts. His best friend was an impecunious baron's second son, and had only his allowance to live on. Lance had attempted to school Jack into making sound investments to boost his income, but the spendthrift had frittered the profit without reinvesting a penny of it. Jack had little prospect of improving his lot unless he married an heiress adept at keeping him beneath her thumb. That apart, their army careers had seen them come through many perils together, watching each other's backs. Those harrowing days alone made the taking of a few liberties barely worth a mention. The two men were closer than brothers.

'Who's taken your money this time?' Lance enquired as he divested himself of his cravat before Reeves could start fussing at his neck. He lobbed the length of lawn on to the bed and his valet went after it like a terrier.

'My sister.' Jack sighed and helped himself to a glass of port. 'I promised Bella I'd take her to the theatre in a new dress and she wouldn't let me forget it.'

'That's sisters for you.' Lance chuckled.

'She was pleased as punch with her frock. She wore it to your sister's salon last week and swears that a baronet noticed her because of it. This fop told her the blue silk matched the colour of her eyes.' Jack narrowed his gaze. 'I'm keeping an eye on him from now on.' He took a gulp of his drink.

'Ruth's holding another tea party soon. I'll watch out for the baronet. Or you could do it yourself if you feel like turning up.'

Jack choked on his mouthful of port. 'You're not going, are you?' He spluttered, thumping his chest, eyes popping in astonishment.

Lance grimaced an affirmative.

'Perhaps I should come, too,' Jack said dolefully. 'Now I'm reduced to begging a bed for the night I'd better find an heiress to sweet talk.' He swiped the banknotes from the coverlet and pocketed them. 'I'm off to run my errands and pay for Becky's coal. No wonder it's so blasted expensive with toffs getting their hands dirty. I might apply at Milligan's for a job.'

It took a moment for his friend's grumbling to sink in, then Lance turned to stare at him. 'What toffs are you talking about?'

Jack came to a halt by the door, looking surprised at his friend's interest in his throwaway remark.

'You said a toff's getting his hands dirty delivering coal,' Lance prompted.

'That's what Becky told me. She said last time she ordered a sack a fellow with a posh voice and nice manners delivered it. She's a cat...probably said it to make me jealous.'

'And this gentleman works for Milligan?' Lance strode closer, his eyes raking his friend's face.

'I imagine so. Becky's a good girl and always searches out the best deal. She said the others pack in too much slack…why…what's the matter?'

'Just curious…' Lance said, but a smile was tugging at a corner of his mouth. 'You're right, coal is damned expensive stuff. I wouldn't mind shares in black gold.'

'You're never *just* curious, Houndsmere. You're not thinking of buying Milligan out and putting me to work on a coal cart to get your ten quid back?'

'Maybe…' Lance said, chuckling, as Jack went out of the door. He slipped out of his shirt and thrust a muscular arm into the fresh one Reeves was holding up. He walked to the mantel and stared into the mirror, doing up his cuffs. 'A coalman, eh?' he muttered, then started to laugh.

'Penny for them, my lord?' Reeves had been watching his master talking to his reflection.

'They're worth more than that, Reeves. I'm not sure even I can afford them.'

'My! How grand it looks.' Mr Sanders turned to the two young ladies squashed beside him on the narrow seat of his gig. 'You'll have a fine time, I'm sure, and make lots of new friends.' He beamed, then carefully clambered down from his perch. He helped the girls alight outside the town house in Belgravia, giving them each an encouraging pat on the arm before releasing them. 'What a wonderful day this is! Mrs Booth is convinced she will receive an invitation soon. And in case she does not, she told me to remind you she'd happily attend with you next time.'

'If there is a next time, Papa,' his nervous daughter whispered.

Mr Sanders wasn't to be denied his optimism. 'Oh…this is the start of many such outings, I'm sure.' He clasped his hands, almost in prayer. 'Now off you go and enjoy yourselves.'

Emma's pensive gaze darted to the line of smart carriages at the kerb that had doubtless conveyed guests already within the house. She inwardly chided herself for feeling tempted to run away. But it had been years since she'd encountered malicious stares and whispers. Only Veronica Gresham now went out of her way to be spiteful. Others simply ignored her or had forgotten about what had happened. But her appearance in such exalted company might give rise to talk and refresh memories. She didn't want that. She had been living a quiet life with her papa and, although it wasn't what she once would have chosen or expected, she had settled into it now. Yet even that modest existence was now under threat since Robin had turned up like a bad penny.

'Ready?' Dawn whispered.

'As ready as ever I will be,' Emma declared and took a deep breath. She'd noticed a liveried footman stationed at the head of the sweep of stone steps and for all his poker face she knew he was watching them. Unobtrusively, she brushed down her creased skirts and straightened her shoulders.

The girls waved to Mr Sanders as he called a farewell, then flicked the reins.

'I wish I had worn something not quite so heavy and dark.' With so little time to prepare an outfit, Emma had simply stitched pretty pearl buttons on to the bodice of a blue-cotton day dress to brighten it up. Her bonnet had received a new trimming, too, but of the two of them Emma knew she looked the dowdier—not that she begrudged Dawn her pretty sprigged muslin or her opportunity to enter a new social circle. But in a corner of her mind lurked understandable envy and a sadness that her friend might soon move away from her.

'I told Papa we would hail a cab to take us home. Don't worry, Em, if we don't want to stay long then we will not.'

'We shan't leave until we've found you a fine

gentleman to marry who will whisk you away from your future stepmother's clutches.'

'We are about to attend a tea party, my dear, not Almack's,' Dawn returned wryly.

'Of the two I think I'd sooner be here,' Emma said. 'At our age we'd be seated with the chaperons in the assembly rooms.'

'What a relief to put the marriage mart behind us.'

'It isn't behind *you*. You said you'd take any man rather than live with Mrs Booth after your father marries her. Michaelmas is fast approaching.'

'Enough!' Dawn groaned.

Emma knew they were bantering to gain some time. She wasn't alone in feeling overawed, or in having butterflies circling her stomach. Even in her heyday, she had never received an invitation to socialise at such an address and, to her knowledge, neither had Dawn. 'Come! We can't dither out here.' Emma gave her friend's gloved fingers a squeeze. 'They'll all be very nice to us, I'm sure.' Linking arms with her friend, they approached the grand portal and mounted the steps.

'Miss Dawn Sanders and Miss Emma Waverley,' Emma announced clearly when her friend appeared tongue-tied in front of the servant and simply thrust her invitation at him.

Joshua Gresham had been approaching in his

carriage at the very moment Mr Sanders had been helping his daughter and Emma Waverley alight from his gig. So astonished was Joshua by what he saw that he slid forward on his seat to press his nose against the window and get a better look. As Mr Sanders set off, Joshua rapped urgently on the roof of the vehicle to bring it to a halt. Before the wheels had stopped turning he jumped in an ungainly fashion to the pavement, twisting his ankle in the doing of it. That was no deterrent to him rushing back along the street. He concealed himself behind an overhanging branch of a mulberry bush and watched the two young women ascending the steps to the Sweets' mansion.

Joshua's eyes popped in rage. So he was right in thinking that there was more going on between Bernard Waverley and the Earl of Houndsmere than a financial deal. But if Houndsmere had lecherous intentions towards Emma he'd be a fool to introduce her to his sister. Something odd was afoot and Joshua was determined to get to the bottom of it.

Having limped back to his carriage, he moodily banged his spine into the squabs, grimacing as his sprained ankle throbbed. But what pained him most was the idea of losing his grip on the Waverleys. At the moment he had Bernard pinned beneath his thumb, but that could change if Houndsmere became his ally.

Veronica would be livid when he told her what he'd just witnessed. She had been unsuccessfully angling for years to procure an invitation to one of Mrs Sweet's salons.

Joshua bawled out an instruction to be taken to Primrose Square. He'd make a diversion on the way home and speak to Bernard in the hope of finding out what was going on.

Chapter Eight

In between being a perfect hostess to her guests, Ruth Sweet had been sneaking out of the graceful rose salon where she held her afternoon gatherings to keep watch for her brother's arrival. Peering over the banisters for the umpteenth time, she finally spotted his tall athletic figure entering the house, followed by that of Jack Valance. Closing the drawing-room door, she swept down the stairs to accost him before the opportunity was lost.

'Really, Lance! What is this all about?' she hissed, trotting over the marble flags towards him.

Sure his friend was about to be reprimanded, Jack took himself off, sliding a look of mock sympathy over his shoulder. The Earl of Houndsmere deferred to no man...but his big sister was a different matter.

'What is what all about?' Lance responded mildly. He gave his sister a peck on the cheek and fondly tweaked one of her brunette ringlets.

She slapped away his hand. 'Don't mess my hair and don't play the innocent with me,' Ruth warned him, though she found it hard to stay angry with Lance when he smiled in that boyish way he'd had since childhood. The Earl of Houndsmere might be revered as a powerful aristocrat by others—to her, he was just her younger brother and not too important for a well-deserved thump. 'Miss Sanders is here. She is a very nice respectable young lady and I won't have you stalking her in my house.'

'Why would I do that?'

'Because I know you!' his sister returned bluntly. 'Why did you ask me to invite her and her friend? You said they were kith and kin of one of your acquaintances. You hinted that they were ladies of advanced years who rarely socialised, but might like to get out more.' Ruth narrowed her eyes, giving him an old-fashioned look.

'All of it true, as far as I'm aware,' Lance replied innocently.

'I concede they are not debutantes, but they are both considerably younger than you or I. Hardly the matrons I was expecting. So what about Miss Sanders interests you?'

'I can't yet say as I've never met her,' Lance said truthfully, turning Ruth about and steering her towards the stairs.

Ruth pulled away from him. 'Never met her?' she echoed suspiciously. A look of enlightenment lifted her brow. 'Ah! I see. So Miss Sanders is an unsuspecting beard, is she? You crafty so-and-so!'

'Still don't know what you mean.'

'Oh, yes, you do!' Ruth plucked at his sleeve to stop him ascending to join the others. 'I want some answers from you and I will know if you're fobbing me off.' She flapped her hand in exasperation. 'I should have known that Miss Waverley was your target. She is the prettier…a real beauty in her quiet way. She's had problems in the past, too, hasn't she, the poor girl? Ruined, as I recall, by an unwise love affair.' Ruth dragged her brother down two stairs so they stood together. She went on to tiptoe to meet him eye to deep blue eye. She wanted her answers now. There wouldn't be a chance to quiz him in company…as he well knew. 'What on earth do you think you are doing inviting Emma Waverley to my house if you intend to—?'

Lance put a finger to his sister's lips to silence her. 'That's enough! You're jumping to conclusions. I just want to talk to her and doing so anywhere other than in polite company such as this is damned difficult.'

'Aha! She doesn't want to talk to you, you mean. I could tell that she is nobody's fool after speaking to her and her friend. I heard an opera singer was next on your list of conquests, not a shabby-genteel spinster with a sorry past. Anyway, good for her. I hope she holds out against you. That'll be quite novel, won't it, Lance?' she archly teased him.

Lance muttered beneath his breath and asked tonelessly, 'Have you finished now?'

'No, I haven't,' she retorted. 'We've enough scandals to contend with already. Our wretched stepmother and her daughter are always creating a stir—' Ruth interrupted herself to add, 'Have you yet discovered where Augusta has disappeared to?'

'No…but investigators are looking for her, for the last time. I've told Sonia that I wash my hands of them both.'

'I'd heard you'd been out of town. You went to Hertfordshire to see her?'

'I got back a few days ago.'

'And?' Ruth demanded to know. 'Has the dratted woman succeeded in luring you back to her bed?' Ruth was aware of his romantic history with their stepmother and that Sonia would very much like to breathe new life into it. 'What has that hussy been doing this time to get your attention?'

'Nothing new,' Lance replied with finality and grit in his voice. He allowed his sister her impertinence because he'd always loved her more than anyone else. But she sometimes overstepped the mark. As she opened her mouth to start again, he hiked a dark eyebrow at her in a way she understood.

Ruth pressed her lips together and resorted to glaring at him in retaliation. Lance tickled her cheek before turning and taking the stairs two at a time. Ruth picked up her pretty satin skirts and chased after him.

'Anyway, it's time you settled down,' she hissed at his back. 'You need a wife and a nursery, then you won't have so much time and money to squander on demi-reps.' When that elicited nothing more than an unintelligible mutter, she added, 'There is a sweet girl called Miss Caroline Lovat just out. She is the rage this Season and all the gentlemen adore her. She will be at Almack's on Wednesday… Why not come? You might fall in love.'

That brought Lance to a halt halfway up the stairs. He turned to his sister with a grin. 'Fall in love? When did that come into it?'

'*I* married for love…our parents married for love,' she said firmly. 'It is what we do in our family. Why should you be any different?' A gleam of optimism lit her eyes. 'So you will come to Almack's?' Ruth knew that if he did he'd be surrounded…not just by debutantes, but by astonished people wanting to know what was up with him. He hadn't been seen in an assembly room for years.

'No, I won't come. I'm sure Miss Lovat will do very nicely without me.' He arrowed a look up the stairs as though eager to get to the drawing room.

Ruth linked arms with him so they could ascend the remaining treads together. She slanted an astute look up at his handsome face. 'Have you already got somebody in mind to marry, Lance?' she asked.

He shot a look at her, but it was seconds later that he laughed, then said, 'Don't be ridiculous… you know I'm not the marrying kind… Have you got a whisky decanter out or am I expected to drink tea?'

'Oh, there's my brother Jack.' Bella Valance clapped her hands in delight. 'I thought he was joking when he said he'd see me later. He rarely takes afternoon tea, even at Ruth's, and she does provide a nice time.'

'I expect he's come for the cake, not the tea,' Emma said on a chuckle. The wonderful array of pastries and confectionery that their hostess had provided was astonishing to see. Emma had only ever encountered such lavish hospitality at debutante balls. She glanced at the fair-haired gentleman who'd just entered the room, seeing at once his similarity to the sweet-faced young lady ensconced beside her on the sofa. Jack raised his hand to his sister, then started towards them through the throng.

Emma had expected this afternoon gathering to comprise perhaps a dozen ladies quietly chatting over tea and biscuits. Perhaps a game of cards might score highest for excitement, she'd thought. How wrong she was! There were easily fifteen gentlemen in the room and several well-attended gaming tables. At one end was a raised dais on which a string quartet made soft music. A couple of young ladies were partnering one another to practise their dance steps, encouraged by their mamas. In all, it was a wonderfully relaxed and informal affair, far removed from her expectations of fusty manners and knowing looks.

'I have made some new friends, Jack.' Bella jumped up to embrace her brother as he came to a halt in front of them. 'This is Miss Waverley, and Miss Sanders is over there talking to somebody who knows her future stepmother.'

Jack politely bowed to Emma. 'Very pleased

to meet you, Miss Waverley. Are you a friend of Mrs Sweet's?'

'Unfortunately, I can't claim to be. I've only just made her acquaintance,' Emma explained. 'She has been most attentive to us, though. I accompanied Miss Sanders today.' She nodded to where Dawn was standing with a tubby fellow. 'It came as a surprise to Dawn to bump into one of her father's future in-laws.'

'A nice one, I hope.' Jack was watching Dawn edging away from where she appeared to be hemmed in against a bureau.

Emma had also noticed that her friend looked uncomfortable and she'd been about to go and rescue her when Jack Valance turned up.

'I think I should like to be introduced to Miss Sanders,' Jack said and set off in Dawn's direction.

'He likes to help damsels in distress,' Bella said insightfully. 'He's always rushing up to butt in when I talk to gentlemen. Sometimes I wish he wouldn't.'

'Brothers can be very protective of their sisters,' Emma said with a hint of ruefulness.

'I suppose it's a good thing.' Bella sighed.

'Yes…mostly it is…'

Bella leaned closer to whisper, 'While Jack's occupied I wish I could talk to somebody I like very much.' She rolled her sparkling eyes to indicate a handsome young man stationed by the fireplace, sipping tea. 'Sir Paul Nixon is over there. Have you seen him?'

Indeed, Emma had seen him and had noticed that he frequently looked at Bella.

'He told me my eyes are as pretty as blue cornflowers.'

'And so they are,' Emma said gently. She recalled being Bella's age and thinking every compliment was heavenly to have. But sometimes selfishness lay behind a gentleman's pretty words, as she'd learned to her cost. Nobody, other than Robin, had warned her to tread cautiously with flirtatious gentlemen and in her tender years she'd seen little of her twin. He'd been away at school or at university a lot of the time. Her papa had believed matters of female decorum women's business and had dragooned his elder sister to take on the duty of overseeing his daughter's come out. Her late aunt had made it plain she resented being dragged from her home in the shires to nursemaid a girl she barely knew. The woman had thus put little effort into tutoring her niece in dainty manners. At balls and parties her aunt would find a hidden spot somewhere and snooze with a bottle of sherry close by, leaving Emma to her own devices. At the time she had thought how wonderful it was to be allowed such freedom. A lot of the other girls had envied her, they'd said, because their own female relatives hovered at their shoulders, monitoring their every move.

And so Emma had been easy prey for a man like Simon Gresham. He had been courting her in secret for four months before finally persuading her that they must elope because her father would never accept him. He'd argued that his lack of prospects and good connections would put her father off and had refused to be swayed by her protestations that her papa wasn't a snob and only wanted her happiness. Later she'd realised Simon had been reluctant to approach Bernard and be thoroughly quizzed in case his hidden-away wife came to light. But she believed that Simon had loved her in his own way.

'Sir Paul is coming over,' Bella whispered excitedly, jerking Emma out of reflectiveness. 'Oh, do I look nice enough?' The girl brushed cake crumbs from her skirt with frantic fingers.

'You look lovely,' Emma replied truthfully. The blush in her young companion's cheeks gave her complexion a becoming glow.

'Would you care to stroll on the lawn, Miss Valance? It is quite warm in here, is it not?'

Sir Paul courteously extended a hand, and immediately Bella allowed him to draw her to her feet.

'Are you off outside?' Jack was all amiability as he materialised by the sofa with Dawn on his arm. 'We shall accompany you as Miss Sanders has kindly agreed to walk in the garden with me.'

'Will you come, too, Em?' Dawn asked, not wanting to leave her best friend on her own.

'Thank you, but I would rather stay here and enjoy another slice of delicious honey cake.' Emma had no intention of being a gooseberry. She gave Dawn a twinkling smile of encouragement, thinking how wonderful this afternoon would turn out to be if her friend met a bachelor she liked who was equally smitten with her.

Once the couples had moved off, Emma got up and went to the double doors, slipping just outside to the terrace to breathe in the spring air. The balmy atmosphere was filled with the scent of early blossom and bluebells and freshly mown grass and she sighed, feeling happier than she had in a long while. How easy it was to forget about her family's troubles while cocooned in the serenity that luxury provided. She watched as her friends descended the steps to some lawns interspersed with pathways. She chuckled softly, having noticed that Jack had kept behind his sister and her admirer, tracking them meticulously as Sir Paul weaved from pathway to pathway in an attempt to shake him off.

'This is a pleasant surprise, Miss Waverley.'

Emma whipped about at the sound of that familiar drawling baritone. Her full pink lips parted in astonishment before she recovered her composure and glanced to and fro to spot if they had an audience. There had been an ironic inflection in his tone and a thought struck her like a thunderbolt. '*Is* it a surprise, Mr Harley?' Too late, she remembered he wasn't a commoner at all. Neither did he look it in his outfit of black tailcoat, buff breeches and top boots gleaming like glass. She would have liked to put distance between them simply so her old blue gown didn't appear even shabbier next to his sartorial splendour.

'Actually it is.' His mouth slanted wryly in a way she was coming to recognise. 'I couldn't be sure you'd come along with Miss Sanders. I hoped you would.'

'Why? Why have you gone to the trouble to procure an invitation for us?' All her quiet enjoyment of a moment ago was lost. Her heart was beating furiously. 'Are you still *curious* about me?' she asked in a voice suffocated with indignation.

'Oh, yes, I'm curious about you, Miss Waverley, and your brother.'

Emma turned pale beneath the stare she could sense singeing the top of her head. So her father's suggestion that they throw caution to the wind with this man was indeed a dangerous one. 'There's no need to be curious about us, sir.' She proudly met his gaze. 'Most people find the Waverleys beneath their notice and that's how we like it. So please leave me alone and my father, too.' She attempted to slip past into the room, but he stopped her.

'And your brother? What of him?'

'My brother is where you can't reach him.' She again made to enter the salon.

'Is that right?' he said and smiled. 'Let's take a walk.' His voice was gentle, at odds with the uncompromising grip on her wrist. 'You can let me know what it is about me that you find so disturbing. I might be able to remedy it.'

'I've no need to go anywhere with you to tell you that you are insufferably overbearing and arrogant. How dare you humiliate me, or my friend, in this way! Miss Sanders believes her invitation genuine and even I, fool that I am, believed my welcome sincere.'

'Has anybody by word or look insulted you or your friend this afternoon?'

'No, but...'

'And neither will they,' he said. 'You are both most welcome here. Now, take a walk with me... please...' he added in a way that made it clear begging a favour was uncommon to him.

Their eyes clashed in contest. She knew he

was daring her to defy him again; some long seconds later she ceded, dragging her molten gold eyes away from his challenge. The tension in her limbs lessened. She was unwilling to make a scene and draw attention to herself and he knew that. When he placed her hand through the crook of his arm her fingers curled into a fist, but she went with him. As they descended the steps she realised she felt betrayed, not by Houndsmere—she doubted he would care about trampling on her feelings—but Mrs Sweet must have helped him engineer this ambush. The opportunity to meet new friends, the chance for Dawn to be introduced to a nice gentleman… it was just a fantasy. Perhaps Lance Harley enjoyed pulling strings and watching people dance to his tune. At first she'd been reluctant to come here, but, her loyalty to Dawn notwithstanding, the tantalising glimpse of social acceptance had lured her in, proving false her claim to embrace ostracism.

'Come…relax… I've nothing in mind to harm you,' he said as they stepped on to springy turf. 'You should feel flattered. I've annoyed my sister in my wish to speak to you and she can be quite the virago when roused. She is offended by my methods.'

'As am I,' Emma said through her teeth. 'Your

sister?' She suddenly glanced up at him, having put two and two together. 'Mrs Sweet is your sister?'

'She is…'

'Is she also an actress?' Emma enquired sourly. 'I have not once suspected that I'm here under sufferance this afternoon.'

'You're not… I am,' he said drily. 'I shouldn't be at all surprised to have her chase after us in a moment to rescue you from my dastardly clutches and throw me out.'

'Well, why get involved in the plot in the first place if now she regrets it?' Emma reasoned.

'Don't blame Ruth. I asked her to issue the invitation and she did so, believing Miss Sanders and her friend to be somewhat different people.'

'Different? In what way?'

'Older…plainer…'

'Is that how you described me?' Emma gasped. He'd made her sound as though she were ugly and approaching her dotage.

'I suppose I might have played down your charms a little bit,' he said, his voice gruff with amusement. So Emma Waverley was sensitive about her age and looks. She'd no need to be where he was concerned. She was easily the most naturally beautiful woman he'd ever clapped eyes on. Even here on a day out—the first in a long time for her, he guessed—she'd not embellished her looks with powder or rouge. Neither did she need to. Her black hair looked thick and satiny, making him long to unpin the simple chignon at her nape to run his fingers through it. Her eyes, tawny and watchful as a woodland creature's, made her perfect skin look peachier. As for the slender curves beneath the modest dress she wore… He dragged his mind away from dwelling on her body as his loins reacted to it.

'Now Ruth's met you and seen how young and beautiful you are, she rightly suspects I've misled her on purpose.'

So he thought her young and beautiful. Though he'd spoken rather roughly, his words sang in her head…a siren call of disaster. Simon had praised her looks. He'd banked on playing to her vanity and it had worked. She was too wise now to fall for that again.

'I think I'd better trust your sister than you, sir. She obviously knows you of old.'

'So she just told me,' he admitted ruefully, leading her towards a tall yew hedge. 'Just over there is a seat where we can talk without fear of disturbance.'

'There is no need to hide. I have nothing to add to what I've already said.' She peered into the distance for a sight of Dawn, but the little party had disappeared from view behind some apple trees. 'When my friend returns from her walk I know she will want to leave as much as I do.'

'Perhaps not, if she enjoys Jack Valance's company more than you like mine.'

'Mr Valance is your friend?' Emma made a hopeless gesture. She had rather liked Jack Valance, too, but feared he was also privy to this conspiracy. Bella had said her brother never usually attended afternoon tea parties. Neither did the Earl of Houndsmere, Emma imagined. Little wonder he believed she should be flattered by his attention! She certainly hoped that Dawn wouldn't like Valance too much and be disappointed when he made no attempt to contact her again. 'Did you also arrange for a member of Dawn's future stepfamily to come and occupy her in case your friend didn't turn up?'

'I'm innocent of meddling in anybody's stepfamily. I have strife enough dealing with my own.'

That sour remark surely referred to his search for Augusta. Emma's skin prickled in alarm. He was angry with his stepsister. How much angrier would he be with Robin when he found out the girl was increasing? Emma removed her hand from his arm and took a step away from him. Her legs were trembling, she realised, as the lawn wobbled beneath her feet. She was terrified she'd say something wrong and betray her twin to this man who could be his ultimate downfall...hers, too. Yet she knew what Robin was doing was foolish and wrong. He couldn't hope to keep it all secret. If the Earl didn't catch up with them first, how long would it be before Augusta's disgust at living in a slum killed her feelings for Robin? She'd bolt back to the high life, taking her excuses with her...her baby, too, if the expected child wasn't a figment of Robin's imagination. Augusta would beg her powerful stepbrother to sort things out for her and he would, to protect his family's illustrious name. Where then would Robin end up? Prison? The gallows? Would he bolt back to France to escape Houndsmere's revenge? So grim and all-consuming were Emma's thoughts that she jumped at the sound of his voice when he spoke.

'We have something in common, you and I, Emma Waverley.'

A bitter laugh scraped her throat. 'Is that so? I can't imagine what it is. I should like to go back now, sir.'

'We are alike in that we are burdened with relations who are a constant trouble to us.'

Emma strove to keep her expression neutral. 'I'm sorry to hear you have such problems. I should like to return now, sir,' she repeated firmly.

'And I'm sorry to hear that your brother is reduced to working as a coalman.'

A dousing in icy water would have come as less of a shock. Once she remembered to breathe she wanted to quickly dismiss his remark with a laugh and a lie, but nothing came. The ghastly imaginings she'd just had of the consequences of Robin's love for Augusta seemed horribly real and imminent. Had the girl run home already, telling tales and blaming her coalman for everything?

Emma was riveted to the spot by a pair of mesmerising eyes that engulfed her and made her head spin. He was patiently waiting for her to say he must be mistaken so he could present more proof that indeed he wasn't. She'd no sophistication for this, Emma inwardly wailed. What was she to do now? She forced herself to think calmly and a part of her mind registered the empty seconds ticking by. She didn't think he'd had Robin apprehended...yet. Perhaps he hadn't managed to locate his quarry. He wouldn't have bothered with this farce here today if he had.

Finally, he took pity on her and broke the awful silence with, 'So you knew about his employment at Milligan's. What does your father think of it all?'

She *chose* to remain quiet now, in defiance of

his penetrating blue stare and the latent power that she knew he could unleash at any time. She wouldn't utter a word that might assist him in bringing them down. Her eyes, bright and hard as precious stones, called his bluff, demanding he do his worst or leave them alone.

A moment that seemed suspended in time passed by in which she prayed he would be lenient. His smile strengthened. He turned and strolled on without her, taking the path that led out of sight.

Emma could feel tears of frustration in her eyes, but she furiously dashed them away with the back of a hand. She moved on slowly at first, then with rapid steps. He'd won. Yet more galling was that he knew she'd follow him without a single word of persuasion being necessary.

Chapter Nine

Emma turned the corner to find herself in a trellised arbour, heavy with honeysuckle just breaking into leaf. She took little notice of the pleasant vista. The racing of her heart had left her feeling light-headed, but she was aware of him watching her approach. He might have gained a small victory, but he hadn't humbled her and she wouldn't be toyed with as a cat plays with a mouse. Let Lance Harley make his strike or set her and her family free.

He had seated himself on the bench and unfolded two muscular arms along its iron back. He didn't stand at her approach, but patted the vacant place beside him. She didn't think he intended to insult her, rather to let her know he wanted no formality between them. Well, she did!

She traversed the granite flags towards the

bench, but stayed on her feet, at a distance. 'What are you intending to do?' Despite the maze of emotions miring her intelligence, she'd retained enough to know to demand answers rather than give them.

When he remained silent, gazing into the distance, she insisted, 'Will you tell me, my lord?' It was the first time she'd called him that and, from the quizzical look he slanted at her, guessed it hadn't pleased him.

He stretched for her hand then pulled her closer to him. His bowed head was just a little way from her abdomen, his glossy chestnut hair begging one of her palms to cup it.

Abruptly, she snatched her fingers from his and sat down beside him.

'Where did you meet Simon Gresham?'

'What?' She swivelled to stare at his lean profile. 'Of what importance is that now?' she cried and made to jump up again, but he caught at her arm, drawing her back.

'Of some importance, I'd say, as your life was blighted from that day. Your father and brother also paid the price of Gresham coming into your life.'

She couldn't deny any of that. And if he wanted to know, why not tell him? Rather do that than be bombarded with questions about her brother. 'We met in Hyde Park,' she informed stiffly. 'I was walking with my aunt. Her hat blew off in the breeze and I dashed after it and tripped over. Simon was riding past and stopped to pick me up from the grass.'

'Ever the gentleman…'

'Did you know him?' Emma wondered why he sounded so contemptuous about Simon.

He grunted a negative. 'Nor his brother. What hold has he over you?'

'I've already told you about that.'

'I remember you told me your father owes him money. What else?'

Emma felt heat rising in her throat and turned away from him. 'Why must there be something else?'

'You're wary of him.'

'No more than I am of…' Her small teeth sank into her lower lip and she left the rest unsaid.

'You've no need to fear me. I meant what I said. I won't force you to do anything you don't want to do. You believe me insincere…a selfish rake with wicked motives and coercion on his mind.' He laughed low in his throat as she blushed and averted her face. But he mocked himself, not her. Just that morning he would have said his description wasn't a million miles away from the truth. He'd got his own way. He'd trapped her alone to offer his protection in return for her becoming his mistress. And now he wasn't sure whether his conscience was bothering him. She wasn't like other women he'd approached, playing coy to heighten his interest and strike for themselves a sweeter deal.

Before he made his move he'd wanted to discover if the obsession he had with her was as real as it seemed. It was… His loins pulsated uncomfortably from just being this close to her, so he'd got some paltry satisfaction out of his manoeuvres. He smoothed his palms on the cold iron of the bench top, cooling the urge to touch her, kiss her, start the seduction that he'd come here for. In his arrogance he'd never before imagined a woman of straitened circumstances might not take what he offered. Usually, once the chase was done and they were settled in one of his houses they were keen to show him just how grateful they were for his favour. He was generous to his lovers and they were envied and admired for the riches and status he gave them. Then when it was over he made sure they were nicely pensioned off. But Emma Waverley wouldn't know any of that. Neither, he guessed, would she care to. Reports of his largesse wouldn't impress her. She'd withdrawn from the fringes of society long ago, still naive despite her ordeal. Her deceitful swain hadn't been a practised womaniser and he'd taught Emma Waverley nothing of how the *beau monde* played its games.

Lance knew he could teach her…he could start right now with a kiss…and finish with… He swore beneath his breath, blocking out the rest of that train of thought. He pushed to his feet and prowled to the pathway. 'Why haven't you told your father Gresham's harassing you?' he asked over a shoulder.

'There's no reason for him to know. I can deal with that man on my own.' A tremor in her voice belied her boast.

'Not as well as I can. Does Gresham suspect your brother is alive and close by?'

'No!' Emma sprang up. 'He has no idea of it and it must stay that way.' That unguarded remark had obviated any further denials on Robin's existence. 'Joshua would have an even greater hold over us if he did know.'

He turned back to face her. 'The matter can't be left as it is to fester. It will only get worse for you all, Emma.'

'I know…' The gentleness in his voice as he'd spoken her name was her undoing. A small sob broke in her throat and she shielded her distress with her slender fingers. He was approaching to comfort her. But she knew they mustn't touch… not in an intimate way. She was too conscious of him…too aware of every single thing about him from the way strands of his long hair curled over his collar to the unyielding strength in the dark fingers he sometimes fastened on her. Swallowing her tears, she returned hastily to perch on the edge of the bench.

Lance walked towards her, stopped close by, muscular thighs, narrow hips, in her line of vision. She wanted to escape, but knew she'd graze herself against him in standing up. She could feel his warmth, sense fragrant tobacco on the idle hand inches from her face. A sparrow bobbing on a gnarled branch of honeysuckle close by suddenly became fascinating to her.

'So, all in all, you're in a mess and need outside assistance. But you consider Joshua Gresham to be a safer bet than me, is that it?' he suggested drily.

'I never gamble,' she said, making him mutter something she guessed to be sarcastic.

'I do…everybody succumbs to vice, Emma.'

'Especially women like me, you mean, who often have little option in the matter.'

'There are worse things for a woman to endure than being generously taken care of. Which leads me to ask, what's Gresham offered you?'

Her gasp of outrage preceded, 'I find your impertinence astonishing. And I won't answer another one of your questions when you have rudely ignored the only one I have asked you.'

'That's something you hold the answer to. What am I intending to do? Whatever it is you want me to do, my dear. I'll engage lawyers to represent your brother in court, pay your father's debts and provide anything else you can think of that you desire.'

Emma did think. Her mind pored over all he'd said and she concluded with a surge of joyous relief that he couldn't possibly yet know about Robin and Augusta. If he did he'd promise to shoot her brother dead, not provide him with an expensive attorney. There was still time to warn Robin that he'd been unearthed and must get away immediately. But she'd tread carefully. She mustn't underestimate Lance Harley for a second.

'I desire none of that,' she said quietly.

'Why not?'

'It isn't necessary.'

'What is necessary, Emma?' He moved one of those long fingers close to her face, trailing it down the side of her warm cheek.

Emma's eyelids fell beneath that first caress, so deceitfully sweet. She blinked, flicked her face aside so his finger fell away from her. 'It's necessary that you promise never to tell our secrets. It's necessary that you swear to leave me and my family alone to make what we can of a bad situation in our own way.'

'And what does such benevolence get me, apart from a place in heaven?'

'My sincere thanks and my good opinion.'

'I think you know I was hoping for more besides,' he said wryly. 'So why would I not demand it?'

'Common decency, sir,' she said huskily. 'Something I still credit you with and know Joshua Gresham has none of.'

He was quiet and still for some minutes, as was she, and just as Emma felt she couldn't bear the mounting tension a second longer he spoke.

'I'll not cede for compliments any more than I imagine you will. So it's time for plain speaking. I want you as my mistress. In return for your agreement to that arrangement I'll sort out the considerable predicament your family is in. I also want to know what has taken place in the past between you and Joshua Gresham in your attempt to keep him at bay.'

'Indeed, it is time for plain speaking, sir,' Emma whispered, wondering why she felt wounded hearing him quantify his lust. She had guessed for some time that he would bargain with her like this. She had seen desire in his eyes when he'd accompanied her indoors after rescuing her from the footpads and again when he'd returned to ask after her well-being. He had more finesse, more generosity, in his approach than Joshua. But their aim was the same: to have her in a bed they'd paid for.

'I have no intention of becoming your harlot any more than I have of becoming Mr Gresham's. And that is all I will ever say on this subject. Please do not insult me again by bringing it up.' She felt a fool for having believed even for a second that his single act of gallantry was complimentary, or might make him treat her with respect for ever.

'Offering you anything you want is an insult?'

'Yes!' she stormed. 'I know you don't understand. How could you? You believe it is your prerogative to ride roughshod over others' feelings, careless of hurt and humiliation caused.' Emma stood up, carefully, steadying herself against the bench. Her eyes were lifted to meet his and she floundered beneath that cool blue gaze, feeling stupidly that she might plead with him to be kind. She swallowed the lump in her throat and slipped past. Soon, she was composed once more and when she judged the space between them great enough she turned back. He was waiting, his expression impassive—he wasn't going to beg her pardon for upsetting her. What he'd proposed would make such a difference to all their lives that she *had* almost been tempted to accept. If her father knew of what was at stake, would he choose her wishes over his son's? Robin had always been her father's favourite. No matter what scrapes his son got into he would always make excuses for him. But she mustn't contemplate her father pressing her to take the Earl's sordid offer. Her twin would deliver her himself into Houndsmere's clutches if he thought that way lay his freedom. Robin would believe her selfish for refusing. Was she being selfish? Was she putting too high a price on her pride when one single word from her now would melt away all their ills?

'I think it best that we both forget about what happened between us this afternoon and no hard feelings. I regret if at any time I unintentionally led you to believe my answer would be different.' She strove to sound sophisticated. 'We inhabit different worlds and have different codes of conduct. And now, it is time to go back and thank your sister for her hospitality before I leave.'

'When you've had time to think about this logically and wish to find me you can send word to Grosvenor Square.' He thrust his hands in his pockets while prowling along the path. 'It would be as well to act soon while you're still in a position to dictate terms.'

So much for her attempt at conciliation and diplomacy! She took a few paces in his direction to ensure he heard every low, vibrant word she said. 'I will never need to know where to find you,' she vowed, eyes sparking angrily. 'It is my greatest wish that I never have to see or speak to you ever again, my lord.'

'Well…if you really mean that then it is time for a final goodbye. I agree…let's have no hard feelings and shake on it.'

As though he'd grown bored of it all he strode towards her, then extended a hand. From his sudden energy she imagined he'd remembered somewhere more interesting to be and was keen to get to it. Emma stretched out her fingers, but they were ignored as his angled upwards and were joined by his other hand in cupping her face.

'Sometimes it's nicer parting company the Continental way. I believe the French kiss *au revoir…*'

Before she could avoid him he'd lowered his head to slide his lips over the cheek she'd hastily presented. She tasted salty from the tears she'd tried to hide from him and lavender scent wafted from her soft warm skin. With thumb and forefinger he turned her sharp little chin so her mouth was available and lightly touched together their lips.

Emma had immediately thrust her hands between them when he took hold of her, but his delicate salute wasn't painful or disgusting. When Joshua Gresham had forced himself on her he'd rammed his slobbering mouth against hers with such force he'd made her lip bleed.

Lance continued lulling her with a sweet kiss until he sensed a lessening of the tension in her fists jammed against his chest. His mouth swayed against hers with just enough pressure to part her lips and allow his tongue tip to penetrate further, tasting their silky linings.

From the moment he had spoken to her on the terrace, Emma had felt as though a coiled spring was tightening within that might snap and make her do something unwise. It *had* snapped and she *was* doing something unwise. But she wasn't fighting him, as she'd imagined she would. Quite the reverse. *It's just clever seduction on his part*, was the alarm call running amok in her feverish mind, but nevertheless she couldn't stop feeling entranced by the cool movement of his skin on hers. She was still in control, she told herself, even as her back arched, pressing her breasts to chafe on his chest. She could stop this at any time…any time she wanted she could push him away. And he would release her; he wasn't Joshua Gresham…he'd told her he wouldn't force her to do anything, and she believed him. He had pride, too…far too much to persist in kissing an unwilling woman.

Her reason still occupied a corner of her mind even as a release of breath sighed from her, leaving her quite enervated. She pushed her hips forward, needing his strength as her limbs weakened. But it was more of the sweet honeyed pleasure he was bestowing that she really craved. She'd not expected this. Simon had not kissed her with such lazy tenderness, yet she hadn't minded his rougher loving. He started to unseal their lips, but she followed his mouth, tempting him back with a light touch and this time he wasn't so restrained in his wooing. He manoeuvred her jaw, using rhythmically stroking fingers so her mouth was open and he could erotically deepen the kiss, plunging his tongue to tease hers. He eased her forward between his spaced feet so her slender hips were snug against the apex of his thighs. Leisurely, he undid her bodice buttons, so slowly that she could have brought it to a halt at any time. He inserted a finger beneath her chemise, running the back of it with tantalising softness against the swell of a breast, nudging a hardening nipple with circular strokes until she whimpered and squirmed against him. One of his hands moved to her buttocks, locking her against the rigid muscle in his groin.

A sound of laughter and muted conversation finally reached Emma through the blood thumping in her ears. Her lashes flicked up and met a narrowed blue gaze. He was watching her… scientifically…as though gauging her reaction to his taming game. With a little gasp, she pushed at him, mortified to have passed his test and failed her own. She took two stumbling backward steps, then swung away, hurrying towards the path.

'It's your friend and Jack Valance...they're still a distance away,' he soothed, reaching for her again.

She slapped away his hand, giving him a warning glare. He wouldn't make a fool of her twice, she impressed on herself. He thought he'd shown her what he could do...if he wanted to. Oh, it had been a clever lesson, but she imagined he knew how to act the beast as well...if he wanted to. She swung away from him, intending to walk back alone. But in a couple of long strides he'd caught up with her, slipping her hand on to his arm as he had earlier when in the role of gentleman instead of philanderer.

She knew it was better they appeared to have been strolling harmoniously rather than sneak out one by one. She let her fingers hover on his sleeve and took a peek from beneath her lashes at him. From the thrust of his mouth she saw he was frustrated by the interruption, but with a cool insouciance she could only admire he led her from the arbour into view.

Jack Valance still had Dawn on his arm. He

raised a hand and immediately started towards them to introduce his companion to the Earl.

'Miss Sanders has kindly agreed to take a drive with me in Hyde Park tomorrow.' He glanced at his friend, then at Emma. 'Perhaps Miss Waverley would like to come, too.'

'Thank you, but I shall be occupied…my father has been unwell.'

Emma knew that Dawn was looking at her, trying to guess what had gone on to make her immediately decline such a nice offer. The Earl of Houndsmere had seemed on the point of agreeing to an outing for them all.

Meeting their friends had given Emma an opportunity to slip away from his side. Dawn let go of Jack's arm and joined her in walking back to the house ahead of the gentlemen.

'Are you ready to leave now?' Emma asked quietly.

'Of course…if you are. I told Papa I would not be back late in any case,' Dawn said. She had immediately sensed her friend's tension even though Emma had linked arms with her in a casual way.

'You seem a little overset. Has the Earl said something horrible to you?' Dawn asked sotto voce.

'No…he is just a little…'

'Intimidating?' Dawn supplied.

'Yes…though he'd say otherwise,' Emma added ironically.

'Gorgeous, too, though, isn't he?' Dawn giggled.

'He'd agree with you on that,' Emma murmured and urged Dawn to a quicker march.

'I've a favour to ask,' Jack hissed when the ladies were out of earshot.

'You can borrow the landau,' Lance said wryly, knowing his friend didn't own a decent carriage to take a lady out in.

Jack gave his friend's arm an appreciative thump. He followed it with a speculative look. 'So…how well do you know Miss Waverley?'

'Not as well as I'd like to,' Lance said and strolled off to say hello to Bella and her beau, who were dawdling some way behind them all.

Out of earshot of Jack he cursed himself for handling it wrong. There was much he could have said, but hadn't. He wasn't sure why he hadn't other than to protect his pride taking a battering if still she rejected him after he bared his soul. And now it was too late to tell her he wanted to protect her and her family not just in return for her agreeing to lay with him, but because when he was with her he felt tenderness as well as desire. He arrowed a look over a shoulder just as she did…and quickly whipped her head around.

He smiled to himself. He was on her mind just as much as she was on his. And he wasn't so conceited that he thought he could masterfully seduce a woman who really didn't want to be seduced by him. So that was a start…

Chapter Ten

'You were gone a long time, Emma.' Mr Waverley greeted his daughter with a complaint rather than enquiring whether she'd had a nice time at Mrs Sweet's. 'Joshua Gresham called while you were out and said he was sorry to miss you.'

'Well, I'm glad I missed him.' Emma made sure to mutter that beneath her breath while loosening her bonnet strings. She never allowed her father to know too much about her ever-increasing antipathy towards Joshua in case he quizzed her over the reason for it.

As her papa approached, Emma noticed that his limp seemed worse and his cheeks flushed. She immediately dropped her gloves and bonnet on to the console table and took his arm, steering him towards the parlour. 'Come, you must sit down and rest your leg.' She guessed he'd been pacing for some time in the hallway, waiting for her to return.

'I want to rest, but I cannot!' He whirled a nervous hand. 'Since you told me this girl Augusta wants to marry my son I'm in a tizz. I can think of nought else. I don't know whether to be happy or sad to know my boy is involved with Houndsmere's stepsister.' He wriggled free of his daughter's hold. 'Oh, what's to be done? He cannot remain a coalman; he is a gentleman's son. You must take me to him, Emma, so I can talk to him myself and counsel him.'

'You mustn't go there, Papa. Robin will be angry. You are tired. Come and sit down.' She again took his elbow, worried by the change in him. When she'd left the house he had seemed preoccupied, but well enough. He'd been in his study, writing paper in front of him, adding to his list of ideas to raise funds to help Robin. Something had started him fretting and she imagined it had been Joshua's visit. The swine had probably again threatened to call in his loan, just for the fun of it.

'I should speak to this Augusta,' Bernard insisted querulously. 'She might be able to persuade her stepbrother to be our saviour. Houndsmere would surely assist in settling things to our mutual satisfaction. He has a crucial reason to do so and would bear the cost of it all to spare the girl's reputation. He'll not have a coalman as a brother-in-law.' Having rattled that off, Bernard took a breath and turned to his daughter. 'The Earl has shown you nought but consideration so can't be such a bad chap, can he?'

Emma couldn't give an answer. Sometimes when she thought of Lance Harley she believed she hated him, but after what had passed between them this afternoon she knew that was far from the truth. And so was her father's belief that the Earl had only noble intentions towards her.

'What did Joshua want, Papa? Has he said something to upset you this afternoon?' She changed the subject to distract her father from returning to his need to visit Robin.

'It was the other way around, my dear.' Her query had brightened up Bernard, making him chortle, 'I was doing the upsetting for a change.' He allowed his daughter to ease him into a chair in the parlour, patting her hand as she sank to the rug to sit beside him. 'I thought Gresham might have come to talk business although he was limping almost as badly as I. He said he twisted his ankle on the kerb and didn't seem to like my commiseration. Anyway, he was more interested in finding out where you were this afternoon.' Bernard grimaced, flexing his knee as the leg ulcer pained him. 'I swear if that fellow were not married he would propose to you again, he speaks of you so often.'

Emma gave her father a sharp look. 'I'm glad

he is married, then, for I dislike him. He is a deceitful individual. I haven't forgotten how just after the duel he pretended to be sympathetic to us to gain our trust. He seemed to change into a Janus after I refused to marry him. He is out for himself, Papa.'

'He has certainly tricked me into borrowing more from him than I ever intended to,' her father admitted. 'But tell me if he has said something bad to you and I will go after him. He might have lost his brother, but *you* were the innocent in it all. And I'll remind him of it!'

'No…it is nothing…just his attitude. There is no need to say anything to him, Papa,' Emma quickly interjected. She didn't want her father ever to know how disgustingly Joshua Gresham had behaved towards her. She feared what her father might do if he did find out. And he was too old and too frail to challenge a man almost half his years.

'Well, we both have no fondness for him, but I can't deny it might solve our problems if you *did* have a well-to-do husband, Emma.' Bernard stroked his daughter's glossy dark hair. 'Don't fret about him. His nose was out of joint because he'd spied you entering a mansion in Belgravia.' Bernard chuckled. 'He tried to make out he'd little interest in it, but I know he was ferreting for information. He was incensed to think we are favoured with such acquaintances when his wife has never received an invitation from a top hostess.' He tutted. 'In the end I told Joshua your friend was the chosen one just so he'd go away and leave me in peace. He seemed satisfied thinking Mrs Booth was the means of Dawn's new popularity.'

Her father's final comment held no truth, but Emma wasn't about to enlighten him. 'Let me see that hand, Papa.' While her father had been gesturing she had noticed blood on his fingers from rubbing his sore leg.

'Blast!' Bernard muttered, seeing the stains. 'I must have knocked the wound. Little wonder it's paining me so.'

Emma put the back of a hand to her father's brow. He was flushed as much from a fever as his agitation. A fluttering of anxiety started up in her chest. Quickly, she inspected the place below his breeched knee, noticing that the dark material was tight over the swelling and damp to the touch. She scrambled to her feet. 'I'll go straight away and fetch the doctor.'

'There's no need,' her father barked. Then admitted, shame-faced, 'I have nothing to pay him with.' He bitterly regretted having used his last sovereign gambling on the Faro pot earlier in the week. 'I have an appointment at the bank in the morning and am quite confident the nice chap at Coutts will forward me something. I can offer collateral,' he added reassuringly.

'What collateral, Papa?' Emma believed all their assets had been pledged by now.

'They can have the deeds to this house…'

'But Joshua told me he has them.'

'He had no right saying that to you!' Bernard struggled up from his chair. 'When next he comes make sure you stay out of his way upstairs. I will not have him discuss my affairs with my daughter.'

Emma attempted to make him sit down again, but he fidgeted free. 'I am a useless fellow,' he cried self-pityingly. 'I cannot do a thing right! Every gaming table is against me.'

'You *must* sit down, Papa. Your leg is bleeding.' Quite firmly, Emma took hold of his arm and forced him into the chair. 'You should let a doctor attend you. I still have Mama's locket. It is of some value…'

'No! You will not sell it!' Bernard again made to rise, but this time his daughter had no need to restrain him. He fell back with a groan against the tapestry upholstery as his leg buckled under him.

'I can pawn it, Papa, and then get it back again when our fortunes improve…' Her voice tailed off. When *would* that be? Some time…never…? Oh, there were times when she felt exasperated with her father almost as much as she did with Robin. How could he have got himself into such a parlous financial state? 'A physician must examine your ulcer, Papa. Tomorrow, I will pawn the locket in Cheapside.'

Her father took her hand and squeezed weakly. 'We'll see about that. Perhaps tomorrow I might be on the mend. For now, a bathing with salt water might do the trick and I can attend to that myself. It is as good as any cure these charlatans will offer.' He sighed, resting his head back against the cushions. 'I'll have an early supper… some bread and mutton will suffice, then off to bed for me. I do feel tired.'

'I'll ask Mrs O'Reilly to prepare it before she goes home.' Their servant lived out and was usually gone by six o'clock in the evening, leaving their meal prepared on the cooking range.

'I have spoken to Mrs O'Reilly. She will come in just thrice a week in future.'

'But, how will we do without her when I cannot…?' Emma didn't finish what she'd been about to say regarding her lack of housekeeping skills. She'd have to learn to cook and clean, she bluntly told herself. Making a stew or wielding a broom and duster a few times a week wouldn't hurt her. Needs must…and she'd rather they put Cathleen off than found they were unable to pay her. Their maid had other clients she went to and hopefully she'd be able to make up her lost wages doing extra work elsewhere.

'I have been thinking, Papa, that I can find employment—'

'No!' he immediately interrupted. 'You are a gentleman's daughter and will not!'

They'd had this conversation before, just after Joshua Gresham had propositioned her and it had become obvious how dire was her father's financial state. Her father had jumped down her throat when she'd mentioned finding a suitable position, insisting that he could soon bring everything right. But nothing was right. Just as her father had insisted that his son was too good to be a coalman, he thought his daughter was above being a governess, or a wealthy woman's companion. But she wasn't. And Emma would sooner have her self-respect and a job than be a rich man's toy for a short while until he grew bored of her and threw her to the wolves.

Once her father had eaten his supper, Emma helped him upstairs. While he undressed himself she went to the kitchen and filled a basin with warm water, stirring in a generous amount of salt to dissolve before returning to his chamber with it. Unusually he allowed her to nurse him rather than insist on bathing it himself.

The wound was inflamed and obviously infected, but Emma managed to keep from him how greatly the sight of it distressed her as she gently wiped away the mess. She put on a fresh bandage and helped her father into bed. Then when he seemed settled she drew the curtains against the early evening light. 'Goodnight, Papa. Sleep well,' she whispered on closing the door.

She disposed of the dirty water and went to sit in the parlour, but she couldn't concentrate on reading, or attending to the linens in the mending box. Her mind was jumbled with worries about her father's health and Robin's fate. She got to her feet and paced to and fro, hoping to banish from her head the memory of somebody else. He could wreak more havoc on her peace of mind than her selfish twin or her poor foolish papa put together. Lance Harley might even now have detectives looking for his stepsister and, in truth, she couldn't blame him for wanting to find the girl to protect her. But when he found Augusta he'd find Robin, too. Then all hell would break loose, not the civilised alliance that her father was hoping for between their families.

Even if she acquiesced to his terms and sent word to him at Grosvenor Square, it might not be enough to save any of them from his wrath. How generous to her would he be on finding out what Robin had been up to with his stepsister? How sweet would be his kisses then?

Emma quit her pacing and went to the window, peeking round an edge of curtain into darkness. Her mind was made up. She didn't want to leave her father tonight, of all nights, when he had a fever. He might wake and need her if his malaise worsened. But she knew she must warn her twin that Houndsmere was on to him and the net was closing fast. She'd also tell her brother that their father was ill. With any luck the news might stir in Robin some filial loyalty. Instead of being a burden on their father, he might realise he must sort things out for himself. Neither would she be a burden on her father. Whatever he said to the contrary it was high time she drew an income from somewhere to pay for her keep. There was a ladies' employment agency that advertised in the *Gazette*. She would take a look in the paper tomorrow and note the address.

She went upstairs and listened at the door of her father's chamber, straining her ears. There was not the slightest sound to hint at him being awake, or in pain. Dusk had fallen now and she knew she must leave at once or not at all. She'd no intention of being from home as long as she had been last time and wanted to return before midnight. She speedily went downstairs and taking her cloak from the peg left the house by the side door. Pulling the hood forward about her face she set off. When a good distance from Primrose Square and any neighbours' prying eyes she hailed a cab.

'You be wasting your time, m'dear. Young feller ain't in up there.'

Emma had been ready to scoot up the stairs, but didn't make it past the first creaking tread. With a startled gasp, she swung about to see a withered face with crafty eyes behind the glow of a candle. The crone's gap-toothed simper did nothing to soothe Emma's frayed nerves. 'Oh... are you sure he is out?' she stammered. It hadn't occurred to her that making this risky trip again might be a squandered effort. 'Will he be back soon?'

'I'm sure he *won't* be back.' The woman snorted and straightened her mobcap. 'I evicted him. Ain't paid me no rent in weeks, the villain.'

'To whom are you referring?' It was a vain hope, but a possibility that the landlady had another lodger owing her rent. Emma recalled that there were several rooms just along the landing from Robin's.

'I'm meaning the coalman. I spotted you with him once before, m'dear. Didn't make meself known on that occasion, as you was embracing him on the landing,' the landlady added slyly.

Emma's spirits plummeted. If her brother had left here, how on earth would she quickly find him again to warn him that Houndsmere was on to him? 'Do you know where he has gone?'

'No, I don't! To hell for all I care,' the woman said nastily. 'So who's Charlie Perkins to you?' She thrust forward the candle so it illuminated the visitor's face.

The strong flame hurt Emma's eyes, making her turn her head aside. It had taken her a second to remember her brother used an alias. She thanked the lord she'd not mentioned his *real* name, or her relationship to Robin. The harridan might expect a relative to pay her lodger's debt and Emma had only enough in her purse for her ride home. She stepped quickly towards the exit with a nod and a murmured farewell.

The landlady wasn't to be put off. She squeezed alongside Emma in the narrow corridor and eyed the slender brunette up and down. 'You're his fiancée, I reckon. The blonde's too young for him, though she says she's his wife. I told 'em I run a respectable place here so he bought her a brass ring to wear. But it don't fool me.' She patted Emma's arm consolingly. 'He'll tire of her and come back to you, I expect.'

'What?' Emma breathed in confusion.

'That girl he's been living with. No better than she should be, her. But the swell wot come looking for Charlie didn't mention her. I didn't neither, 'cos I've got me reputation to think of.'

'Swell?' Emma had come to an abrupt halt. Had Houndsmere already caught up with her brother and Augusta, too?

The woman smirked. 'Upper crust and wot a looker. Might have been Charlie's brother…dark-haired and handsome. But handsome is as hand-some does, that's what me mother used to say.'

'Did he ask for Charlie?'

'Called him Mr Perkins. I asked for *his* name, but he wouldn't say.' The landlady hadn't in-sisted on knowing in case she upset him and he pocketed the coins jingling in his palm.

From the woman's cocked head and inquisi-tive slits of eyes Emma guessed she was pre-paring to fire more questions at her. 'Thank you for your assistance…good evening.' She hastened from the shadowy hallway into dark-ness. It hadn't occurred to her that Lance Harley and her brother looked alike, but on reflection, she supposed they did. The Earl was taller and broader than her twin. But Robin had been a fine figure of a man in his heyday when well groomed and well fed.

The awful realisation that Harley was not only hot on her brother's trail, but knew about his alias, too, made her speed up along the cobbles and renew her search for a ride home. Robin's employer would know him as Charlie Perkins. The Earl had obviously been to Milligan's to make his enquiries, then easily put two and two together about who Charlie might really be. Thankfully, it seemed he could still be in ignorance of his stepsister's whereabouts.

Her preoccupation was rudely curtailed as a woman swayed past, drunkenly bashing into her. Emma politely said, 'Excuse me,' but got only curses in return.

Her Good Samaritan wouldn't be about tonight to rescue her if she got into a scrape with belligerent locals, she warned herself. Well, not unless he was visiting his *chère amie*. She allowed herself to think of that faceless mistress. Did she look like her? What would become of her? Did Houndsmere plan to discard her? Or had he the wealth and stamina to keep a harem at various addresses? She felt a dart of pain beneath her ribs at the thought of sharing him with others. But as she never *would* submit there was no need to give it another moment's thought, she chided herself.

A clop of hooves made her jerk up her head. She waved at the squat silhouette of an approaching hackney, sighing in relief as it slowed down. Having clambered aboard she gave the jarvey directions to drop her at the top of her road. She settled back, closing her eyes, realising with a sinking heart that tomorrow she would need to return to this eastern quarter to pawn her locket. And do it she must, though it broke her heart, because she feared that salt water and a good night's sleep wouldn't cure her poor papa's ills. He must be examined by a doctor. Her father would insist on doing business with a pawn-broker himself. But Emma couldn't allow that to happen. The locket was hers and the money from it must be used sensibly, not staked at the nearest gaming table in the futile hope of dou-bling its value.

She glanced out into the menacing blackness. She felt apprehensive in this area. But it would seem so much better during daylight. So much less dangerous than when only the gleam of a misshapen moon lit the snarled streets.

Emma wasn't convinced it was the best she could do and she wouldn't be stampeded into accepting the paltry amount she had just been offered for her locket. She closed the door of the pawnbroker's and set off to look for another.

The necklace was heavy and of good quality gold, and it was the most precious thing she'd ever possessed. Her father had given it to her as a birthday gift on the year she made her come out. She had worn it every day since, beneath her bodice, loving the feel of the warm metal laying against her skin. Her mother would have felt the very same sensation against her breast and that gave Emma a closeness to the woman she'd never known. Nestling within the locket had been a miniature of her mother and father, painted to mark their wedding. She had carefully removed those precious portraits and stowed them away before coming to Cheapside. Sarah Waverley had had Spanish blood and Emma's father had always said that his daughter had inherited her dark-haired beauty from his beloved wife. Though not conceited, Emma knew it was true: she saw her mother's likeness every time she looked in a mirror.

Spotting another set of brass balls set high on a wall, she crossed the road towards that shop, wanting to get this business over with and return home to her father. He had still been asleep when she slipped into the house last night and she had gone to bed herself thankful that nothing had happened in her absence. But he had been up early that morning, flushed and complaining of a headache. Emma had again bathed his leg, worried that the wound showed no improvement. If she'd told him she was going to pawn the locket it would have upset him, so she'd said she was off to post a note to thank Mrs Sweet for her hospitality. She had done that. But her main reason for leaving him on his own had been to raise some cash.

Emma slowed down by the second premises and peered in the window. She could see little beyond the jumble of clocks and assorted gold and silver wares piled up. So in she went. At once she regretted having done so. This fellow looked shiftier than the other one who had been straightforward, if curt.

'What have we here, then, miss?' Solomon Pope purred.

'I'd like you to tell me its worth.' Emma brought a hand out of a pocket with an enticing gleam of gold swaying on a chain.

'Its worth, or its value to me?' he countered.

'I will pawn it if the price is right.' Emma met his sly eyes.

He patted the wooden countertop, inviting her to put the item down for inspection.

Pope pushed the circlet of gold links this way and that, then tested its weight in a cupped hand. 'Very nice…but I have several already in the window.'

'I don't want you to put it into the window. I will collect it very soon. Actually, I made a mistake. I've decided to keep it.' She'd sooner go back to the other fellow and haggle rather than deal with this one who seemed crafty.

'How does two guineas sound?' Pope's fingers snapped shut on the locket.

Emma had put out her hand to take back her locket, but she slowly withdrew it. It was a good deal more than the previous offer.

Seeing her hesitation, he slipped two gold coins her way. 'I'll keep your locket safe in here.' He pulled open a drawer behind him and deposited the necklace inside.

A few minutes later Emma was outside and hurrying towards home with the receipt for the locket tucked in her pocket. She brushed away the tears beading her lashes. Her mother would have wanted her to put her family's well-being above sentiment. But even so a lump had formed in her throat.

Once sure that his customer was out of sight Solomon Pope retrieved the locket. He'd not made a sale yet today and before closing up could do with something fresh to draw the eyes of passing trade. He knew Miss Shabby Genteel wouldn't be back to redeem her property. The likes of her never were for they only came to him when they'd hit rock bottom. He made some room in the window and displayed the necklace at the front on a scrap of velvet.

Sensing he was being watched, he looked up and scowled. He knew that particular skinflint of old. He was a regular customer, buying cheap geegaws for his fancy women. Solomon hoped he'd pass on by. The bell clattered even before he had made it back behind the counter.

The fellow strutted up to demand, 'What price is the gold locket?'

'Three and a half guineas, Mr Gresham.'

'I'll give you one and take it off your hands now.' Joshua was desperate to have it, but hoped he was hiding it well. He knew from experience that this old miser was hard as nails when doing business.

Joshua had thought he must be mistaken when he exited his lawyer's office and spotted Emma peering into a pawnbroker's window. He'd quickly taken cover in the dim hallway and from his vantage point had watched until she emerged from the shop a short while later. Joshua had deduced that Waverley must have been telling the truth. If Houndsmere *had* loaned him money, Emma wouldn't be reduced to visiting a pawnshop. Either that or the old fool was still running through all his borrowed funds before they'd spent one full day in his possession. But Joshua feared that the Waverleys' prospects could improve, courtesy of their friendship with those social climbers, the Sanders. So he ought to strike immediately. When he'd visited

Bernard, after observing Emma and her friend entering the Sweets' mansion, the older man had been working at his desk. Ever inquisitive, Joshua had manoeuvred into a better position to glimpse Waverley's scribblings. It had made little sense to him. A coalman called Charlie seemed to be on Bernard's mind, as did a woman called Augusta.

The locket would be of sentimental value to Emma. If she still refused to sleep with him, even with the gift of her locket as a final inducement, then he would present it to his wife for her birthday and take the house in Primrose Square, as was his right.

'I said a guinea for it,' Joshua renewed his offer.

'And I said three and a half, Mr Gresham.' Solomon returned with the locket retrieved from the window display.

'Two, and that's my final offer.' Joshua pushed the gold away on the splintered counter as though it hadn't impressed him.

'Good day to you then, sir.'

Joshua's chest swelled in rage, but he wanted Emma's necklace so burst out with, 'Two and a half guineas and you will take my money, you scoundrel!'

Solomon extended a hand to seal the deal.

Joshua grabbed coins from his pocket, throwing them down in frustration, then snatched the locket and, refusing to shake hands, was soon gone.

Chapter Eleven

Had Emma not been blinded by tears as she hurried along towards home she might have noticed a sleek black curricle stop at the kerb up ahead. But though she had the comforting weight of cash in her pocket, her heart felt empty. Now separated from her mother's precious locket, the finality of what she'd done had sunk in. She knew it was unlikely that she'd ever be able to recover her keepsake within the time she'd agreed with Mr Pope. The last personal link to her mama had gone for ever. Already she felt bereft. More than that, she had to tell her father what she'd done. With all their other troubles occupying him, he might have forgotten they'd talked about pawning it. If he brought the subject up, she couldn't lie…yet the truth would undoubtedly distress him.

'Hello, Emma.'

Emma jerked her head up at that husky, intimate greeting, looking into a face of raw-boned masculinity. So absorbed had she been in her woes that she hadn't noticed a gentleman alight from the splendid curricle, then lean against it, waiting for her to draw level with him. She was forced once more into awareness of how breathtakingly good looking Lance Harley was.

He glanced past her at the row of office buildings and commercial premises she'd walked past. 'I wouldn't have expected to see you here. Were you meeting somebody?'

His comment was light, but she knew he wanted an explanation and, with tension simmering between them on matters of great import, it would be silly to antagonise him over something trivial. 'I had some business to conduct, sir.'

'With your brother?' he asked.

She decided to use her tactic of deflecting his question by asking one of her own. 'Have you business here, sir?'

'My lawyer's office is along the street.'

A half-smile moved a corner of his lips, confirming her worry that she might have made it too obvious she believed he had been with his East End mistress. His attitude bucked her up. Discreetly, she smeared tears from her lashes, then put up her chin. 'I have to go now…my father is ailing. Good day to you, sir.'

He held out a hand. 'I'll give you a ride and take you quickly to him.' Her hesitation made him add softly, 'It is broad daylight, Emma, you will be perfectly safe.'

'Indeed?' she parried, matching his ruefulness. 'Last time I rode in a carriage with you I feared for my life.'

He gave a soundless laugh. 'Today I'm stone cold sober and will be a model driver, I promise.'

She nibbled her lip, in two minds whether to take the hand he had held out. She would get home that much sooner…but…

'What can I say to make you trust me?'

Emma didn't want him to think she was too timid to accept. It would be a boon to quickly return before her father began fretting and questioned her absence. Besides, she'd noticed they were drawing attention. Instinctively, she went to him, extending her hand.

'Where are we going, sir?'

'For a drive. Don't be alarmed,' he added. 'I just want to talk to you. We were interrupted at my sister's and there was more I wanted to say.'

'But I have nothing to add, sir, so please don't waste either your time or mine.' She slanted a look at his rugged profile. They had been on the road just a few minutes when she realised he was taking a circuitous route to Marylebone.

'A quick drive round Hyde Park and you will still be home sooner than if you had walked.'

'I would have hailed a cab.'

Lance threw his head back and groaned. 'Will you never stop thwarting me, Miss Waverley?'

'No, sir,' she said, but met his smile with one of her own. It was the first time they'd engaged in light banter and she liked it. But her happiness faded as memories of families and problems crowded into her head. This burgeoning harmony wouldn't last.

He drew the curricle to an abrupt halt with Hyde Park nowhere in sight. Neither was much else about. A row of cottages and an area of heathland, much like the one she walked and talked on with her brother, was the only vista. But this grassland was shielded by a windbreak of scraggy hedging.

'This will do.' He threw the reins to the tiger, then sprang down and came round to help her alight. He nodded at the deserted park. 'Just a quick stroll…please?'

There was a light in his eyes she'd not seen before. And something inside her melted into tenderness. It would be so easy to very much like this handsome, charismatic rogue. But she must never let him mean too much for that could only end in heartache. For now, though, she must concentrate on being practical. She had no idea where Robin was. But Lance Harley might know and if she were clever she might find out.

'Just five minutes, then,' she said huskily.

In fact, they walked hardly at all. Once behind the screen of hawthorn Lance drew her to a halt, turning her towards him with firm fingers that caressed her shoulders.

'You look upset. What business did you have in Cheapside? A matter concerning your father's financial problems?' His thumbs gently brushed the tear smudges on her cheeks.

'I'm afraid so...' She wouldn't admit they were reduced to selling family heirlooms; rather let him believe she'd also had a meeting with a lawyer.

'Why be upset over it when I can easily help you?' he asked softly.

'I need no help, thank you. I was upset... because I'm worried about my father's health. And I was thinking of my mother, too. I have been a long while without her.'

'How long?' he asked.

'All my life. She died the day my twin brother and I were born.' Her voice broke on a sob.

Lance leaned in, gently pressed his lips to her cheek in comfort. 'That is indeed a tragedy. My own mother passed away when I was fourteen, so I have very fond and vivid memories of her that I cherish.'

'You are lucky then, sir.' Emma smiled up into his warm blue eyes and that entangling of gazes seemed to be the signal he needed to softly mould together their mouths.

'I could have been slower and more tactful in my approach to you at my sister's house,' he said. 'You don't know much about me other than I like you, but I'm not a patient man.' He paused as though regretting what he'd said. 'When I say I'm not patient, I can be very giving and considerate and tender...' He hung his head, looking almost bashful. 'What I'm trying to say is that I'm not a selfish lover and I don't want you to fear that I'm a debauched reprobate. I know I've gained a reputation that might shock some young ladies, but honestly, you shouldn't believe half of what you hear, Emma. It's just people making up stories.'

'I haven't heard anything,' Emma said, sounding taken aback. She freed herself, stepping back.

He turned his head and choked a regretful laugh. 'Forget I said that, then.'

'I don't think I can. What stories? Never mind,' she followed up briskly. She'd made herself sound an ingénue. Of course the Earl of Houndsmere would have a certain reputation and the gossip would concern his carousing and his women. 'It is not my concern whether you conduct yourself in a way likely to make tongues wag, my lord.' It was her turn to smother a sour laugh. 'Yesterday you said we were alike and in that unfortunate respect we seem to be. My reputation stands no scrutiny either.'

'You've been thinking about what I said… that's a good sign.' He reached for her, holding her still as she would have turned away at his gentle mockery. 'I've chosen to flout convention from time to time from arrogance and privilege. You have nothing to feel ashamed of, Emma. You were dragged into something bad.'

'But you still allow your arrogance and privilege to affect your behaviour, don't you?' She swung her face around to challenge him with a bold golden gaze.

He tugged her yet closer so their bodies touched and rested his head against hers. 'I want you. I can't help how I feel. I'm offering you anything you or your family want. Am I so repulsive that you can't bear the thought of letting me love you?'

Emma knew how easy it could be. But what did love mean to him and to her? Different things, she was sure. Love to her meant a life-long relationship, not a liaison lasting months. She twisted from his embrace and walked away a few steps. 'You know very well I do not find you repulsive, but…'

'But…?' he demanded.

'But there are complications and consequences…'

'All of which I am aware and can cope with.'

'No…' She shook her head vigorously, turning to give him a fierce stare. 'No…you cannot put everything right…buy everything you want with your money. I told you, we are from different worlds with different ways.' She swung away and quickly went back into view, waiting by the curricle. When he joined her, she demanded politely, 'Please take me home now without further delay. My father will be worried about me.'

Lance helped her up and, having leapt agilely aboard, set the magnificent beast to a fast pace. But he kept to his word about not driving recklessly although Emma was aware of his frustration. It was like a solid wall between them. She'd thwarted him, as he called it. And he didn't like it because he wasn't used to not getting his own way. In truth, she wasn't sure whether she wanted him to get his own way, too…and devil take the consequences…

It was as he helped her down at the corner of her street that she realised she had completely forgotten to try to winkle out of him whether he knew where her brother might be.

* * *

The elderly butler's expression did not betray his loathing for the stylishly dressed woman who moments ago had swept into the house as though she owned it. But indeed he did loathe her and had done so for many a long year. When Wilkins had served William Harley he had in equal part despised and pitied that man for having brought shame on his name by marrying her. Now she was William's widow and no less of a thorn in the side of the young master than she'd been a pain to his father. But Wilkins knew his place: it was carrying out the Earl of Houndsmere's instructions. And those instructions were that if the Countess showed up unannounced she was to be treated with courtesy…and asked to wait in the hall.

'Please take a seat, my lady,' Wilkins intoned. 'I will see if his lordship is at home.'

Sonia bristled and would have barged past, but two footmen materialised as if from nowhere to block her way.

Wilkins gave a tiny derisive smile. He indicated a high-backed chair for her to use, then a moment later had disappeared to inform his lordship of his stepmother's arrival.

Learning that Houndsmere would grant her an audience did little to lift Sonia's petulant expression. She sailed past the slow-paced butler and theatrically threw open the door to Lance's study, posing on the threshold.

'What do you mean, making me wait for your time as though I'm some common visitor?'

'That is precisely what you are, ma'am,' Lance said curtly. He had a hand braced against the casement and was idly watching the street scene. He turned to ask wearily, 'What is it you want?'

Sonia unpinned her hat and tossed it towards his desk. Lance was close enough to intercept the flying feathers before they disturbed his papers. He lobbed the bonnet on to the seat of a nearby chair.

'I have done as you suggested. I have come to London to make my daughter behave. Have you discovered where she is yet?' Sonia flounced to the chair and sat down with the feathered concoction on her lap.

Before Lance could reply the butler was back. With a discreet cough Wilkins entered the room.

'Excuse me, my lord…another visitor has arrived. Mr Clunker asks to see you urgently.'

'You may show him in.'

Sonia burst out, 'How dare you interrupt me! I will not wait in another room while you speak to some minion. I was here first.'

'His arrival is timely. He is here on your business, not mine, so stay and listen to his report.' After Wilkins retreated, the Earl explained,

'Clunker is a detective and I'm hoping he's discovered your daughter's whereabouts. Whether he has or hasn't, from today you can deal with him now you're in town. Augusta is your responsibility.' Lance knew that, rightly or wrongly, turning up Robin Waverley, or Charlie Perkins as he now was, had taken precedence over finding his stepsister who, unless incarcerated, was likely to abscond again.

According to Waverley's landlady, he'd missed the fugitive by more than a few hours. Lance hadn't yet decided what to do with the man when he did find him. It would be no easy task even for a skilful team of barristers to sort out the Waverleys' multitude of problems. For Lance, the main concern was keeping Emma's name from being dragged through the mud again. She was the source of the scandal that had wrecked her family, just as he was guilty of introducing the woman who had been his father's downfall. William had been dead for years, yet the effects of his son's juvenile dalliance with Sonia Peak were ongoing. Lance knew he had money and influence enough to weather his storm, whereas Bernard Waverley was sinking fast and taking his daughter with him. And Joshua Gresham, and no doubt others, were circling, waiting for the right moment to pounce. Was he any different? Lance thought with a tinge of self-disgust.

Did his generosity and standing make his lust cleaner? But it wasn't just that any more. He couldn't ignore the tenderness she invoked in him. He turned his mind from sentimentality. He'd thought he'd fallen in love before and been wrong, and made a fool of himself and his father because of it. He'd done nothing other than offer Emma a life free of want. What was wrong with that? At his sister's he'd tricked her into a kiss… and started to seduce her…

Why had he done that? Had he lost control? Had it been an audition? If it was the latter, she'd passed with flying colours. He imagined he had, too; she'd responded to him sweetly. Inwardly, he smiled at the memory of her soft mouth tracking his, her body grinding innocently against his. Even in that she'd been too inexperienced to attempt to dupe him…keep him waiting for surrender. But then earlier today when he'd seen her rushing along with tears in her eyes his only thought had been to scoop her up and shield her from harm… Well, perhaps there had been a stirring in his loins as well as his heart. He thrust his back into the chair, impatient with himself and where his thoughts were heading.

His mistresses were rarely middle class. They were from the lower orders…or similar to himself in status. Several of his paramours had been young, titled widows. But all of them had been seasoned game players and he'd preferred it that way. Business as usual suited him. That's why it was strange, and maddening, that no other woman interested him at the moment. God knew he wished he could turn his attention elsewhere and forget Emma Waverley. His conscience was bothering him, that's all it was, he told himself. Perhaps hers would, too, in time. She'd turned down a better life not only for herself, but for her family…so would she eventually choose to change her mind? Lance could be patient…for a short while…after that, what was he going to do? Give up gracefully? He wasn't sure he knew how. Leave her to go under with her father? He couldn't. So his conscience *was* bothering him…

'What is keeping them?' Sonia sprang to her feet and paced to and fro in front of the desk. Once sure she'd regained her stepson's attention, she sat down again, pondering on what engrossed him. She knew it wasn't her or Augusta putting a frown of intense concentration on his face.

She immediately rewarded his attention with a sugary smile. It did nothing for him other than start him wondering how he ever had been in her thrall. She was a blowsy blonde now, but when he'd first met her she'd been a beauty with a clever tongue. She'd kept him aroused and amused. Youth was to blame…innocence and an inability to see bad in people led the young into all sorts of trouble. Emma might not agree with him on much, yet she'd not deny that. She'd fallen into the same trap. But she'd been a victim as well as an instigator. He wasn't sure he could claim to have been. Although Sonia, for all her sham modesty and claims to be eighteen, had turned out to be older and more experienced than him when they'd first met. He'd fallen under her spell and now…now he couldn't tolerate her company for more than a short while. So much for falling in love.

The study door opened again, interrupting his brooding.

'Take a seat if you will, sir.' The Earl indicated the vacant wing chair.

Mr Clunker looked surprised to find his lordship had company, but he gave the woman a polite nod, then perched on the chair with his hat secured beneath an arm.

'Let's have your news,' Lance said without preamble.

'I have located your stepsister. She was lodging in Whitechapel, but has recently moved from there.' Clunker glanced at the woman, unsure of how much to disclose in her presence.

'You may speak freely in front of the Countess as she is Augusta's mother.'

'Very well, my lord.' He paused. 'Firstly, your

stepsister is apparently now going by the name of Jane.'

'Perhaps it's occurred to her to exercise discretion,' Lance observed scathingly.

'I think it is more to evade detection, my lord. She has…umm…got involved with a low sort of fellow, I'm afraid.' The detective peered beneath his brows at the girl's mother for her reaction to that.

'Doubtless she feels at home with him,' Lance muttered, gesturing for Clunker to carry on.

'The fellow is a coalman named Charlie—' Clunker's hat dropped from beneath his arm to the floor as he abruptly shrank into the upholstery. The Earl had lunged to his feet to stride round the desk.

Sonia was also startled by Lance's reaction. A moment ago he'd looked as though he'd found the matter tedious, now he appeared greatly interested in it. It pleased her that he appeared angry to learn his stepsister was consorting with riff-raff. Perhaps the damage to his name was hurting his pride. It was certainly hurting hers. A coalman as a son-in-law! She hadn't clawed her way from the slums of Wapping to the position of Countess to endure that! 'You must arrange her immediate marriage, Houndsmere,' she snapped. 'There are gentlemen willing to take her, I'm sure…'

'Beg pardon, ma'am, but it might be too late for that,' Clunker interjected, swooping on his hat. He would sooner have just dealt with the Earl, but soldiered on. 'A neighbour of theirs knows them as a married couple. Whether the union is valid—'

'Thank you for your report,' Lance cut the man off. 'You may leave now and I will be in touch about any further enquiries.'

After Clunker had withdrawn with an obsequious bow, Sonia flew to Lance and tried to embrace him. She was still convinced she could seduce him if he'd let her close enough. Impatiently, he disentangled himself.

'Will you relish having the likes of a coalman as your brother-in-law?' she taunted, furious at having been rejected again. 'This must be hushed up.'

'Are you staying at Larkspur House?' Lance interrupted. The property was in Chelsea and had been bought by his father after his first wife died, for use by his mistresses. In a final snub to his wanton second wife, William had bequeathed to her use of it until her death. The insult was clear. But Sonia was thick-skinned and besides had nowhere else to stay when in town. She left her daughter there most of the time, in the charge of various matrons she employed as chaperons.

For herself she preferred country living and entertaining her gallants in relative obscurity.

'Well, unless you intend to invite your stepmama to stay here with you in Grosvenor Square I suppose I'll have to go there,' Sonia replied, peeking archly at him.

'Go home, then, and I'll attend to matters and send word of what's been done in due course.'

Sonia angrily rammed her hat on her head. 'You had better do it quickly and discreetly. If they are married, it must be annulled and I'll accept no less than a viscount for my dear girl—it's the least she deserves.'

Lance gave a hard smile, but it wasn't Sonia's hypocrisy, or his stepsister, that caused it. He'd be interested to discover how much of this Emma had known when they'd been together earlier. Most of it, he imagined. And he wanted an answer from her. But there was something else he had to do first.

'Is it all right if I borrow the landau again?'

Lance raised a quizzical eyebrow.

'Miss Sanders has agreed to go for another drive with me. Alas, Mrs Booth is also coming along. *Again…*' Jack added funereally and rolled his eyes.

Lance's expression mingled humour and disbelief. 'Are you courting?'

'How can I look for a wife? I've nothing to offer.' Jack grimaced. 'Perhaps it was a bad idea, asking her out for a second time. I don't want her to think that I'm willing or able to take things further. She's not an heiress and that's what I need to set me straight. I just like her company, that's all.'

'Right…' Lance said wryly. 'Well, you're welcome to take the landau and enjoy more of her company.' He pushed open the door to Boodle's and immediately their arrival was met with a volley of greetings from gentlemen stationed within the fug of cigar smoke and alcohol fumes.

'Nixon's over there,' Jack said. 'He called on my sister a couple of days after Ruth's tea party. He's taking Bella and my mother to the theatre this week. They're quite excited about it.'

'Sounds serious. Nixon seems nice enough.'

Jack gave the young baronet a piercing look. 'I'll get to know him better before making my mind up on it.'

'No time like the present,' Lance advised, his attention already elsewhere. It seemed luck was on his side, providing him with a perfect opportunity to corner somebody. As Jack set off to cross-examine his sister's suitor, Lance ordered a cognac from a passing steward. When he had it, he took a swallow, then strolled towards a table where a game of Basset was in progress. The circle of spectators standing behind the gamesters' chairs indicated that a serious amount was at stake. As he got closer, Lance spied the banknotes, coins and assorted items of gold and silver on the table. In among the jumble were visible edges of papers, denoting IOUs had been pledged by those who'd emptied their pockets, but still weren't prepared to admit defeat. Lance stood at the back, staring at one player in particular until the fellow sensed his observation. Others in the audience had deferred to the Earl, making a space for him to move forward and get a better view. Usually he wouldn't have bothered; today he did.

Joshua Gresham puffed out his chest, a smug smile tugging at his lips, at the honour of having been singled out for recognition by the Earl of Houndsmere.

Lance transferred his attention to the young man seated in front of him. He was sweating and his hands were trembling as he pushed his solitary crown over the baize. He was wasting his time staking it as far as Lance could see. The luckless young buck had been given a set of duds. When the hand was played out Lance lowered his head to speak to him. Peter Rathbone peered over a shoulder, looking terrified to see the Earl close behind him, considering how they'd parted at that tavern. But he was soon listening intently. His jaw dropped as he digested what was being said. A moment later he nodded vigorously, then shot up from the table to push a path through the crowd.

'I'll take Rathbone's place…and his debts…'

'Highly irregular…' the banker trumpeted, knowing the Earl for an excellent player.

'Is he in his cups? Why'd he saved Rathbone?' a different gentleman hissed, knowing full well that Houndsmere would bet high, drunk or sober.

'He knows that cub's father,' somebody else rumbled. 'Saving young Rathbone from embarrassment, I expect.'

'What are you lot worried about?' Lance enquired of nobody in particular as the muttering continued to ebb and flow around him. 'I'm the one starting off down a hundred.'

'You can make that nearly two,' the banker snorted. 'Rathbone put vowels in as well.' He glanced from one gamester to another. 'Any objections to Houndsmere sitting in?'

Not a word was said, although nobody looked content at the substitution.

Lance shrugged and emptied his glass, then immediately signalled for a refill before slouching into the vacant chair. 'I'm feeling generous and in need of some diversion, so deal the cards.'

'We were all sorry to hear the Countess has just arrived in town,' a tipsy voice crowed from among the spectators. 'Not as sorry as you though, eh, Houndsmere?'

A tense silence followed; most of the men present believed that such gross impertinence warranted a request for an apology at least, a meeting, at worst. The Earl had avenged himself pitilessly for less of a slur in the past. This time he shrugged. 'Commiserations accepted. But don't mention her again.'

The fellow with the big mouth sidled off towards the bar. Lance emptied his glass the moment the steward put it down. Before the man could retreat he'd offered it back to him for another refill. Then he drew from his pocket a roll of cash.

Joshua had been watching and listening to what went on. He'd never before sat at a card table with Houndsmere. The Earl usually chose to gamble with an exclusive elite comprising Valance, his brother-in-law and other close friends. They often had a table set up especially at the back of the room. But Boodle's was rarely graced with his illustrious presence. Watier's or White's were his lordship's usual haunts. The banknotes at the man's elbow drew Joshua's sly eyes. In common with the others he had heard of the harlot who'd married the late Earl and he'd heard of her equally troublesome daughter. If they had

distracted Houndsmere with family woes, Joshua
would be delighted to capitalise on it.

Other gamesters seated around the table were
thinking the same thing, concealing subtle smiles
by rubbing their chins. Joshua deemed himself a
skilful player; a stack of cash at his elbow proved
it no idle boast. He was ahead and was confident
he'd manage to stay that way. What a feather in
his cap it would be if he cleaned out his lordship's pockets this afternoon. His smirk was
swiftly controlled. What he'd really like to do
was foster a proper acquaintance with Houndsmere: it would open all sorts of doors. Veronica
had been a shrew of late, but she would be as
nice as pie to him if, through his new friend the
Earl of Houndsmere, he secured her an invitation to Mrs Sweet's.

For himself, an insight into the Earl's dealings
with Waverley was what he wanted.

Chapter Twelve

'Oh, would you please pursue yonder vehicle? And hurry!'

As soon as he knew his passenger was safely on board, the jarvey put his nag to the test, weaving in and out of the traffic and fully entering into the spirit of the chase. The coal cart was going at a cracking speed with just a solitary hundredweight sack on the back.

Inside the cab, Emma was shaken and swayed while struggling to stay upright. The whirlwind ride reminded her of the first night she had met the Earl and he had brought her home. She tried to concentrate on this pursuit, but the more she banned Lance Harley from her mind the more persistent a fixture there he became. The memory of his arms holding her, the hint of sandalwood on his skin as it abraded her jaw when he kissed her, wouldn't be denied. Neither would the sweet words of comfort he'd given her over the loss of her mother. A little involuntary noise broke in her throat as a phantom mouth seemed to skim hers, touching and tantalising, making her forget her sadness.

She mustn't imagine he really cared, she sternly told herself. He was a skilful charmer and she was in the throes of some absurd infatuation. His attention and offers of favours in return for hers should not flatter her into dreaming that he might feel affection for her. She had piqued his pride and now he had something to prove, to her and to himself. He was no better than any rake strutting around town and might easily forget about her if he managed to gain his victory and soothe his ego. She knew she'd never forget him, though. If she never again saw Lance Harley, the memory of their brief, tempestuous acquaintance would remain with her until the day she died. No man...even the one she'd once hoped to marry...had ever made such a deep impression on her.

She gasped and clung on as the vehicle careered round a corner. The wheel found solid ground, knocking the breath from her and focusing her mind again on Robin. Sliding to the edge of the seat, she forced open the stiff window to poke her head out. A rush of cool damp air battered her flushed face. The cab appeared to be gaining ground on the cart, thank goodness. She'd hoped to bump into Robin for days and had imagined that he would be equally keen to see her. Today she had decided to lose no more time in warning him of danger and to go to his place of work. In the event she hadn't needed to run him to ground. She had been on her way home after settling some merchants' bills out of the money she'd got from selling her locket when she'd spotted one of Milligan's carts. Spontaneously she'd charged after it in a most unladylike fashion. Fortunately it had stopped a short way along the road and she'd put on a spurt once sure Robin was doing the deliveries. But off he went again, and Emma hadn't relished keeping up the chase on foot, or calling out to him. When it had started to spit with rain she had hailed a cab.

Emma closed the window and sat back against the lumpy squabs. With a surge of relief she picked up on something positive: if the Earl *had* caught up with the couple, Robin wouldn't still be going about his business. He'd be in gaol, or in deeper hiding if he and Augusta had somehow evaded her stepbrother's clutches.

'He be stopping up ahead,' the driver yelled.

'Oh, pull over now, please,' she instructed, seeing the cart turn in through some open gates.

The jarvey steered to the kerb and Emma immediately jumped down and paid him. Pulling up her hood, she dashed to the gates to peek around an edge of timber. The horse and cart were stationary, but Robin had disappeared. A ramshackle stables ran the length of one side of the yard and a dilapidated hut flanked the other. Emma imagined her brother had gone inside, perhaps to collect his wages. She wondered whether to go to find him, but Robin wouldn't want her to make herself known. Neither did she like the idea of it. The fewer people who saw them together, the better it would be. But she had come this far and didn't want this chase to end up as fruitless as her visit to his lodging house. Concealing her face in the folds of her cowl, she proceeded hesitantly into the courtyard.

'Wot you after, then, miss?'

Milligan had emerged from a stable to see what he supposed to be a customer. If ladies needed coal they sent a servant to put in an order. Startled, she'd swung to face him and he could see she wasn't quite a servant, but neither was she proper Quality.

'Who are you?' Emma demanded, backing away from a sooty-faced individual who reeked of tar.

'Who are *you*, more like? D'you want a coal delivery?' He cocked his head, giving her a thorough look. Beyond the shadow of her hood he could just make out a pale, heart-shaped face and a pair of pretty catlike eyes.

'No...thank you. I...' Emma hesitated, but knew she'd no option but to state her business. 'I want to speak to your employee, Mr Perkins,' she said firmly.

'He's a popular feller...everybody be seeking Charlie.'

'Who?' Emma immediately twitched back her hood to better hear his answer.

'Not sure I should say...' Craftily, Milligan started massaging his chin with his grimy fingers while steadily regarding her. Now he'd got a better look at her he could see she was black-haired and beautiful, if hoity-toity.

He was waiting for her to bribe him, Emma realised. She pulled out a few pennies from her purse and held them out as an inducement.

Milligan snorted in derision, but took them all the same. 'He give me hundred times as much as that.'

'He?' she immediately pounced. 'Was he a well-to-do gentleman? Tall with dark hair?'

'Trying to remember...'

In desperation, Emma held out a shilling even though she knew she couldn't afford to waste one penny on this wretch. The money she had got from selling her locket should be put to better use than this.

Milligan took the coin. 'Now I think on it he didn't give his name, but he was top notch. That's all I know.' Milligan didn't intend to cross such a man and had already said too much. The swell had told him never to mention their conversation, especially to Charlie, and had paid handsomely for his silence. Milligan reckoned Charlie was in deep trouble to attract the attention of a man like that.

Emma's pent-up breath was released. It was no real surprise, yet news she'd been dreading to hear. Houndsmere had told her himself that he was aware her brother worked for Milligan. 'I must speak to Mr Perkins urgently.'

Milligan extended a palm.

'I'll not give you another farthing!' she fumed.

He accepted the rebuff with a shrug. 'I don't reckon Charlie's wife knows about you. Jane'll have yer eyes out.'

'Jane?' Emma parroted. Had her brother taken up with another woman?

Milligan's eyes travelled to her belly beneath her enveloping cloak. He shook his head, smirking. 'The randy so-and-so has got you in trouble, too, has he?'

Emma's indignation soon suppressed her scarlet-cheeked embarrassment. 'Please tell me where he is!' She really wanted to head home now it was pouring down. But in for a penny, in for a pound…she'd have to persevere if she were to find her twin.

She had made a split-second decision to pursue her brother, knowing that Mrs O'Reilly would stay with her father until she returned. For all her brusqueness, Cathleen was a kindly soul and had insisted on sitting with poorly Mr Waverley so Emma could go out on business. Their maid had offered to resume her normal hours for no extra pay, but Emma had declined that offer. The woman had to earn her living as did everyone else. Nevertheless, Cathleen kept turning up every day on some excuse or another.

'Charlie's finished his shift so you'll find him at home, I reckon.' Milligan smeared rain from his face, jogging off to find some shelter in the stable. 'He's got lodgings round the corner in Rowley Street, next door to the bakery.' That last was sent over his shoulder.

Emma called her thanks and pulled up her hood.

'That way's quicker, miss.' Milligan pointed helpfully to a side door that led from his yard.

Emma set off, huddled into her cloak, and soon found Rowley Street and the bakery.

She used a hand to shield her rain-battered vision, blinking at a small mullioned window that was ajar on the first floor. She could hear the sound of an argument. The deeper of the two voices was definitely her brother's. Emma banged on the door, hoping one of them would hear her over the noise they were making. Just as she was about to raise her fist to thump the panels again, the door was yanked open with some force, sending Emma skittering backwards.

'Hell's teeth! What are you doing here? How did you find me?'

'That's not a very nice way to greet your sister.' Emma sounded equally terse. 'I've put myself to some trouble today on your account, Robin. I wouldn't have done so unless the matter was urgent. I followed your cart here. You passed me by earlier in the High Street and I've been trying to catch up with you to tell you some bad news.'

'Sorry, Em…' He sighed, sending a sheepish glance up the stairs. 'You've caught me in the middle of something.'

'So I gathered. I could hear you outside,' she warned. He still hadn't invited her in out of the rain so she helped herself, stepping into the hallway. 'Will you take me to your room so we might talk in private?'

Somebody had emerged from a doorway further along the dim passage. The stout fellow planted his hands on his hips.

'We live upstairs,' Robin hissed. He had also noticed the belligerent landlord and hastily steered his sister out of sight towards the staircase.

Having climbed the bare treads, carefully avoiding the lethal-looking splintered areas, Emma went into the room her twin indicated. The dismal, cluttered space seemed vacant. Her encompassing glance took in a small table edged by two stick-backed chairs, a battered sofa and a bed pushed against the wall. A petticoat and stockings hung on a string suspended below the ceiling so it was quite obvious a woman lived here with him. Emma closed the window as a draught blew on to her rain-soaked complexion, making her shiver.

'Augusta might as well come out from wherever she is hiding,' she said bluntly. 'It's too late for any of that now her stepbrother is on to you.'

'What do you mean?' Robin demanded. He'd gone pale and grabbed her elbow to hasten her reply.

'I mean that the game is up. I've come to tell you the Earl of Houndsmere will catch up with you and Augusta before long. You must warn her, too.' Emma liberated herself from his clutch.

'She can hear you. She wouldn't have dived for cover if we'd known it was only you, Em. I had a feeling Houndsmere would send investigators after her so everybody knows her as Jane Perkins.'

'That won't fool him for long,' Emma said flatly. She thanked heaven that Milligan knew Robin's wife as Jane. If he'd uttered the name Augusta to Houndsmere it would surely have rung alarm bells in his head.

A scurrying sound preceded a fair-haired young lady emerging from beneath the bed, dusting herself down.

'Does my stepbrother suspect we're together?' Augusta asked, her tone a mix of annoyance and nervousness.

'Your stepbrother's been looking for Robin, but of course he'll get two for the price of one when he catches up with you both,' Emma replied, giving the girl a sorrowful smile.

Augusta was pretty and petite and looked very young. But she was old enough: Emma could clearly see a tell-tale bump beneath her creased skirt. Her brother had not been exaggerating the seriousness of his situation then. 'You really should not risk your health squeezing under the bed like that, my dear. You might hurt yourself,' Emma said in genuine worry. 'As Robin has forgotten his manners and omitted to introduce us… I'm Emma Waverley and I imagine you are Augusta Harley. I'm very pleased to meet you. I just wish circumstances were better for us all.' Emma clasped the girl's hands in welcome, giving them a squeeze.

'I'm pleased to meet you, too. But I'm just Augusta Peak. My stepfather didn't give me his name. As for my real father...well, I'm not exactly sure who he was. My grandma says my mother probably doesn't know either as she was a tavern wench at the time with lots of gentlemen friends. We spring from lowly folk in Wapping, you see. But I like my grandma,' she finished stoutly.

Emma was taken aback by the girl's frankness. She also felt a twinge of pity for Augusta, growing up in such awful surroundings. It made it the more astonishing that she'd chosen to come back to them.

'There's no need to trouble yourself over my health, I'm very robust,' Augusta said proudly. 'Grandma says our family's born to hard labour and hardship. But thank you for your concern.' She gave Emma a spontaneous hug, but quickly broke away. 'Oh, you're all wet. Take off your cloak and bonnet or you'll catch a chill.'

Emma indeed felt as though the damp had seeped through to her bones. She took off the sodden wool and hung it over a chair back, then rubbed warmth into her goose-pimpled arms before removing her dripping hat.

While the girls had been talking, Robin had been pacing, anxiously whittling away a thumbnail with his teeth. Suddenly he burst out, 'I can't understand why Houndsmere is taking such an interest in me if he doesn't know Augusta is here. How does he know I'm even alive?' He shot a look at Emma. 'Did you tell him something?'

'Not intentionally,' Emma replied with a hint of apology. 'He questioned me and guessed from something I said that you were alive and hiding in the East End. After that…' She sighed. 'His curiosity hasn't waned at all. I have asked him to leave us all alone, but…'

'But?' Robin demanded, looking perplexed.

'But…he doesn't want to.'

'Does he intend to be a friend to us?' Robin sounded optimistic.

Emma couldn't tell her twin that Houndsmere indeed would be a very generous friend if she agreed to share his bed.

'He's a devil of a nuisance to shake off. He never gives up because he's used to everybody doing whatever he says,' Augusta helpfully interjected. 'My stepbrother always finds me in the end when I run off. Yet I've told him to leave me alone.'

'Why *do* you run off?' Emma was at a loss to know what Augusta didn't like about her pampered life.

'My mama is…not very nice…' Augusta said, pulling a face. 'She has more time for her gallants than for me. And she is always plotting a way to get Lance to love her when he never will again.'

After a stunned silence Emma whispered, 'Again?' She had listened with mounting disbelief to Augusta's explanation. 'Surely your mother was married to the *late* Earl?'

'She was. But she always wanted Lance because she was with him first. I don't blame her… he is nice…although strict…and so handsome. Mama hoped he'd marry her, but he wouldn't. So she married his father instead.' Augusta had reeled that off airily, then added, 'She still wants him back even though she knows he has other women and they are much younger and prettier than she is. One of them is called Jenny. I've seen my stepbrother out in his phaeton with her. She has hair even fairer than mine.' The girl twirled a flaxen curl around a finger, then seemed to notice the strain on Emma's face. 'I'm sorry… I know I shouldn't be so vulgar and outspoken. I'm always getting told off for it. We are quite scandalous, aren't we?' She shook her head. 'My grandma works as a char and she says that the Quality have no reason to think they're above her, the way they carry on.'

Emma could only agree. Her heart felt as though ice had surrounded it, freezing it solid and restricting its beating. He was a rake, she knew that, but not that he was so thoroughly debauched. Little wonder he had asked her not to believe all the gossip about him! He had shared a woman with his father. Now that man had died was Lance Harley her lover again? Emma imagined pretty, blonde Jenny was the *chère amie* who lived in the East End.

'I should be going now.' She refused to think more about it. 'I have done what I came to do. Now you must do what you think best, Robin, to keep you both safe. I won't come back again. I intend to find some work and it might take me away from London.'

Robin didn't appear to be listening. He interrupted with, 'Has our father sent some money to help get me out of this place?'

'He has nothing left!' Emma shouted angrily, then clamped her lips together, ashamed of her outburst. 'Goodbye, Augusta.' She embraced the girl. 'Please take care of yourself.' She quickly donned her damp cloak and fastened her bonnet.

'I shall. Thank you,' Augusta said politely. 'I hope I'll see you again,' she called as Emma approached the door.

'Will you accompany me downstairs, Robin?'

Her brother led the way along the landing.

'I'm sorry I shouted,' Emma said when they were again standing in the hallway. 'But you should know that our father is not well. As soon as he is feeling more himself and able to cope without me I will find employment. But he never will improve unless you leave him alone. The worry of all this makes him fret constantly. He wants to see you and Augusta.'

'Well, let him come!' Robin snorted. 'When he sees how we go on he will want to help us before his grandchild is born.'

'He cannot help!' Emma exploded through her gritted teeth. 'He has nothing left…not even his health.' She paused to rein in her temper. 'The doctor attended Papa earlier in the week. He was surprised at how our father has deteriorated since his last visit.' Tears glittered in her eyes at the memory of the doctor's grave expression when examining his patient. Before the doctor left he had told Emma to ensure Mr Waverley had as much rest as possible, handing over some powders to ease his sleep and some ointment for his leg.

'That's a blow…' Robin looked despairing. 'I've been relying on his assistance. Augusta is utterly fed up with living like this.'

'Is that why you were quarrelling earlier?'

Robin nodded, then his face drooped towards his breastbone. 'I wish I'd died out in France… I've come back to nothing and can't bear living any longer as a pauper.'

'Don't ever say that!' Emma spontaneously threw her arms about him, hugging him fiercely.

He smelled of coal and sweat, but nevertheless she held him as though she'd never let him go and dried her tears on the coarse cloth covering his shoulder. Eventually she pushed him away to arm's length. 'I understand why neither of you want to carry on like this. Especially Augusta, in her delicate condition. You should send her home to her mother, Robin, for her own good.'

He wiped the back of his hand over his teary eyes. 'I've tried to make her go for she is holding me back finding better work. I can barely support myself, let alone a wife. But she won't leave me. You heard her. She says she is strong and she likes it better with me than with her mother. She just wants somewhere nicer for us to live.'

'I don't blame her for that.' Emma's voice cracked with emotion. She embraced her brother again, kissing his cheek in farewell. 'Do you really love her, Robin?'

He nodded. 'But for how long will it last when all we do is argue? Being poor isn't romantic, Em. It's hell.'

'I know and I'm truly sorry,' she said huskily. There was nothing else to be said...she had nothing more to give. So before he could try to wheedle and pluck at her heartstrings Emma turned and hurried away into the wet evening.

At the end of the street she stumbled into an alley. Blinded by tears and rain, she rested against a wall to compose herself for the journey home. She folded over at the middle, arms crossed at her abdomen, allowing sobs to rack her for there was no more holding them back.

When she had quietened she smeared wet from her face and took stock. Getting work as a governess or lady's companion would never solve their problems. Her wages wouldn't come quickly, nor would they be enough. But there was a way and whether she owed it to her family to abase herself no longer mattered. She could see that now. On the day Robin had ambushed her by the heath and frightened the life out of her because she'd thought a ghost accosted her, he had told her he'd sacrificed his future for hers. Unnecessarily…recklessly…he had tried to avenge a wrong done her. A wrong that she, in *her* stupidly trusting way, had invited. Now she must make amends.

Her conscience and her love wouldn't allow her to watch her father's decline and her brother's misery…not when in her heart she knew she was the fount of all their ills. So she must swallow her pride and her hopes for her future. She must be a bit more like Augusta, she realised. The girl might be many years younger, but she was strong and courageous and took pride in her lowly roots and her grandma's coarse wisdom. Emma realised she'd immediately warmed to

Augusta…more than she had allowed herself to warm to the girl's stepbrother. But change her attitude to him she must if she were to be his mistress. And the worst of it was that she knew she could do it quite easily. It would be when he expected her to turn off her feelings and forget about him, as he'd forget about her, that she would struggle.

Veronica Gresham could tell her husband was enraged about something. Five minutes ago their manservant had appeared with a letter for him. He'd torn it open, then had grown redder and redder in the face while growling out a curse. Even before receiving it he had been in an odd mood, snapping at her for no reason.

Now he was pacing to and fro with the paper shaking between both sets of his fingers as though he might rip it asunder. Securing her needle in her embroidery, she pushed the tambour away to stand up.

'Oh, for heaven's sake, be still! What ails you, Joshua?'

He ignored her and went to the window as though seeking a solution to his problems outside.

'Have you had a business setback, my dear?' She was hoping he had not. She had ordered a new gown without his permission and hadn't yet owned up to it.

He shrugged her off his shoulder as she attempted to comfort him and stormed out of the parlour. A moment later she heard the door of his den slam shut.

Now the atmosphere was peaceful Veronica returned to her seat and started weaving her needle into the tapestry once more. While sewing she brooded on the woman who had enthralled and divided Simon and Joshua. Emma Waverley would end up a lonely old maid, as she deserved to.

In his study Joshua sat at his desk with his head supported in his palms. His plot was in tatters. He pulled open his desk drawer and reluctantly withdrew a parchment secured with red ribbon.

The deeds to Waverley's house were no longer his—he'd lost them in that confounded game of Basset. The letter he'd received had been from the victor's solicitor demanding the document be taken to his office in Cheapside without delay. Joshua still couldn't fathom why the Earl would demand payment this way rather than in hard cash. The spectators who'd gawped at the play until the bitter end had been equally puzzled. None had commiserated with him; he'd received congratulations. Those gentlemen had believed the inebriated Earl had been uncharacteristically lenient, taking on Waverley's debts in payment rather than emptying the loser's bank account. But Joshua wondered if there was more to it... something that concerned the Earl's recent visits to Primrose Square. Houndsmere hadn't looked like a man mellow with drink when he'd got up from the card table and walked away in a straight line. But they'd all seen him sink a bottle of brandy. Too late, some late arrivals, cognisant with the Earl's ways, had chortled that they'd never game with him drunk or sober because he played like a professional card sharp. If he had cheated, Joshua hadn't spotted it and neither had anybody else. Now it was too late in any case. The deed was done.

Joshua had hoped to sell some stock to pacify the Earl. But the letter stated he must immediately comply with specific terms. He snatched up the deeds, tempted to hurl them to the floor. He couldn't risk a lawsuit with one of the wealthiest aristocrats in the land. Especially as a score or more gentlemen were witness to what had gone on at Boodle's that afternoon.

He still had Emma's locket to tempt her with. It would be some time before news filtered through to her or her father—whom he'd heard was ill in bed—that the deeds had changed hands. Emma might succumb before discovering that his threat to make them homeless carried no weight.

Joshua decided not to take a carriage to Cheapside; he needed the air and some exercise to work off his fury. As he marched, he cursed his brother to damnation. But for Simon he would never have become obsessed with Emma Waverley. He'd never liked his younger brother: too handsome, too popular. As children they'd fought over toys and would far sooner play with friends than with each other. Even the woman Joshua had eventually agreed to marry had come under his little brother's spell. Veronica was wont to bring up from time to time that she'd preferred her first husband. After the duel Simon was finished. But Joshua was still waiting to even up one final score with his brother: deflower the woman Simon had loved and risked everything for, but had never managed to bed.

In truth, Joshua had little real affection for Emma. But he'd enjoy breaking her in. Apart from that it was the battle of wills he craved and the taming. He'd already had a taste of her squirming against him…hitting and kicking to be free. The memory made his breeches feel uncomfortably tight and his panting breath momentarily deafened him to a greeting from a passer-by.

Joshua spun about to see Roland Sanders,

swinging his cane, proceeding along the street without a backward glance. He hurried up behind him, inquisitive to know how Mrs Booth had managed to cosy up to Mrs Sweet. 'Sorry, my dear fellow…was lost in thought.' Joshua clapped Sanders on the back.

Roland had only greeted him from courtesy. He didn't like the man and couldn't bring to mind anybody who did.

'How have you been? Not seen you about for a while, Sanders.'

'Arthritis playing me up.' Roland flexed his knobbly-knuckled fingers. 'Mrs Booth has been making me rest at home. She's very good to me like that.'

Joshua was glad that Sanders hadn't been in the gentlemen's clubs recently. He wouldn't have heard about the deeds changing hands. 'And how is Waverley doing?' Joshua asked, all sympathy. 'Heard he's ailing, the poor old soul.'

'On my way to see him. Bernard has much on his mind, that's his trouble. My good friend shouldn't have entangled himself with money grubbers.' Roland made a pointed reference to Joshua's extortionate interest rates. He doffed his hat, ready to move on.

'I'd say that damned Charlie the coalman's the cause of his worries.' Joshua threw that in as a last resort, hoping to pique Sanders's inter-

est and make him tarry awhile to talk about Mrs
Sweet. It had the desired effect. Roland immediately strode back to him.

'Charlie? Coalman?' he whispered, his eyes
darting to and fro. 'What do you know about
that?'

Instinctively Joshua knew he'd hit upon something. 'Why, everything...he told me everything
about it.' He licked his lips, sensing something
of note was about to be revealed. 'I'm his main
creditor and he can't keep anything from me.
Waverley told me about Augusta, too.' He recalled seeing both the names on the list Bernard had been writing. The effect this all had
on Sanders was peculiar and amazing. The
older man stumbled back and leaned heavily on
his cane to keep himself upright. Immediately,
Joshua inwardly cursed that he'd not taken more
notice of Waverley's scribblings.

Roland steadied himself on his feet, wondering if Bernard's infection had left him brain sick.
'Well...shocked, I have to say,' he mumbled.
'Waverley told me it was all to be kept under
my hat and nobody else must know any of it.'

'He told me the same thing.' Joshua played
his part, adopting an alarmed expression. 'Let's
have your opinion on how he should go on,
Sanders, then I'll tell you what I think on it.
Between us we might be able to come up with

a solution to help him.' Joshua determinedly steered Roland towards the wall so they could talk without being overheard.

Chapter Thirteen

'Please do come for a drive with us, Em,' Dawn urged. 'I know you're fretting about your papa's health, but we won't be out too long. You look as though you need a little relaxation. You're quite wan, you know.' Dawn gave her friend a hug.

'Of course I will come and I'll attempt to keep Mrs Booth occupied so you can get to know Mr Valance a bit better.'

'We had a lot to say to one another despite her constant interruptions.' Dawn rolled her eyes. 'My father must be in his dotage to consider getting leg-shackled to her.'

Emma smiled. She'd heard her papa muttering that his friend was a shrewd individual, more enamoured of the widow's bank balance than he was of her. He'd sounded envious, his daughter had thought. Her mother had been gone a long while and Emma was surprised that her father hadn't remarried for companionship, if not love. But Bernard Waverley and Roland Sanders were good friends and very alike: widowers with spinster daughters still at home and a propensity to spend money they didn't have.

'I think I rather like Jack Valance, Em, even though I hardly know him.' Dawn sighed, breaking into Emma's reflectiveness. 'But I'm not quite sure what he feels about me. At times he gives me a very intense look, then at other times he seems quite casual. But he's always polite,' she hastened on. 'I just can't be sure what he's thinking.'

'At this moment he is probably thinking he's very lucky that you have agreed to go out with him again,' Emma said loyally.

'I am looking forward to it so I'd best be off,' Dawn said. 'I want to sort out something nice to wear.'

Emma accompanied her best friend into the hallway.

'We'll call for you at half past four, then,' Dawn said as she skipped down the front steps.

'I shall be ready and waiting.' Emma waved before closing the door and then her eyes, leaning her forehead against the panels. She hoped Dawn wouldn't lose her heart too quickly to Jack Valance. It remained to be seen whether he was sincerely smitten or was simply the Earl of Houndsmere's ally. Emma couldn't air her suspicions. Dawn would be mortified and she would do anything rather than hurt her. Besides, at the moment she had nothing to go on other than a suspicion that had sprung from her misgivings about Lance Harley's character. Now she knew about his relationship with Augusta's mother it seemed she'd been right to be dubious about him from the start. When he'd taken her for a drive and they'd talked about their mothers, she'd thought they were growing closer… perhaps close enough for confidences and family problems to be shared and a solution found. But she shouldn't trust him.

But Jack might be a different sort of man. Why would he not genuinely like Dawn? She was a lovely person and Emma was sad to think that at some time she might lose touch with her best friend.

Emma had grown used to being shunned, yet Dawn's friendship had been unwavering. In future things might be different. Without a husband's name to shield behind, a gentleman's mistress inhabited a twilight world and did not mingle even on the fringe of polite society. Emma would sooner steer clear of Dawn than have her sweet, loyal friend blighted by an association to her. But it hadn't come to that yet.

Last night Emma had tossed and turned the

night through, trying to arrive at a decision on what to do. Just before dawn, when every bleak thought about her papa and Robin had seemed at its darkest, she had risen to light the candle stub. She had found pen and paper and dashed off a letter to Houndsmere. Her acceptance of his terms had comprised just two stark lines and she'd been on the point of sealing it when instead she'd suddenly crumpled the note in a fist, then hurled it into the fireplace. She couldn't yet take that final step when she knew she was still susceptible to falling in love with him. She didn't know him well enough to trust her future and her body to him. She needed to learn more about his ways…good and bad…and perhaps bad might be better. Knowing he was thoroughly reprehensible would help her harden herself against him. He'd promised to love her sweetly with unselfishness and consideration…but how did she know…?

'Will you be going out with friends later then, miss?'

Cathleen had emerged from the kitchen, interrupting Emma's inner turmoil.

Having received her mistress's answering nod, the maid offered, 'I can sit with your papa and let him read the paper to me like he did before.'

'It's good of you, but he seems a little better

today. You can get straight home at your usual time.'

'Oh, go on wid yer...' Cathleen flapped a hand. 'I know he likes a bit of company while he's stuck in bed, twiddling his thumbs. He played a hand of Rummy with me as well and I enjoyed it, so I did.'

Emma smiled. 'Well, if you're certain it's no trouble, thank you. I shan't be gone long anyway. I'll pop up and see my father now and let him know I'll be out, but that you're keen for a game of Rummy.'

The woman smacked her hip, clucking her tongue. 'I forget to say...your friend's pa came by when you were at the apothecary yesterday.' Cathleen paused. 'I know Mr Waverley likes that feller, but I sent him away as your pa was fast asleep.'

'Mr Sanders won't mind calling another time.'

'Later on that Mr Gresham paid a visit as well. It was a pleasure, so it was, shutting the door in his face.' Cathleen pursed her lips on a smirk. 'I wasn't going to tell you about that. I know you've no liking for him.'

'Indeed not,' Emma said with some conviction.

A rap at the door cut off Cathleen's next comment. 'If it's the nasty fat feller come by again he'll get the same answer as yesterday from me.' Cathleen marched to open up, saying over a shoulder, 'Mr Waverley shouldn't see any visitors yet a while.'

A moment later Emma was relieved to hear the voice of the postman rather than Joshua Gresham's hateful tones.

She took the letter from Cathleen, her smile fading, having recognised the script.

'Your father won't want to be upsetting himself reading that!' Cathleen also knew Mr Gresham's hand from previous correspondence.

'Indeed he won't be reading it,' Emma said decisively. 'Not until he's fully recovered.' She opened the drawer in the console table and dropped it in. Her father was making good progress, but any worry was likely to set him back and she would never allow that to happen.

'It's a very fine day for a drive,' Emma said brightly to break the quiet. Jack Valance's smiling eyes were on Dawn, making her cheeks turn rosy beneath his lingering regard. Mrs Booth was eagerly watching them both, as the stylish landau in which they were all seated proceeded at a sedate pace towards Hyde Park.

'It is a fine afternoon,' Jack agreed, squinting up at the clear blue sky. 'I'd like to stretch my legs. Perhaps a walk towards the water would be nice when we stop?' he suggested as the landau turned in through some open gates. He glanced at Dawn for her answer.

'How nice that sounds.' Mrs Booth had spoken over Dawn's reply, making the young ladies exchange a subtly pained look.

Politely, Jack helped them all down. Dawn was the last to quit the carriage and he kept hold of her hand, placing it on his arm. Immediately, Mrs Booth appropriated the use of his other elbow. The little party had not gone more than a few yards along the path winding though green parkland when Emma spotted somebody guaranteed to distract the older woman's attention and allow Dawn and Jack to carry on alone.

'We had a very nice time at Mrs Sweet's house. I expect you heard all about it,' Emma rattled off, then strolled to stand in the shade of a nearby tree. Her ruse worked. Julia relinquished Jack's arm to join her and gawp at an elegantly dressed lady holding the hands of two handsome children. Ruth Sweet had seen them, and as the youngsters ran off to play chase she waved a greeting at Emma.

'Heavens! She remembers you,' Mrs Booth gasped. 'Dawn told me Mrs Sweet was so very nice and friendly to you both, but I've been disappointed not to receive my own card. It was my influence that secured Dawn that invitation, I'm sure.'

Emma knew differently and felt her cheeks heating as the memory of what had occurred that afternoon infiltrated her mind. While Mrs Booth continued chattering about her ambition to be Mrs Sweet's friend, Emma watched the strolling couple. Dawn and Jack had managed to gain quite a start on them. Emma had felt reassured on meeting Jack again. He seemed an open character. Perhaps later she'd get a chance to chat to him properly and find out more about his feelings for Dawn. If she had to speak out of turn then she would, rather than see her best friend bamboozled by a rogue.

'Oh, look who has arrived. I would sooner see that fine gentleman pay attention to Dawn,' Mrs Booth lamented with such feeling that Emma again took heed of what she was saying. 'But he can have his pick of dukes' daughters when he decides to settle down whereas his friend must fortune hunt for a bride. There can be no future for Dawn with Mr Valance unless he improves his prospects.'

An investigative glance Mrs Sweet's way caused Emma to emit an involuntary gulp, quickly smothered by a cough. The Earl of Houndsmere was leading a beautiful pale-flanked horse towards his sister's carriage... while staring directly at them.

'Oh, goodness! He also remembers you!' Mrs

Booth hissed as his lordship's gaze remained turned in their direction. 'If you smile, my dear, he might come over. I should *so* like an introduction.' She nudged Emma in the ribs.

Emma's eyes veered away from him. She did indeed want to talk to Lance Harley...but not here in public. What she had to say should be uttered behind closed doors...if she ever found the resolve to begin that conversation.

'Dawn will wonder where we've got to.' Emma sounded calm despite suffering the sensation of a sardonic stare boring into her profile. 'Let's go and meet them by the lake.'

'But we cannot move on *now*! He *is* coming over and Mrs Sweet is with him.' Julia tugged Emma backwards as she would have set off towards the path.

'How very nice to see you again, Miss Waverley,' Ruth said with a warm smile.

'It's nice to see you, too, ma'am.' Emma bobbed politely. 'Might I introduce you to Mrs Booth?' she quickly added, having received another prod from her companion.

The polite formalities over with, Ruth gave her brother a twinkling smile. 'I imagine you remember the Earl of Houndsmere, Miss Waverley. I believe you strolled with him in my garden.'

'Yes, of course...' Emma murmured, executing a small bob in his direction. Well, she'd wanted to distract Dawn's nemesis so her friend could escape. She'd managed to do so in some style, Emma realised, feeling quite hysterical. Julia seemed about to swoon in pleasure and hadn't once looked to see where her future stepdaughter had got to.

Everybody was watching them. Passing carriages were slowing down, promenading couples were bumping into one another as they keenly observed what was going on.

'I think I've spotted Jack Valance and your friend up ahead.' Lance had thrust his hands into his pockets and was staring into the distance. 'Shall we catch up with them, Miss Waverley?'

Before Emma could formulate a polite reply in the negative Ruth spoke. 'While the young people tire themselves out walking, let me introduce you to my children, Mrs Booth.' She took a plump elbow, steering a beaming Julia over the grass.

'I find your high-handedness rather too much!' Emma said in a suffocated hiss. He had hold of her wrist and was leading her in the opposite direction.

'And I find your guile rather too much,' he returned in an equally flinty tone. 'So we have lots to talk about.'

'Please explain what you mean by that.' Emma

imagined she already knew what he meant, but waited with bated breath for his answer.

'Why didn't you mention that my stepsister and your brother are not only in cahoots, but lovers?'

So there it was…out in the open. And though her heart felt as though it might batter its way from between her ribs there was also a modicum of relief in the knowledge that she need no longer be tortured by the imminence of him unearthing that secret. There was nothing left for him to discover…unless he hadn't yet located the couple. But she suspected he had, even if he hadn't yet been to Rowley Street to confront them.

'Are you going to answer me?'

'Yes… I'll answer you. I knew I didn't have to tell you about Robin and Augusta. I knew that before long you would find out for yourself, because nothing escapes you, does it, my lord?' She sounded bitterly resigned to his victory.

'I think perhaps you might, Miss Waverley.'

His harsh self-mockery made her glance up at him.

'Indeed, I shall try to if you don't turn about, sir. I thought we were to meet our friends.' She had believed they were to head to the lake; instead, he was traversing the greensward at an angle, his pace steadily increasing in the direction of a copse.

'We have unfinished business that needs to be dealt with somewhere private.'

Emma valiantly kept up with his long stride, her small fingers fidgeting beneath his cool palm, settled on top of them on his arm. But he was unrelenting until they reached the shelter of the trees, then he immediately set her free. He walked away from her a few paces before pivoting on a heel and assessing her with a pair of deep blue eyes. 'Don't look so terrified. I have no designs on your virtue…leastways not in Hyde Park in the middle of the afternoon.'

'I'm not scared of you.' Emma elevated her chin to a proud angle, her stare clashing with his.

'That's a good start at least.'

His cruel-looking mouth softened into a smile as his gaze slowly roamed over her, making Emma feel unbearably hot. He never leered at her in the way that Joshua Gresham did. But she was just as aware of Lance Harley's desire for her body. Joshua turned her stomach, but the pull of attraction between her and this man was so strong that it seemed to solidify the atmosphere, making it hard for her to breathe. Only a short while ago she hadn't known the Earl of Houndsmere existed. Now when she was out she was watching for him, longing, yet dreading to meet him by chance again as she had on the day she'd sold her locket. Today that had happened.

And that first glimpse of him had been enough to start butterflies dancing in her stomach.

'Have you thought about my offer of assistance?'

'I've thought of little else,' she admitted. There was no point in pretence. It was too late for any of that.

Her honesty made his smile deepen. 'And?'

'And...now that you know about your stepsister's involvement with Robin, will you still be prepared to help him?'

'Help him escape the minx, you mean?' he asked.

Emma wasn't sure what to make of that. He'd sounded scathing of his stepsister, but not because she had shackled herself to a coalman. Rather the other way around, as though her brother were the one deserving of pity. At first she'd been flustered to be unexpectedly brought face-to-face with him. Now she was coming to understand that this might be a perfect opportunity to agree to a plan of action with him...if he were amenable to co-operating. Her father would be so content if she could return home and tell him that the Earl wanted to get involved in remedying the situation affecting both their families.

She sighed, gesturing her sorrow as a prelude to a frank discussion. 'What a mess it is for us all!'

'You have a nice way with understatement, my dear.'

He'd sounded sarcastic, which wasn't surprising, or auspicious, but she persevered in hoping that this conversation could bear fruit. 'Have you been to their lodging to speak to them?' She took a few tentative steps closer to him.

'Have you?' he countered.

She nodded. 'I saw them recently and warned them you would soon catch up with them.'

'To give them a chance to abscond elsewhere?'

'Yes…if that's what they want to do.'

He shook his head, mouthing an oath, before saying to the branches swaying above his head, 'God in heaven, you're a child, Emma, no matter your age.'

'What do you mean by that?' she snapped indignantly as her cheeks flamed. So being candid had gained her nothing but his disapproval.

'I mean that you're old enough to know better and this game has to stop.'

'It might be a game to you,' she stormed, 'but to us it is deadly serious. My father is ill with worry over it and has no way to put things right. How dare you say it is a game to *us*!' She marched right up to him, tawny eyes afire. 'It is *you* who think it all sport…who think *me* sport.' Her vision became blurred by angry tears.

'You're wrong. I don't…'

She slapped away the hand he stretched towards her, turning her back on him. 'Of course you do. I'm nothing to you...just an opportunity there to be taken. My family's nothing to you. Your own family is nothing to you. Even knowing that your stepsister is enduring hardship in a slum while increasing with child hasn't moved you...' She bit her lip and swung back, seeing immediately that he hadn't known that.

'Is she indeed?' He grunted a sour laugh. 'That might complicate the matter of an annulment if indeed the marriage is valid or has yet taken place.'

'Whether it has or hasn't, an annulment matters little because Augusta vows to stay with him. She loves my brother and he loves her.'

'Poor fool...if she is anything like her mother he won't for long.'

His cynicism infuriated her into rashness. 'Well, you would know about her mother, wouldn't you? It is a shame that I didn't realise at once what sort of a degenerate you are or I would never have accepted a ride home with you on that first night. I'd sooner have fended for myself against those men.' She immediately regretted having blurted that out. She *had* acted childishly now. Worse still, she had sounded like a jealous shrew...a rival for his affections. And she wasn't, she inwardly impressed on herself.

His stepmother and his other women were welcome to him. She didn't want him…and she'd never fall in love with him. Their relationship must remain purely business and any rogue emotion disturbing her when he was around must be mercilessly quashed. No more silly fantasy of growing closer and sharing their worries.

He was walking towards her. Outwardly, he didn't seem angry, yet something bad was blackening the colour of his eyes, making her backpace with his advance.

'Who told you about that?' His query sounded idle as though her reply was of scant interest.

But it wasn't; as she felt the bole of a tree behind she tried to shift aside, but he rammed a fist on bark, barring her way. 'Who told you about that?' he repeated.

'Let me pass,' Emma requested coolly. 'I thought we might talk sensibly about troubles besetting our families, but I see now that is impossible. I want to join my friends.'

'And so you shall after you've answered me. Did Augusta mention that I'd been in a relationship with her mother?'

'Yes, she did.'

'It was a long time ago… I was eighteen and shamefully naive…'

'You need not explain to me.'

'I'm aware of that. But you wouldn't have brought it up unless keen to know more about it.'

'I think your conceit has misled you, my lord. I have no interest in any of your sordid liaisons. Now let me pass,' she demanded, her voice wobbly. Whenever he was this close to her she felt tempted to sway in his direction. She yearned to have his warmth and the rock-like strength of his body pressing into hers. The memory of how he had made her feel when he kissed and touched her kept her awake at night, too aware of her patched cotton nightdress scraping her skin. She had skimmed her fingers over her own body in the way he had touched her while wishing the hand to be his...firmer, more insistent than her own.

She jerked her mind from the drugging memory and turned towards freedom. Before she could escape he'd planted his other hand on the oak, imprisoning her. Grabbing at his forearm, she attempted to physically remove him, but achieved nothing other than him flexing the muscle she'd dug her fingernails into. She flung her spine against the tree trunk, then glared up at him. She realised she shouldn't have done that... shouldn't have made lengthy eye contact at all, let alone in a way that challenged him. Before she could break their gazes he'd moved closer, his thighs grazing her pelvis and his weight pressing her back against wood. He untied her bonnet, letting it drop to the earth. His mouth lowered, so slowly that she knew he was giving her time to avoid him, but she couldn't summon the willpower. Already, her lashes were fluttering low, her breathing slowing in anticipation of his lips touching hers.

Why had Simon never kissed her like this was a phrase that wailed in her head. She had been in love with him, yet had never been treated with such tenderness that it felt as though her bones might melt. Never before had she deliciously shivered beneath male fingers trailing her nape, her collarbone, her ears, every available exposed part of skin, while a careful onslaught of caressing lips and teasing tongue on her mouth made her sigh at its seductive sweetness. In her fevered state she believed she might crumple to the ground if he stopped what he was doing. *You're losing your mind*, she told herself, and, drawing a shuddering breath from his mouth, she forced her hands between them.

For a moment she was sure he would let her go. The long fingers that he'd thrust into her hair withdrew to curve over her fragile shoulders. Their mouths unsealed, his tongue tip lightly trailing her lower lip as though in parting salutation. Then his mouth was back on hers, hot and hard. This was no subtle wooing but blatant carnality and the more she twisted her face to free it, the more erotic the assault became. He pulled the pins from her hair so ebony silk coated one of his hands while the other breached her cloak, caressing with skilful sensuality over her hips and breasts, teasing and tantalising the flesh swelling beneath his touch. Finally, he lifted his head to look at her.

Two small palms flattened against the muscles in his chest, then pushed. She put the back of her hand against her throbbing mouth. 'I can tell you are a practised seducer. There's no further need to prove that to me.'

'Am I? Well, you could have fooled me. So what suits you? How did Simon Gresham win you over?'

'He gave me his heart, that's what he did!' she cried in outrage and one of her small hands arced up to crack against his face. She knew he could have stopped her if he'd wanted to but he allowed her to hit him, simply turning with the blow that left an imprint of her fingers on a lean cheek.

'He gave you his heart, did he?' he mimicked with brutal mockery. 'It's a damn shame he didn't give you his honesty before he bedded you at a tavern on the Great North Road.'

'He did not! He wasn't like you! He was a decent man and treated me with respect and consideration.'

'That's good to know.' He pushed himself off the wood, swooped on her bonnet, handed it to her then walked away and stood with his back to her. 'Decent men don't commit bigamy with unsuspecting virgins, Emma.'

She winced beneath the undeniable truth in that and, though she longed to retaliate, she couldn't find the words. With trembling fingers, she located a single pin still fixed at her nape and did her best to neaten her hair.

'Do you pine for him still?'

For a moment she wondered if she'd misheard him. What did he care if she still had a broken heart? Perhaps his ego couldn't bear rivals, even if they were ghosts. 'It's none of your business,' was all she said and rammed her bonnet back on her crown to conceal her dishevelled locks.

A moment later he turned to her. 'Come… I'll take you back to the others now.'

So he wanted to go, did he? He'd lost interest in the game because he thought he'd bested her and there were no more kisses to be had. Well, she wasn't ready to go! He might have started this today, but she would finish it. When he walked towards her she blocked *his* way this time. And when he reached out to draw her into his arms, believing she'd come to him in surrender, she slapped his hands down. Her small fingers could only partway encircle his sinewy wrists, but she did her best to anchor them at his sides so he couldn't touch her.

'You will listen to me,' she whispered to the sapphire pinned in his neckcloth. It resembled his eyes so she gazed over his shoulder instead. 'You might think you may treat me as you want, but you will not. I'm not your stepmother, or your Jenny or any other of your fancy women. Nor will I ever be.' She paused, her throat throbbing with tension. She'd been expecting him to step past her, pulling her with him once he realised she'd arrested him for no pleasurable reason. But he didn't. He stood quite still, his body a hair's breadth from hers and his hands where she had them pinned. Abruptly, she released him and took two hasty backward paces.

She raised her eyes, but his expression was inscrutable. She couldn't tell if he considered her impudent, or pitiable. Or even if he felt some amusement for the way she'd stood up to him. She believed what Augusta had said about few people crossing the Earl of Houndsmere. He was used to people kowtowing to him, not telling him truths about himself. And they were truths, she realised, as a flicker of some emotion twisted his mouth. He didn't look guilty, but he looked thoughtful.

'Are you going to spoil what little happiness your stepsister has found with my brother? Are you going to hound them until the strain of it all makes them turn on one another?'

'Augusta is no sweet innocent and will go her own way whatever I do.'

'I'm not surprised she is no sweet innocent. How could she be with you and her mother colouring her life? What shining example has she had to follow when growing up? Given what she has been through, I'm surprised she is as lovely as she is. You may mock her, but with a callous libertine for a stepbrother and a mother who rarely has time for her I think she has turned out remarkably well. How lonely and sad she must have felt and little wonder she yearns to find some company with strangers. You should admire Augusta. I do. And I like her. Before you condemn her, or my brother, or me for that matter, you should look to your own morals, sir.' Emma clamped her lips together, having rattled that lot off, wishing he'd say something instead of regarding her with that relentless hooded gaze.

'Have you finished?'

'For now,' she replied haughtily, straightening her bonnet.

'For good. I think you've said enough, don't you?'

'Have I? Well, what will you do if I find more to say? Ruin me or my family with your revenge and your riches?' She laughed bitterly. 'You cannot…it is already done. So go ahead and do your worst, my lord.'

Emma swung about and started back the way she had come, her eyes tigerish and her cheeks flushed in terrified exhilaration. She knew he was walking behind, but he didn't attempt to catch up with her until some promenading people hove into view. Then in an easy stride he was again at her side, placing her arm on his as though they were just like any other harmonious couple enjoying a stroll. She would have loved to rip her hand away, but daren't make a scene and worsen a very bad situation.

She was trembling, though she tightened every muscle she possessed to try to steady the fingers on his arm. She didn't want him to know how anguished she felt now the full force of her audacity had finally caught up with her. She had gone too far. She had been unbelievably ill-mannered and presumptuous. How he went on with his family was none of her concern…but she had made it so, and intentionally challenged and provoked him in the doing of it. Her father would be horrified if he knew how disgracefully she'd behaved. So would her brother. She had just worsened their lot instead of securing Lance Harley's help in finding a solution to it. What excuse had she to offer to those people she loved? None! She could have…*should* have…bitten her tongue rather than comment so insolently on the Earl of Houndsmere's private business.

An apology was on the tip of her tongue and she battled inwardly to suppress her pride and force herself to issue it. And then it was too late. Her friends were in sight and Dawn had spotted her, raising a hand to wave.

Warily, Emma lifted her eyes to a profile that might have been hewn from granite. She wanted to say a farewell at least, but he removed her hand from his arm and, without a word, but with an unfathomable, if penetrating look, walked away.

Chapter Fourteen

'A gentleman is here to see you, my lord.'

Wilkins glimpsed a tic-ridden jawline and a deep frown as his master strode past, a sure sign that he was immersed in some inner turmoil. Wilkins had seen him angry on many occasions. But never had Houndsmere appeared quite so absorbed in stormy thoughts as now. The manservant hobbled in his wake to repeat his message.

Conscious of being pursued, Lance halted, bringing the old fellow up short.

'A visitor has arrived,' Wilkins puffed out. 'I have put him in the library anteroom with a footman outside the door. The fellow insisted that you have urgent business to conclude.'

'His name?'

'Mr Joshua Gresham, my lord.' The butler gave his employer a circumspect peer, wondering whether the caller had lied about having an appointment; the Earl didn't look as though he'd been expecting anybody. Gresham had acted pompous, but often the lower orders attempted to bolster their courage with bluster when presenting themselves at this grand abode. 'I can have him shown out, your lordship?' Wilkins ventured.

'Not at all. I'll see him now.' Lance had entered the house so fast that he'd almost gained the foot of the stairs, but he changed direction, heading to the library. He'd been about to get some cash from his chamber and take a trip to the East End to see the hapless lovebirds, but he could delay that for a short while. He was in just the right mood to deal with Joshua Gresham.

Lance paced along the spacious corridor aglitter with chandeliers, gesturing for the footman to remove himself. Even with the prospect of a fight on his hands he couldn't put out of his mind a woman, tawny eyes ablaze, castigating him for his wickedness. Emma had forced him to examine something about his character and he didn't like what he'd found. He'd believed himself fair and ethical, but he hadn't been where his stepsister was concerned.

By the time the old Earl had been bewitched into marrying again and became Augusta's stepfather, she had turned fifteen. At her mother's insistence, her come out had taken place the following year. Sonia had wanted to offload the responsibility of her child to a son-in-law so she could live her own life even then.

Pretty as she was, Augusta received no acceptable proposals. At sixteen she was already a rebel, outraging rather than charming eligible gentlemen. Some fortune hunters stepped up, hoping the elderly Earl might be desperate enough to settle his wayward stepdaughter with a pot of gold. But before the end of her debut Season William Harley didn't care what happened to the girl or her mother. He had uncovered his second wife's greed and adultery and had ejected her and her daughter from the main house to live elsewhere on the estate. People assumed Augusta was from the same mould as her mother to constantly be in mischief. Lance had held the same idea. But he was wrong. Had he taken the trouble to really get to know his stepsister, he might have discovered that for himself. But the disgust he felt for her mother had made him prejudiced. Instead, Emma had brought to his attention something that should have been obvious to him: Augusta was nothing like Sonia and that was why the desperate girl kept putting distance between them. She wasn't bad, she was lonely and neglected…not just by her mother, but by him, too.

Lance had believed his contribution to his

stepsister's well-being had been met with his money and nothing else was his concern. But his responsibility to her went beyond food and clothes and allowing her to reside in his properties. And bringing her home when she absconded from them, to dump her back on her mother's doorstep.

He felt ashamed. Not only of his cavalier attitude, but that a wonderful, caring woman who barely knew Augusta had needed to bring her virtues and his faults to his attention.

Lance pushed open the anteroom door, and immediately Joshua Gresham sprang to attention. He'd been prowling about while waiting, but now snapped a bow.

Lance went to the decanter on a side table, pouring a measure and stoppering it without offering his visitor a drink. He looked at Gresham over the rim of his glass, wondering if the man had resembled his younger brother in looks and character. If he had, God only knew what had attracted Emma to Simon Gresham. Not that Joshua was ugly: he was of adequate height and breadth and had regular features. But he had an air of unpleasantness, endorsed the moment he opened his mouth.

'You are wondering why I have taken the liberty of presenting myself like this, but I think you will welcome the imposition on your time, my lord, when I explain—'

'There was no need to deliver the deeds here. My solicitor was briefed to deal with this matter.' Lance cut across Joshua's waffle.

'I haven't brought them, my lord.'

Lance elevated a quizzical eyebrow, putting down his depleted glass. 'The document is with my solicitor?'

'I intend to keep hold of Waverley's debts.' Joshua's attempt to sound confident floundered beneath a pair of glacial blue eyes.

After winkling every astonishing detail out of Roland Sanders earlier that afternoon, Joshua had decided against meekly relinquishing the deeds. He had turned for home, happily depositing the document back in his desk. Then he had set out for Grosvenor Square, whistling. Now he was feeling far less chirpy. The moment he'd set foot in his lordship's magnificent world was the moment his bravado began to sap. His opponent's power and wealth was evident in every piece of furniture and every artefact reposing on polished surfaces. The porcelain bowl, the jade figurine, the rare ancient tomes under lock and key behind the leaded glass of the bookcases... all were testament to Houndsmere's wealth and exalted station in life. Joshua had been restlessly pacing while waiting, casting envious, resentful glances to and fro. At one point, he'd been about to bolt, but had talked himself out of it. Being allowed into this opulence was a privilege to be drawn out to its fullest and bragged about.

His sweating brow and hoarse voice had betrayed his anxiety, though. The Earl was looking at him with a faintly amused expression that was harder to endure than would have been a bawled demand for an explanation. 'I have news, my lord, that I believe you will find extremely concerning,' Joshua gabbled out into the heavy silence. 'Once recounted, my gambling debt to you will seem as nothing compared to the reward and gratitude due to me in bringing this to your attention. Naturally you will have my utmost discretion on it all.'

'I can't wait to hear it.' Lance refilled his glass, then shot the whisky back. He gestured with the empty vessel that he was growing impatient for the yarn to be started.

Joshua turned ruddy beneath the Earl's insouciance. He was hoping to soon wipe the disdain off his face. 'I have it on good authority that your stepsister is embroiled with a criminal absconded from justice. It is the same individual who murdered my brother in a duel. Namely Robin Waverley.' He ended on a high note, vibrating with triumph.

'And you think that information is worth the price of his father's house to me?'

A dawning realisation that Houndsmere was not only already aware of the news, but was also unmoved by his hint of blackmail, caused Joshua's jowls to sag towards his chest.

'I will not ask for the deeds again. Take them to my lawyer today or I will sue for costs and damages and also have your own house from under you. And never think to mention my family's business to me or to anybody else or I will make you wish you had never been born. Do you understand?'

Joshua licked his arid lips. He had believed this information so shocking that Houndsmere would meet all his demands to keep it secret. But pieces of a puzzle were falling into place. The reason for Houndsmere's visits to Bernard Waverley became clearer. The men were allies in this. And Emma was in on it, too. She'd always been close to her twin brother and would do anything to save his hide…including sleeping with the man who could buy Robin's freedom.

A while ago Veronica had recounted some gossip that Houndsmere had been spotted at just after dawn, assisting Waverley's daughter from his phaeton. Joshua had dismissed it as fallacious scandalmongering arising from the Earl's unexplained visits to Primrose Square. Now he believed that Houndsmere *had* delivered the little harlot home after a night of fornication and had not done so as discreetly as he might.

'I said…do you understand?' Lance enunciated, bracing a hand against the doorjamb.

Joshua gave a stiff nod of agreement, yet frustration was starting to boil in his chest. After leaving here he had planned to call on Emma. He'd already sent Bernard a letter telling him he knew all about his secrets. He supposed the fellow must be very ill indeed not to have immediately responded to such an alarming missive. Not that he expected Bernard to worry his daughter with the new threat Joshua intended dangling over them. But *he* intended to. Once aware of his increased power, Emma would surely put up no further resistance. So Joshua wasn't quashing his lust for her, not when he was so close to achieving his goal of having her.

As Houndsmere approached to loom over him Joshua whined, 'I would not go against you, my lord, but I have every right to demand recompense from Bernard Waverley. His son killed my brother.'

'And you think that gives you the right to hound the family long after the event?'

'Bernard owes me more than those deeds…'

'He owes you nothing. His house and his debts

are mine. You will never again trouble Waverley or his daughter at their home or anywhere else.'

'His daughter?' Joshua pounced at once.

'The family is under my protection and that is all you need to know. Now remove yourself and deliver those deeds today before you are in default.'

Joshua's pinched features turned florid at that blunt dismissal. The writhing in his gut wouldn't be calmed, although he tried telling himself to keep a cool head. 'She interests you, doesn't she?' he burst out. 'I'm not surprised. She has a way of being most obliging to her father's creditors.' He sneered. 'I've tasted her, too…sweet as wine, isn't she…smells of lavender…'

Lance took a single stride, grabbing him by the throat with one large brutal hand. He shook him as a terrier might treat a rat. 'You're lying… you've never got close…unless you've forced yourself on her. Have you?'

'I didn't need to…she's a wanton…' Joshua gasped out the lie through barely moving mauve lips.

Lance thrust him away so he fell against a side table. Unbalanced, Joshua crashed to the floor, winded, his hands wrapped around his aching throat. He knew he'd gone too far now to backtrack. His lordship's perilous rage was evident in every taut angle of his face and that stony black stare that seemed to nail him to the floor. Joshua scrambled to his feet and puffed out his chest. Inwardly, he was quaking, wishing he'd approached things differently. He was no match for this man in a fair fight or anything else. But still the thought of losing his grip on Emma was deranging him. He plunged a hand into his pocket, scrabbling for metal. 'I'm not lying about that harlot. Look!' He thrust the gold locket out on a flat palm. 'She left it in my bed over a month ago. And when I'm done here I shall go and return it to the little strumpet. I'll wager she'll wrap her legs around my neck as she did before to thank me.'

Lance scooped the gold into a fist that carried on to make heavy contact with a smirking mouth. Joshua collapsed without knowing what had hit him. This time he had assistance finding his feet. Lance hauled him up by the collar of his coat then dragged him by it to the door, slamming him face front into it.

'You might think yourself an able villain, but you're an amateur, my friend,' Lance said close to his ear. 'But if you wish to try to cross me and test my capacity for revenge…go ahead. It'll be a pleasure teaching you a lesson.'

Lance opened the anteroom door with one hand and shoved Joshua into the hall with the other. For good measure he hurried him on

his way with the toe of his boot, sending him
sprawling. He left him where he fell, bleeding
on a priceless Persian carpet, and strode past to
the stairs, taking them two at a time.

'Show my visitor out.' Over a shoulder, he
calmly addressed two footmen who had started
to sprint from the vestibule on hearing the commotion. The sight of a gentleman nursing his
bloody chin while dragging himself upright
against the watered silk wall seemed to bother
the servants not a jot. They stationed themselves
either side of him and bundled him out of the
house.

'Buck up, my dear!' Emma encouraged,
squeezing Dawn's fingers. 'Better that Mr Valance has been honest than upset you by making out he is somebody he is not.' Emma knew
all about how it felt to be tricked in such a way.
She had been led to believe Simon could become her husband and his vile brother had lied
and pretended to be a friend to her and her father. Lance Harley had at first omitted to tell her
he was a nobleman. But she didn't believe *he'd*
misled her…rather that he hadn't wanted to boast
about his status. But she mustn't think of him
or revisit their passionate argument. Apologise
for her impertinence, indeed she must…but how
and when to do it…that was uncertain. For now,

commiserating with Dawn must stay uppermost in her mind. And then she must hurry home and see how her father did.

'I know Mr Valance acted correctly telling me he hasn't the means to take a wife.' Dawn sighed. 'It was just a little dream I had that we might become more than friends. We got on well together for so short an acquaintance.' She shrugged. 'I hope we keep in touch.'

Instead of being dropped outside her house, Emma had asked to be set down with Dawn, saying she could walk the short distance to Primrose Square. On the journey back from Hyde Park she could tell that her friend was in need of a shoulder to cry on, despite Dawn's brave face. Mrs Booth had snatched at Ruth's invitation to accompany her to a teashop to treat the children when they left the park. The younger ladies had been asked along, too, but had declined. It had suited them both to go straight to Marylebone in the landau with Jack Valance. As for the Earl, he had untied his fine palomino from the back of Ruth's carriage and had ridden off with barely a word to anybody. Emma had imagined that his sister's smile stood as an apology for his churlishness in abruptly abandoning the party. It had been as well that Ruth didn't know the truth of it, Emma thought, or the woman might not have looked her way so sympathetically.

Jack had initiated most of the polite chitchat on the short journey. He had declined Dawn's invitation to take tea, immediately setting on his way after helping them down from the landau.

'Now it's your turn to spill the beans, Em.' Dawn cocked her head. 'The Earl of Houndsmere has paid you a good deal of attention.'

Emma gave a neutral smile. 'Oh, I think this afternoon he invited me to take a stroll to escape Mrs Booth fawning over him.'

'A lot of aristocrats might like to be fawned over. But Jack told me his best friend is not at all big-headed. When they were on campaign on the continent Colonel Harley would muck in with the rest of the men, using a shovel or cooking when needs must.'

So…he'd been a soldier. There was so much she didn't know about him, Emma realised. And why should she? Though their lives had become entangled they were still just acquaintances… nothing more. Unless she became his lover. Even then he might not tell her much about himself. The only personal information he'd ever shared was that of having started an affair with Augusta's mother when he was eighteen. How many years ago was that? He looked about thirty, but could be older…

'Do you like the Earl, though, Em?' Dawn persisted.

Her friend's question put Emma on the spot, making her probe feelings she'd rather not analyse. She didn't hate him, neither did she fear his power over her as she once had. He had told her he'd not harm her or force her to do anything she didn't want to. And neither had he. The kisses and caresses she'd received had been blissful, not hurtful, because in truth she adored the feel of his body, his mouth, pressing hard against hers. The unpalatable facts about her past that he'd brought to her attention had been justified. Just as had those truths about him that she'd laid at his door.

He was a rich aristocrat and she was the spinster daughter of an impecunious gentleman. The Earl of Houndsmere had done what any man in his position would do if finding a woman attractive and in need of financial assistance. He'd suggested a solution to benefit them both. She was conscious that there were a multitude of needy females who would doubtless welcome a proposition from a handsome, generous peer of the realm. She couldn't blame him for thinking she might be one of them.

'Don't you know how you feel about him, Em? Can't you decide if you like him?' Dawn had been watching the changing emotions flitting over her friend's lovely features. Emma's eyes had been sparkling like topaz jewels one moment and clouding the next.

Tempted to prevaricate, Emma instead told the truth. 'Yes… I like him. But it would be foolish to like him too much. You and I must both be sensible about things: you cannot become fond of Jack because he has too little and I cannot become fond of the Earl of Houndsmere because he has too much. So…enough of these unsuitable gentlemen. We should talk of something else while we finish our tea. Then I must get going. Mrs O'Reilly has been a real boon while Papa has been ill, but she will want to get off home.'

'How is Mr Waverley? My father was in a tizzy over not being able to see him earlier in the week. He came back and went straight to his study with a very black expression.' Dawn paused. 'This morning at breakfast he muttered about paying him another visit while we were out for a drive in the park. I wondered if Mr Waverley had taken a turn for the worse and that had upset Papa.'

'No…my father's health has improved.' Emma felt a fluttering of uneasiness. Quickly, she finished her tea and stood up. 'I should get home and see how he is, though.'

Once outside on the pavement she waved to her friend and speedily set off, disquiet still bedevilling her. The families did not live far apart and, walking briskly, she reached Primrose Square in under fifteen minutes. She lightly ascended the stone steps and entered the house to find Mrs O'Reilly in the kitchen, stirring a pot of stew that was steaming a savoury aroma into the atmosphere. Everything appeared calm and peaceful, but Emma blurted, 'Did my father have a visitor while I was out, Mrs O'Reilly?'

'He did, miss. His friend knocked and seemed determined to come in. As your pa is so much better I let him upstairs to see Mr Waverley. I left them alone with the playing cards.' She shook her head. 'And now I'm thinking I shouldn't have. I heard them arguing, so I did. I was about to go and throw the feller out, friend or no friend. But he left with a red face and barely a word. He's not been gone long.'

'Arguing?' Another stab of foreboding tightened Emma's chest.

'I took your father up a powder a little while ago, hoping he'd have a nap before eating his dinner. He was grumpy and said he didn't want it.'

'Why did they argue?'

Mrs O'Reilly shook her head. 'The cards were all over the floor. I picked them up and asked if the other feller had cheated. But your father wouldn't say.' She tutted. 'These men…worse than children with their tantrums, so they are.'

Cathleen put down the spoon she'd been stirring the stew with. 'I'll be off home now. Your dinner is ready when you are.'

'Thank you, Mrs O'Reilly.'

As soon as Cathleen had left Emma ran upstairs. What Dawn had told her led her to believe that whatever was wrong between their fathers had started before that card game this afternoon. She rapped on his chamber door and, when she received no answer, entered.

'What are you doing, Papa?' Emma sped up to him. He was still in his nightgown, but was struggling to put on his waistcoat over it. Unsteady on his feet, he lost his balance and fell backwards on to his bed.

'Roland came while you were out,' Bernard puffed. 'He told me that Gresham is aware of all our business. Every sordid part of my son's employment as a coalman and his affair with Houndsmere's stepsister is known to that blackguard!' Bernard thumped his fists on to the mattress in despair. 'Roland thinks the cunning wretch tricked him into saying more than he should have. Joshua made out he knew everything when in truth he only had a few facts. I bawled my friend out for letting one word slip between his lips. He is supposed to be my most trusted confidant, but blabbed our secrets.'

'You *told* Mr Sanders about Robin…and everything else as well?' Emma cried. 'It was supposed to be just for us to know, Papa!' She bit her lip. She wasn't without fault. She had let slip about her brother on the very first occasion she had met Lance Harley. And now he knew everything, too.

'I couldn't help it… I was so excited…and Roland promised he would keep his mouth shut.' Bernard looked shamefaced. 'But I know it is all my fault. Now I must put things right. I'm going out to see my son before Gresham catches up with him and I'll warrant with a Bow Street Runner at his side to arrest Robin.'

'You must not!' Emma guessed her father was feverish from distress. His face was flushed and perspiring, and he seemed confused to be dressing himself over his nightgown. 'I will go and warn Robin,' she soothed him. 'Please get back into bed, Papa.' His chest was heaving with the effort of gasping in breaths and she feared if he didn't stop thrashing about he'd knock the scab off his healing wound.

'But he will listen to me…not you. You have let me down by taking too long to deal with it, Emma,' her father scolded, struggling to stand up. 'I should have borrowed more money and helped Robin sooner,' he wailed. 'It is my fault he is found out. Houndsmere might have loaned me money, had I asked. I would have done anything that man said to have his backing and save my son…'

'Hush, Papa…' Emma felt tears prickling her own eyes, listening to her father's sobs.

Bernard wiped his face with the sleeve of his nightshirt. 'Why hasn't Gresham been here to taunt me?' He frowned. 'I know that devil: he would have come just to rub my nose in it.'

'He did visit when you had a fever,' Emma informed. 'Mrs O'Reilly sent him away, Papa, but he…' She had been about to say that he had sent a letter instead. Something made her think better of it and stay quiet. Until now she had forgotten about the post she had slipped into a drawer.

She picked the beaker up from the nightstand and agitated the milky water with the spoon standing in it. 'Take your powder, Papa, it will calm you. I promise to sort this out. I know I can.' Inwardly, she prayed that was no empty boast, but it had the desired effect. He meekly drank the concoction.

Handing back the empty cup, he gazed at her with damp, trusting eyes. He caught at her fingers to pat them. 'You are a good girl, little Emma.'

She gave him a shaky smile. It wasn't by being good that she'd bring this right. Quite the opposite behaviour would be needed. At one time she might have been relieved to know that Houndsmere had lost interest in her...now she prayed that he had not. After her insolence earlier it was likely he might not want to see her again. And she couldn't...wouldn't beg.

She helped her father remove his waistcoat and settled him under the covers before going downstairs and straight to the console table in the hall. She had never before opened any letter addressed to her father, but she feared that the content of this one would destroy him. So he must never see it. Quickly, she broke the seal, gasping as her eyes flew over the two paragraphs that crudely gibed at her father.

With brutish candour, Joshua had described what he wanted to buy his silence: Emma to quit her home and move to an address of his choosing to henceforth be his concubine. He had actually written that in a letter to her father! Emma screwed the parchment in a fist and threw it as far as she could. She had always disliked Joshua, even in the early days after Simon had died and his brother had pretended to be sympathetic to gain their trust. But never had she believed he would sink so low as to torture an ill man with the abuse he intended to inflict on his daughter.

She retrieved the paper and stuffed it in a pocket. Praying that her father would stay put in his bed now he'd swallowed the sleeping draught, she donned her cloak and went out. As she walked quickly away she realised she would visit two very different districts this evening: Rowley Street and Grosvenor Square. And the latter trip to Mayfair would require the greatest courage.

Houndsmere had told her not to let things fester, or the matter would only get worse. He had been right. But for her own sake she had prevaricated…and in doing so had risked her father's health and her brother's safety. Now she might have left it too late to be put right. And all because of her stupid pride.

Chapter Fifteen

The loud bang on the door made the couple immediately break apart. Robin had been rocking Augusta in his arms while she tearfully complained of feeling horribly queasy most of the time and wishing she wasn't having a baby if this was what it entailed.

'It's only the landlord,' he reassured, as her startled gaze darted to the door. 'Dry your eyes now. I'll pay him his rent and he'll leave us be. Then, I'll go out and get us some supper.'

'I don't want any food,' she whimpered, rubbing her swollen abdomen. 'And I don't like that horrible old man, Robin. Don't let him in. He tried to kiss me when you were at work… please…let's move from here.'

'Soon…' Robin promised, but his expression had turned grim. Augusta's sweet face and blonde locks drew male attention. It wasn't the first time he'd had to protect her from the low life they were forced to surround themselves with. He flung wide the door, snarling, 'I believe you have an apology to make, sirrah...'

'You took the words right out of my mouth,' came the drawled reply. 'And before I'm done with you, I will have it. As will your sister.'

It took a second or two for Robin to overcome his shock and clack shut his dropped jaw. He attempted to slam the door in the Earl's face, but a strong arm whacked the wooden panels back against the wall.

'Leave us alone!' Augusta cried, intrepidly springing forward to shield Robin from her stepbrother, advancing into the room. 'I love him and I'm staying with him.'

'So I gather,' Lance said in the same mordant tone. He closed the door, running a jaundiced eye over their dilapidated abode. 'Well, it must be love, I suppose, to make you put up with this when you've a feather bed to go to.'

'Such things means nothing to me,' Augusta declared, tilting her chin. 'I'd sooner starve and sleep on straw here with Robin than go back with you to Chelsea.'

'A trifle dramatic—nevertheless, I believe you truthfully would,' Lance replied mildly. 'But if you wish to stay out of trouble, Waverley, you need to leave here this instant and do as I say.'

'What punishment have you planned for me?' Robin had recovered his senses and moved Augusta behind him in a show of manliness. He felt a dolt now for allowing a pregnant woman to step up to protect him. Besides, the Earl didn't look as fierce as he'd expected him to when he apprehended them. In fact, he didn't look *really* angry at all. 'Tell me what you intend to do,' Robin insisted.

'I'll help you. That's the truth. Now quickly, get your things together to set on the road.' Lance gestured to his stepsister to fill up the carpet bag resting against the wall, then turned to Robin. 'Joshua Gresham knows you are alive and is on your trail.'

'Who told *him*?' Robin burst out, turning pale. 'My father wouldn't... Emma!' He thumped a fist into a palm. 'Joshua has always had eyes for her. He and his brother both wanted her, but she avoided Joshua from the start. If I hadn't caught up with the couple on their way to Gretna, then Joshua would have. He found out his brother planned to elope and set out after them to betray Simon. Anybody could see that it ate Joshua up inside, not having her.' Robin agitatedly paced to and fro, thinking things through. 'Joshua proposed to her after Simon died, but she turned him down. Has he been sniffing around my sister again, do you know? He married Simon's widow, but a wife wouldn't stop that lecher going after a woman he wanted. Somehow or other he must have dragged our secret out of Emma—'

'He hasn't,' Lance cut across him. 'Your sister has done her best to save your hide, imperilling herself in the process. When you next see her make sure to show her the gratitude she deserves, or I'll show you some manners.'

Robin didn't like being criticised and threatened in front of Augusta. 'What do you care?' he blustered. A silence followed that made him widen his eyes on his detractor. 'Hell's teeth… you *do* care…' he muttered.

'Get your belongings together now, before I recover my senses and leave you both to your own devices. I'll meet you downstairs. You have precisely ten minutes before I send the coach away.'

'Where are we going, Lance?' Augusta looked much more cheerful now she knew her stepbrother wasn't about to kill the man she loved and drag her back to her mother.

'I'll tell you that somewhere more private.' The glance he cast at the thin walls needed no explanation.

Five minutes later the couple rushed out of the dingy building, Robin carrying their carpet bags, and joined Lance on the pavement.

He'd been prowling impatiently and smoking a cheroot, seeming little perturbed by the rough neighbourhood or the suspicious glances sidling his way from passers-by. The driver on the coach was hunched in readiness to receive his next instruction, the reins slack on the chestnuts' glossy backs. As Lance opened the carriage door for Augusta, the rotund landlord wobbled out after his absconding lodgers, bellowing for his rent. Robin turned crimson with humiliation. He'd had every intention of paying up, but had forgotten about it in the chaos. He dug into his pocket and pulled out a fistful of coins.

Lance decided not to waste more time watching him sorting through silver and copper. He flicked the landlord a sovereign. 'You've seen nothing and heard nothing, is that clear?'

The fellow deftly caught the gold in mid-air in one porky fist while tugging his greasy forelock with the other. For a sovereign he was prepared to forget his own name. He backed off into the dim hallway from whence he came, banging shut the door.

Augusta eagerly clambered aboard her stepbrother's coach as though well practised at it. Robin followed her, with muttered thanks and a peer from under his eyebrows at the Earl's saturnine features. Lance boarded last and, almost before he'd sat down opposite the couple, he rapped for the coach to pull away at speed.

'Are you coming with us to protect us, Lance?' Augusta slid forward on supple hide to catch hold of his hands in persuasion.

A week ago he might have eased his fingers free after allowing her them for a short while. This time he didn't. He smoothed a thumb over the back of her hand. 'I'm not coming with you any further than the Red Dragon on the Cambridge Road, where you can spend the night. I can get a ride back to London from there and you will take the coach on to Yorkshire in the morning where you'll be safer.'

'Oh, thank you!' She lifted their clasped hands, putting her lips to his fingers. 'You're very good to me, Lance.'

'Is he now? Perhaps it's not you he's thinking about.' Robin had been pondering on things and the conclusion he'd arrived at made him grunt a laugh, deep in his throat. 'I know what you're thinking, Houndsmere, but she won't agree to it, you know. Emma's not like that.'

Lance let go of his stepsister's fingers and sat back against the squabs, crossing his booted feet at the ankles. 'I know…' he said, gazing out into the dusk. 'And it's a bit late for you to be playing the protective brother.'

'What's that supposed to mean?' Robin sounded indignant.

'It means that you're right in one respect about Gresham. He has been bothering your sister for some time.'

'I'll kill the bastard if he's harmed her!' Robin shot forward on the seat.

'What…swing for both of them?' Lance queried drily. 'Best not make matters worse, but leave the brother still breathing to me.'

'I didn't aim to kill Simon… I only winged him. He must've been a sickly sort to die of a flesh wound. We all went home and thought no more of it when the surgeon said it was a scratch.'

'Did he?' Lance gave Robin a penetrative look, then slowly he sat forward, giving the other man his full attention. 'Who was the surgeon?'

Robin shrugged. 'Joshua stood second for his brother and he arranged for the fellow to turn up.' He suddenly burst out, 'Applegate…that was his name. I left that confounded common believing that I'd done a good job for Emma. No serious injuries were sustained and I was sure it would all blow over. I thought in time my sister would thank me for bringing her back and doing something to restore her reputation.' Robin thrust his fingers through his untidy hair at the memory of the furore ensuing after that. 'Instead, I ruined my life on that blasted day.'

'Emma's, too,' Lance said with such grit in his tone that Robin glanced warily at him.

'Who stood second for you?'

'Gordon Rabley...good friend of mine at the time...heard he died of smallpox while I was in France.'

'Anybody else present?'

Robin shook his head. 'Wanted to keep it as quiet as possible...delicate situation...'

'Quite...' Lance said.

Robin turned the spotlight on to his interrogator. He was interested to know his lordship's intentions towards Emma, although he doubted he'd get an answer. It didn't really matter anyway; he could guess exactly what a renowned rake saw in a ruined, raven-haired beauty. 'So what are your plans in *that* respect? As her brother I'm entitled to know...'

'Very good...' Lance drawled damningly. 'Rather late with your righteous outrage, but I understand you've been busy with my stepsister.' A sardonic black brow was raised in a pregnant Augusta's direction. She had curled up against Robin's side and seemed half-asleep, sucking her thumb.

'My twin's a grown woman, not a silly girl, and doesn't need mollycoddling. On the shelf she may be, but I can tell you straight that what you've in mind for her…' He inclined forward to hiss quietly, 'You're wasting your time.'

'Well…perhaps I'll think of something else,' Lance growled. 'Now rest your tongue.' He gazed out of the window, frowning.

He'd never before wanted a wife. When Sonia had tried to force him to have her he'd been ready to dash for the hills and that had been before he'd uncovered all the lies she'd concocted about her past and her little daughter. No man should take vows at eighteen, before he'd lived, he'd told her. He'd grown older, but never changed his mind about marriage. Over time he'd watched Sonia reveal her true colours and realised what a lucky escape he'd had. Or perhaps his reluctance to settle down had just been that he'd never *really* been in love. Now he was and he realised it hurt like hell. He might have laughed at the awful irony of it. After years of skirting around mentioning anything a woman might misconstrue as a proposal, he was now desperate to find the right words to say to the woman he wanted to spend his life with. What would he do if she spurned him? Go away quietly? Was he capable of doing that? He knew she didn't hate him…might even like him…but was Simon Gresham's ghost still locked in her heart?

'Where are we going, Lance?' Augusta broke into her stepbrother's brooding with a bright enquiry. She was enjoying the adventure, gazing out of the window of the plush coach. The blackened chimneys and narrow dirty streets were getting fewer and the trees and open spaces more abundant.

'I've a hunting lodge in the Dales. It'll shelter you for now until something permanent can be sorted out.' He plunged a hand into his pocket and pulled out a roll of banknotes, tossing them on to Robin's lap. 'There should be some provisions in the larder and that should see you through for anything else you need. There is a retained housekeeper at the lodge and you can keep my coach and manservant. He'll get word to me if anything is in urgent need of attention. Other than that stay low until I send word.'

Robin stared at the carelessly given cash on his lap, running his thumb over the edges of the notes. It would have taken him a lifetime of toil as a lawyer to earn such an amount. Why had it been given? For Augusta's sake or for Emma's? Augusta had said that her stepbrother had washed his hands of her the last time she ran off. Considering the trial she had been to him it wasn't surprising the man was fed up with her, in Robin's fair estimation. He looked up, meeting a pair of cool blue eyes. Emma had attracted admirers when younger—none as illustrious as this man, though. Nevertheless, it was a tragedy that she had thrown away her future on a good-for-nothing like Simon Gresham when she might have been a wife and mother by now.

Lance watched Robin's expression turning cocky. The fellow thought he was home and dry now his sister had the Earl of Houndsmere wrapped round her finger. And she had…so he'd allow her brother his smirk. 'Get some sleep… we've got an hour's drive in front of us.' He rested his head back against the upholstery and closed his eyes, a smile slanting his lips as immediately a heart-shaped face set with a pair of reproachful golden eyes filled his mind.

When Emma got home from her trip to the East End she unfastened her bonnet and cloak and then threw them to the floor in frustration. She felt like weeping, but knew that would do her no good.

Another wasted journey! Mr Perkins had left and taken his things with him, the landlord had told her. And that was all he *would* say. Despite her hammering on the door he'd refused to open up again, so she'd set off round the corner to Milligan's. He had remembered her and had said he didn't know where Charlie was, but if the fellow didn't turn up on time on the morrow, he'd be out on his ear.

Emma went to the kitchen and listlessly stirred the pot of mutton stew. It had thickened to a rich brown gravy and smelled appetising, but though she was hungry she didn't feel like eating a morsel. She feared that her brother *wouldn't* turn up for work at Milligan's because Joshua had caught up with him. Had the swine had her brother arrested? Had the landlord seemed flustered and reluctant to talk to her because he refused to get involved in it?

She stirred faster while questions to which she had no answer whirled dizzyingly in her mind. Finally, she flung down the utensil and gave herself a stern talking to. Moping would do her no good! She needed to act so must go out again and hope that her second trip of the evening would eventually bring a halt to it all. Lance Harley had promised to put things right and she trusted that he could actually perform that feat. And in return she must uncomplainingly keep her end of the bargain.

First she had to see if her father was awake and could be persuaded to eat some dinner. Approaching his chamber door, she was relieved to hear the sound of his snores. She peeked in, then withdrew noiselessly. The powder was giving him the rest he needed and by tomorrow she might have good news for him.

She stood on the landing, bolstering her courage to set off straight away to Grosvenor Square. The matter wouldn't wait and it was better she deliver her letter at twilight than in the full glare of the morning sun and his servants' scandalised eyes. Should she manage to summon up the sauce to ask to see the Earl, she doubted she would be admitted, even if he were at home. And why would he be? Dissolute bluebloods didn't spend their evenings indoors, twiddling their thumbs. With a pang, she realised this must be how mistresses conducted their liaisons with eminent gentlemen: inconspicuously…at a distance…melting into the background when they were not needed.

She had no *wish* to see him, she impressed upon herself, and would be mortified if she inadvertently bumped into him. Far better that he read about her consent than she embarrassed herself trying to find the words to express it.

She went to her room and collected the letter she'd written earlier, then went downstairs. Gathering her cloak and bonnet from the floor, she gave them a cursory shake before donning them. About to leave the house she hesitated, returned to the console table and, by the light of a solitary candle flame, examined her shadowy reflection in the mirror. She put up her chin, rubbed some colour into her wan cheeks, then encouraged herself with a fierce frown before heading for the kitchen door.

Chapter Sixteen

Emma was turning out of the square when she became aware of fast approaching hooves and the clatter of wheels on cobbles. She tweaked forward her hood to shield her features and hurried on without turning around. An infinitesimal peek over a shoulder revealed the bulk of a coach and a male figure jumping from it. A lone woman drew the wrong sort of attention from gentlemen seeking diversion after dark and Emma suspected he might be up to no good. The sound of heavy masculine footsteps in pursuit made her gather her skirts in her fists and run as fast as she could. There was a narrow lane up ahead and she hoped to hide there. She didn't feel up to a fight. The last time she'd been set about she'd stood her ground. But then she'd been feeling more robust in spirit.

'Damnation, Emma, what do you think you're

doing?' was rasped out by a familiar voice as two hands fastened on her.

She twisted about in a pair of strong, imprisoning arms, panting for breath. Before she'd properly glimpsed his face the scent of smoky sandalwood was tempting her to throw her arms about him. She had raised her fists to defend herself, but let them fall and gazed up at him with huge soulful eyes. The stroke of his fingers on her cheek was lulling her and as she relaxed she realised just how dear he had become. And that wouldn't do. Not when she had in a pocket her terms for their business arrangement.

Now he knew she wasn't about to struggle Lance loosened his grip on her. 'Were you off to visit your brother? If so, you're on a fool's errand.' His exasperation at seeing her once more chancing ravishment and robbery by being out alone at night wasn't easily curbed. But he thanked his lucky stars that he'd managed to apprehend her before she'd got too far.

Emma shook her head then found her tongue. 'I went there earlier. Are you also aware they've fled?'

'Yes... I know...'

She realised he was waiting to hear where she *had* been heading in that case, so she took a steadying breath then blurted, 'I was going to Grosvenor Square.' She pulled an edge of parchment from her pocket to display the letter. She met his eyes proudly, but nevertheless was glad of the gloom concealing her blush. She knew he'd guess why she'd written to him, but she hadn't discerned triumph…or pleasure…in his face. In fact, she couldn't read his expression at all now his thick black lashes were low over his eyes. Her heart continued its rapid thud beneath her cloak; she was desperate to know that he still wanted her after their frosty parting in Hyde Park. For if he didn't…what then?

'Come…we can't talk here.' Lance caught her wrist, leading her towards the vehicle.

'I… We don't need to talk. Please just take this. I can walk home…it's not far.' She pulled away, thrusting the letter at him. He barely glanced at it and made no attempt to take it.

'Don't you want to know what's happened to your brother?'

'Do you know where he is?' she demanded, approaching him.

'Yes… I know where he is.' Lance caught at her hand again. 'Come, get in…please,' he coaxed. 'We've a lot to discuss.'

'Have you seen Robin? Spoken to him?' Emma rattled off.

'Yes…'

'When?'

'This afternoon. Get in the coach, Emma, and I'll tell you more.'

'If I come with you, will you take me to him? I've so much to tell him and none of it good. He is in danger of being apprehended because that devil Gresham has found out he is alive and in London...' Her voice cracked in anguish, preventing her carrying on.

'Your brother already knows all of that, as do I.' He cupped her soft, cold cheeks between his palms, tenderly brushing his thumbs on her skin to soothe her. 'I can't take you to him, but I can assure you he's safe. And so are you. Get in the coach, Emma.'

A sigh of sheer relief escaped her. 'He is truly out of harm's way and your stepsister, too?'

'Yes... I swear. Now I am done asking nicely. Get in the coach or I will put you over my shoulder and bundle you in.' Lance jerked a nod at the vehicle, in a final, implacable command that she alight.

She gave him a mutinous look, wondering if he was joking. Something in the way his dark eyebrows were elevated convinced her he was not. She knew it was unwise to stand talking like this, so close to home. The wonderful news he had given her she believed to be true and she was desperate to discover more about it. His letter was deposited back in her pocket and she held out her hand to let him assist her into the carriage.

Lance leapt aboard, then slammed the door, rapping for the driver to set off as he took the seat opposite her. 'You will never again go out alone at night.' His tone was controlled, but when she didn't answer—although it had seemed at one point that she would snap her defiance at him—he turned her face so she couldn't avoid looking at him. 'I want your word on it, Emma.'

Their eyes clashed through the murk before she jerked back against the squabs so his hand dropped away. 'You have no right to tell me what to do,' she replied coolly.

'Is that so? I'll wager that letter in your pocket gives me every right.'

She felt horribly hot and put into her place by that trenchant remark, but retorted, 'I will not seek your permission for anything, at any time. If we come to…an arrangement…then I will demand certain rules be observed.'

'Will you?'

Emma swung her face away, staring sightlessly at a sombre sky. A throb of tension was now between them and she was as keenly aware of that as she was of him. Shadows had obscured his expression, but she knew a glimmer of amusement would be in his eyes and shaping his mouth. He believed *he* would be the one setting the rules and she would obey them all without question.

It would be as well to act quickly, while you are still in a position to dictate terms.

So he had told her when propositioning her. It was strangely fair advice and she rued having ignored it. But he'd known all along he had the upper hand and could afford to dispense favours. Now things were so much worse for her family, was he conscious he no longer needed to?

She forced herself to focus on Robin's predicament and to speak about it before he asked to hear her rules for sharing his bed. 'Have Robin and Augusta sought sanctuary elsewhere in London?' She prayed that they had and that there was yet time to instigate a plan of action before Joshua caught up with them.

'No…they're travelling to Yorkshire.'

'Yorkshire?' Emma echoed. So astonished by that was she that she slid along the seat to sit directly across from him and gaze deep into his eyes. 'How can that be? Robin hasn't the means to travel to Middlesex, let alone to Yorkshire.'

'They've taken my carriage and will arrive in a day or two. I imagine they're resting at an inn now rather than journeying overnight.'

Emma continued staring at him, dumbfounded, digesting that information. The practicalities of it infiltrated her mind. 'But my brother will have no job to go to and no way to provide for himself, let alone Augusta.'

'He has enough cash with him to tide them over for some time. He doesn't need to work. In fact, it would be better to keep themselves to themselves for now.'

'You have given them money to make a new life together?'

'Apparently so...'

Emma frowned at her fingers, laced together in her lap. She'd not missed the irony in his last remark. So what had brought about his change of heart? Had his conscience pricked him after she'd accused him of neglecting his stepsister? Had he decided to be kinder to Augusta and allow her to stay with the man she loved rather than force her home? If he had, then Emma knew her apology for calling him a callous libertine was long overdue. 'Augusta is lucky to have your protection and so is my brother.' Her pearly teeth nipped at her lower lip before she blurted, 'I'm very sorry I lost my temper and spoke to you the way I did in the park. It was unforgivably rude of me.' Flustered by his silence and steady regard, she carried on. 'I hope Robin thanked you for what you've done for him. I'm grateful, too, and so will my father be when I tell him of this.'

'Does he know why you left the house tonight?'

Emma's wide glossy eyes darted to his face. 'No! He must never know. He has taken a sleeping draught and I pray will not wake before I return.'

'And if he did know? What would he do, Emma?'

'I hope he'd buy bullets for that empty gun he has.'

He grunted a laugh. 'Do you hate me that much? Would you not care if he shot me down?'

She gazed out into the night, feeling ashamed of herself. How could she have uttered such a thing when she'd just found out how greatly he'd already helped her family? 'I'm sorry. I shouldn't have said it. It was just a silly joke…' she murmured.

'Do you regret writing me that letter, too?'

'No…please forget about the gun. I'm sorry… it was a stupid thing to say.' Emma gestured weakly. 'I'm no different to any daughter in wanting a display of my father's love and protection, that's all.'

'He gave you that on the day we first met and he pulled that pistol on me,' Lance reasoned.

'Since then he knows Robin is alive and in need of help…from somebody like you.' She wished she'd not uttered that either, or so sourly. 'Sons are always the apple of their fathers' eyes.'

It was said with finality, to let him know she'd nothing more to add.

Emma wondered if he'd heard the years-old gossip that Bernard Waverley had nothing left to sell but his daughter. Did he believe her father venal enough to do it? She wished she could stop herself wondering the same thing, because the idea of it being true was breaking her heart.

'May I have the letter, then?'

Through the gloom, she watched five lengthy dark fingers unfurl in her direction.

'Yes...of course...when you set me down.' She avoided meeting a pair of black diamond eyes by peering out of the window and trying to ascertain their location. 'Am I quite close to Primrose Square? Can you set me down now?'

'No. You're not close and even if you were you're not walking home in the dark.'

'Where are we going?'

'Round and about...the driver will keep going until I tell him to stop.'

Emma lifted her limpid eyes to a sliver of moon. That's how he lived his life, she realised: giving orders to people to do his bidding. A servant to drive aimlessly until he'd had enough, a woman to pleasure him until he'd had enough... and he'd had the cheek to tell her to stop playing games!

'You may tell him to stop,' she said hoarsely.

'I know where I am. I won't walk. I'll hail a cab. I must go back and tend my father. He's been very unwell.'

'What ails him?'

'A leg ulcer, and the more he frets over his son, the slower his recovery. The news you have given me will greatly reassure him, though.' She gave him a fleeting smile before turning back to the night. 'Will you just stop on the corner, please?'

'Give me the letter, Emma.'

She shot him a rebellious look. 'You needn't fear that I will rip it up and renege on our deal now you have already started to keep your side of the bargain.' How confident he must have been that she *would* succumb to have put things in motion!

'Would you get away with crossing me, do you think?'

'Don't mock me,' she said sharply. 'I know this is a piffling affair for you. You can buy back Augusta's old life in a flash. The problems we have are very different.'

'I wasn't mocking you, Emma, but myself.'

What was he upset about? Wasting time when it could be better spent elsewhere? She slipped unobtrusive sideways glances at him. He looked immaculately attired as though off out for the evening. Had he been on his way to visit Jenny when he happened upon her? Perhaps a delay in meeting his mistress was making him irritable. Emma believed he was genuinely concerned to find her walking the streets at such an hour. 'Were you heading somewhere important when you spotted me?' she asked casually.

'Yes... I was coming to see you and your father,' he returned drily.

That came as a surprise. 'Why? To tell us about Robin going to Yorkshire?'

'Among other things.'

'What other things?' Emma sat forward, searching his face, one profile of which was being dappled to shades of gold by the swinging coach lamp. 'Is there more I don't yet know?'

'There are things *I'd* like to know. One of them concerns the duel that started this confounded mess. Earlier your brother told me something odd: that Simon Gresham's death was unexpected since he only sustained a minor injury.'

'I was told the same thing.' Emma sighed. 'Simon's wound was light, but we heard an infection set in. It was a dreadful shock when he passed away so quickly...' She tailed off into silence.

'Does talking about it still upset you?'

'It was a long time ago,' she murmured. 'But something like that is impossible to forget.' She quickly changed the subject. 'Joshua must have been sniffing around Milligan's, asking questions, and that's how Robin found out he'd been unmasked and needed to bolt.'

'He didn't know. I told him.'

'How did *you* find out?' Emma demanded.

'Gresham came to see me.'

Emma blinked in shock. 'Why did he do that?'

'He wanted me to cancel his gambling debts to me in return for keeping quiet about Augusta's involvement.'

'The villain! He tried to blackmail you? How dare he!' Emma was outraged on the Earl's behalf.

Lance chuckled, disarmed by her spontaneous championship.

'You didn't agree to it, did you?' Emma sounded as though she might call him a fool if he admitted as much.

'No... I did not,' he confirmed gently. 'But I greatly appreciate your concern.'

Emma blushed beneath the heat in his glittering eyes. 'The vile pig shouldn't get away with such behaviour. He might still carry out his threat from spite, though,' she warned.

Lance inclined towards her, taking her hands in his. 'Forget about him, Emma. I told you before he's of no consequence and easily dealt with.'

He paused. 'Your brother didn't have a clue that he'd been betrayed. How did that happen?'

Emma frowned. 'My father confided in his closest friend and Joshua somehow or other managed to trick the secret out of Mr Sanders.' She turned things over in her mind. 'Joshua must have been banking on you punishing Robin and dragging Augusta home rather than helping the couple.'

'Exactly right,' Lance said. 'He was confident I'd thank him and pay him.'

'But you did not.' She gave a contented smile and unconsciously pressed his fingers affectionately.

Lance raised one of her small hands to his lips, rewarding her for that first tenderness. 'Well… I did…but not in a way he liked, or expected.' He recalled his satisfaction on laying Gresham out on the floor.

'What did you do?' Emma's eyes widened in anticipation. 'Did you fight with him?'

'Not exactly…' he replied with studied disappointment. 'He went down with one punch.'

Emma again tightened her fingers on his, pleased at the idea of the swine getting the ending he deserved. Her happiness soon faded. 'But he can still cause such terrible trouble.'

'He won't ever hurt you, Emma, I swear.'

'Luckily, I managed to intercept a letter meant

for my papa. I guessed Joshua's aim in sending it was to taunt my father with threats so I opened it. I know I should not have, but once I'd read it, I was glad I had kept it from him. Papa must never see it.'

'What did it say?'

Emma couldn't tell him. Instead, she wriggled her fingers free of his, then plunged a hand into her pocket. She held out the crumpled paper she'd retrieved from the floor so her father wouldn't find it.

Lance angled the note towards the coach light. While reading it his mouth became thinner and a muscle leapt in his jaw. He looked up at her with a tender expression. 'It was wise of you to have kept it from your father, but I wish you hadn't been bothered by it either.' He folded the letter. 'If you will allow me to keep it, I'll make sure that Gresham gets it back.'

Emma nodded her agreement. She'd sooner the hateful thing was out of the house.

A silence settled on them and Emma wondered if he was brooding on what he'd just read or whether something else occupied him.

'Will you come in and speak to my father tonight about those other matters interesting you? He will want to thank you for what you have done for Robin.'

'No…another time. You say he is fast asleep and I won't wake him.'

'I *am* very grateful to you, sir, for what you've done for my family.'

'I know you are.'

He sounded distant, a touch frustrated even, and she wondered what she had done wrong. A short while ago they had seemed wonderfully harmonious. She'd told him weeks ago about Joshua having designs on her and that she hated the fiend. She was sure he wasn't annoyed at the idea of having a possible rival. 'I didn't mean what I said before about the gun…it really was a joke.'

'I know.'

'What, then…?' Her whispered request for him to explain his mood tailed off.

'What if we forget for a moment about the past and our relations, and talk about what happens now, between us.'

After a strained silence she asked, 'What is there to say about it?'

'If you let me have the letter you've written to me, or tell me what's in it, that might start a conversation.'

She tore her eyes from his to study the silver crescent peeping from behind stringy clouds. Oh, why couldn't they go back to clasping hands and laughing together? For a blissful interlude they'd become friends…confidants…a team battling the ills besetting them.

'It says that you have won, my lord, as you well know.' She had managed to sound composed despite the lump in her throat.

'Won what? An unwilling woman? It's not what I want or need.'

Emma felt bewildered by that. She'd imagined her submission would please him. 'What do you want, then, if not my consent?'

'You know what I want… I've shown you.'

'I'm not a child, I know there's more to it than clever kisses,' she scoffed. 'I won't swoon from plain speaking about our bargain. You want and need me to go with you to a house of your choosing where I will undress and lay with you in return for your money. My letter says that I will do that.'

'If that was all I wanted, I would visit Haymarket and choose a girl.'

'I'm sure Jenny would be disappointed to know it,' she sniped to the night sky.

'Are you jealous of her, Emma?' he asked softly.

'No…nor of any of your other women,' she flung at him hoarsely while mesmerised by a solitary twinkling star.

'Do you want to know more about my past life?'

She whipped her face around to look at him. 'I will never want to hear one word about it!' She was aware he was amused by her vehemence and it made her innards feel as though they were being twisted into knots. 'If you have changed your mind about things, my lord, just say so. It won't surprise me to know your eye has roamed elsewhere.'

'Would that it had…' he muttered.

Why couldn't she feel a glimmer of relief that he wanted to bring things to an end? Fine clothes and jewels…whatever she desired…it wasn't a future she'd coveted. She'd never dreamed that this was how her life might be. Gently reared, indeed she was, but she'd expected to have a normal life in a modest house with a decent man who loved her and their children. That was what she'd once longed for. And before she'd turned twenty she'd damaged the likelihood of it.

Drawing an aristocrat's attention had never entered her head. Yet due to an accident of fate she'd met an earl and aroused his lust. Now she felt peculiarly bereft that it might be over between them before it had properly started. And it wasn't just because he would go and take with him the help Robin still needed…it was because of *her*…what *she* wanted and needed. From the moment they had met she'd striven to keep Lance Harley at bay and now that he was choosing to walk away she no longer wanted him to. She didn't want to lose him.

Everything between them so far had been shadowed by her family and its problems. She had preferred it that way because she hadn't wanted to examine the reality of an emotional involvement with him. She hadn't the sophistication to separate her heart from her body and had known all along that pain would ensue from temporary intimacy with a man she had feelings for. But perhaps it would have been worth bearing that pain...perhaps she should now swallow her pride and try to woo *him*. She was aware he'd been watching her...could feel the weight of his stare on her as she fought to make sense of mores that were foreign to her. Would she manage to harden herself and act in a way that he expected of his mistresses?

'I have no experience in these things, but I accept it is my role to learn how to please you and never to question you, and I will try...' She fell silent and shrank into the seat the moment she heard a string of oaths flow from beneath his breath. He suddenly cradled her hands in the breadth of his, making her jump.

'What I want and need, Emma, is for you to admit there is a strong attraction between us and making love is something we both desire,' Lance differed gently. 'I want to know you feel something for me besides duty and gratitude. Do you?'

Was she about to act the hypocrite and deny she craved his kisses and caresses? She had tossed restlessly beneath his phantom touch through the long nights. But once known as his paramour—and the gossip would spread however discreet their meetings—she must turn her back for ever on a chance of having somebody to cherish her as a wife. For how long would the Earl of Houndsmere feel that *strong attraction* for her? Till her looks faded and with them her chance of having children with a husband? Did she want to risk rearing bastards on her own? But most of all…did she want to love him, in and out of bed, knowing that he felt no such deep or enduring emotion for her?

She was too greedy to have it all, she realised, while watching empty streets speeding by and trying to ignore the pressure of his long fingers entwined with hers. She wanted him to be there in the mornings to talk about their children and how they did with their lessons. She wanted him to sit with her at dinner and talk about their families and their friends. That's what she wanted… but would have none of it. He could have his pick of dukes' daughters to marry, Mrs Booth had said, and Emma knew it was no exaggeration. When that day came, what would she do?

Go gracefully and watch him from the shadows? Plead and weep to be allowed some crumbs of his affection and try not to see despising in his eyes? Had that been Augusta's mother's fate?

How could you have allowed yourself to fall in love with him? Emma inwardly wailed, trying to keep torment from shaping her features. She knew he was reading in her face her girlish hopes for her future. He was feeling sorry for her and giving her a way out to pursue her dreams. Perhaps he had a conscience where she was concerned as well as where Augusta was concerned. But she didn't want his pity, or his charity. And he wouldn't take the only things she had left: her pride and her self-respect.

She pulled her hands from his and folded them in her lap to still their trembling. 'Do you expect me to humiliate myself and plead with you not to leave us high and dry? Have you helped Robin escape to impress on me how powerful you are? If it was just a gesture, it was unnecessary. I knew from the start you wouldn't make empty promises, my lord. And neither do I.' She pulled the letter from her pocket and tossed it on to the seat beside him. 'I do feel more for you than just duty and gratitude. I like you kissing and touching me, as you already know very well. So perhaps hearing me say so will soothe your vanity and put your mind at rest that I have the potential to be value for money. But now you have the letter you may tear it up if you wish and go to Haymarket. And that is all I have to say, so please stop this vehicle and set me down.'

He made no attempt to pick up the letter or stop the coach and after a few pulsating seconds Emma leapt to her feet, prepared to thump on the hood and call an instruction herself.

'He only takes orders from me.' Lance caught at her arm, tugging her off balance so she fell against him. A lazy hand deflected the blows she aimed at him, then imprisoned her so she lay spreadeagled against a broad, hard-muscled chest.

'Well, I don't!' Emma finally found the breath to burst out. She struggled against him, then became still. Tension flowed from her in a single exhalation; she'd wanted to feel his body moulding to hers since he'd captured her when she'd been running away. Despite her indignation at this rough treatment, traitorous heat was starting to flow in her veins in anticipation of his mouth soon on hers. Her breasts were heaving and every breath she took abraded her taut nipples against his chest.

Obliquely, she was aware that the coach was rocking over ruts, bumping her hips against his in a most erotic manner. And then his mouth swooped to take hers in a savagely sensual kiss while a hand plunged into a mass of silky black hair. Long fingers gripped her scalp, keeping her face hard against his.

Emma struggled in earnest to be free of the strong arms around her and sit upright. Was this a lesson in what to expect if he decided her suitable? There was no sweetness in it, but arousal had stirred immediately to life low in her belly and was defeating her defences. Despite the aggression between them her body had responded instinctively to his touch. Of its own volition her mouth was parting beneath the pressure of his.

The bruising weight of his mouth was lifted from hers. Instead, she felt a soft caress sweep her cheek before it trailed tormentingly slowly to bury behind her ear. The hard grip on her scalp relaxed and his fingers slid to straddle her nape, stroking with slow rhythm against the sensitive skin there.

'Let me go, I don't want to…not here…not like this,' Emma gasped even as her eyes closed and she angled back against the soothing feel of his fingers. 'You have proved your point.'

Lance's response was to bring his mouth back to hers. With gentle yet inexorable insistence his lips slid artfully against hers, persuading her to part her mouth for him. The stroking thumb continued working its sorcery on her nape, building a lethargy in her. His kiss remained teasingly courteous, tempting her to invite more from him. And she did. Emma kissed him back. Her bunched fists unfurled against his chest, clutched at his jacket for support as they crept to his shoulders and anchored there. Her back arched instinctively as his hands massaged the delicate bones below her thrusting breasts. The vehicle added its weight to her seduction, swaying her body side to side as it negotiated turns in the road. A gasp broke gutturally in her throat and as though it was the signal he had been waiting for he deftly parted her bodice and cupped a breast. She sighed pleasure into his mouth, thrusting towards his hand when his thumb rotated over a rigid nipple.

With a groan, Lance dragged his mouth from hers and lowered his head. He tantalised the rosy nub with tongue and teeth until her squirming was invitation enough and he drew hungrily.

The pulse in Lance's loins was a nagging agony and, in a reserved part of his mind that was crumbling to desire, he cursed himself for a fool. He'd been desperate to have her tell him she felt something for him and had let his blasted ego take over when she clung to the idea of the passion they shared being one-sided and wrong. But Emma wasn't like Jenny or Sonia or any other woman. He'd never felt this consuming, aching tenderness for any of them. Emma was the only one he'd ever honestly loved and adored. Was he going to insult her and tumble her quickly in a carriage? Her first time should be wonderful... night-long loving in luxurious surroundings. She deserved to be told of his devotion and deepest respect. She should know he wanted her as his wife and the mother of his children, as well as his lover. And he would say all that to her...once he'd conquered the shock of knowing this was no obsession, no infatuation...he had fallen properly in love. From the start he'd believed that his conscience was bothering him where this beautiful woman was concerned. It hadn't been his conscience—it had been his heart.

In a few more seconds he knew he'd be lost in her sweetly innocent response to him and there'd be no way back. And how she'd hate him tomorrow!

Emma plunged her mouth up desperately, seeking his to demand he kiss her back. The slide of his hands on her feverish skin had kept at bay the memory of her family's problems. He'd been right to tell her they should concentrate on themselves; when webbed in sensuality like this it was hard to remember she had a twin brother at all. Shyly, she strove to entice him with little kisses until she sensed his lips form a smile against hers.

'Are you trying to seduce me, Miss Waverley?'

His teasing was tender, but nevertheless chagrin cluttered Emma's throat. 'If I am, it seems I am unsuccessful,' she uttered in a suffocated voice.

'If only that were true,' he murmured in a velvety growl. He was tempted to kiss her again to reassure her, but knew that if he did all his honourable intentions were doomed. Five fingers threaded through tresses that looked like sable and felt like silk skeins. 'Damn our families for miring us in this.'

A faint hope that had valiantly flickered in Emma's breast that they might find peace together extinguished as she listened to his gruff regrets. He wished he'd never met her, just as, not so long ago, she, too, had cursed fate for putting him in her path. But not now. Fool that she was, she had allowed him to mean everything to her.

Her eyes closed and she garnered strength enough to swiftly sit upright, then steal away to the opposite seat. She clutched her cloak tightly about her open bodice rather than fumble with its fastenings. 'Please tell him to turn back now.'

'Emma...'

'Please don't say anything more,' she curtailed him sharply.

He rapped out an instruction for the driver to take them to Primrose Square.

A murmur of thanks escaped Emma. She

could not soon enough escape the crackling tension that once more had wedged them apart.

'I think what you want and need is to marry and have children.' He broke her embargo on their silence. 'Am I right?' Never before had he felt so anxious to have a woman say yes.

'I was resigned to remaining a spinster after Simon died.' It wasn't a complete falsehood. She had imagined that would be her future so thoroughly compromised had she been.

Lance uncrossed his arms and leaned towards her. He planted his forearms on his knees, then raised his eyes, locking their gazes. 'I'm not sure I believe you, unless you've never got over that dolt you eloped with. Do you still love him?'

'Believe what you want,' she whispered and refused to let him see her raise a hand to wipe a tear from the corner of an eye. She allowed it to slide down to settle on a ridge of pale cheekbone.

He touched her face, gathering the brine on a fingertip. 'He can still make you cry. Why don't you just tell me the truth? You still love a dead man, but you think you owe it to your brother and your father to sleep with me.'

'Yes!' she cried. 'I do. I owe it to them. It's all my fault!'

'No…it's not…and I'm not a rapist. I don't want your gratitude or your duty, Emma. You're home.' He got out and helped her down right outside her door. He watched her anxious expression as she saw where they were. Her flitting gaze was inspecting the windows of nearby houses.

'It's too late to worry about what the neighbours think.' He turned her towards her door, then sent her towards it with a gentle push. 'Goodnight, Emma.'

She ran up the steps with a murmured, 'Goodnight.' She let herself in with shaking fingers, then quickly closed the door and leant back against the panels with tears blurring her vision. A moment later she heard the vehicle clatter away.

Chapter Seventeen

'I'm here to speak to your husband, madam.'

Veronica goggled at the visitor before an undignified gulp caused her throat to bob, rendering her incapable of replying.

A moment ago, she'd been seated at her embroidery when she'd heard the door knocker. She'd not been expecting a caller and, to her knowledge, neither had Joshua. He hadn't left the house in days, instead shutting himself in his study with a bottle of port. That had been his routine since the afternoon he'd returned home with his face cut and bruised.

The post had already been delivered and their housemaid had appeared to be dithering at the door so Veronica had sailed up to take charge. She'd proved herself no more adept at dealing with the distinguished gentleman on her front step than the servant.

'Do you want me to repeat myself?' Lance clipped out. Either she moved aside or he'd barge past her. He knew Gresham was hiding somewhere within.

'Of course not, sir,' Veronica burst out, colour rising in her cheeks. His brusqueness hadn't dampened her delight in having such a worthy fellow call on them. She noticed his crested curricle and the tiger at the reins, resplendent in the black and gold Houndsmere livery. The neighbours would be green with envy. 'I'm so sorry… a surprise…a great honour…'

'If you would tell your husband that Houndsmere is here.'

'I believe I recognised you, my lord. Please do come in and you are most welcome.'

Lance stepped over the threshold with a nod for her.

'I shall see if my husband is available,' Veronica said breathily, hoping Joshua would be sober.

'There is no need to, ma'am. I can see for myself that he is.' Lance was staring past the nervous woman at a pasty-faced individual who had stumbled out of a doorway further along the corridor. He set off determinedly towards him.

Joshua turned tail and tried to escape up the back stairs. In his inebriated state he didn't make more than the first few treads before his arm was gripped and he was unceremoniously hauled back down.

'No need to invite me to the drawing room,' Lance snarled close to Joshua's ear. 'In here will do.' He shoved his host back towards the doorway from which he had emerged.

Once inside the wood-panelled den, Lance closed the door and lounged against it.

Joshua eyed him malevolently, rubbing a hand over the graze beneath the days-old bristle on his chin. It was an involuntary sign of resentment that elicited a slight smile from the man who'd caused his injury. Joshua's guts squirmed at his adversary's attitude and he wished himself a pugilist. He'd love nothing better than to batter this man to the ground before kicking him out. The humiliation of being tossed down the front steps of Houndsmere's mansion in Grosvenor Square would always haunt him.

'I've the deeds here,' he muttered, yanking open the drawer in his desk, then hurling the parchment at the Earl's feet. 'Take them!' He had been holding on to the document in the vain hope that Houndsmere would change his mind about doing a deal once he'd had time to ponder the seriousness of it all.

But no such luck! Joshua's scheming had come to nought. He had gone to the East End seeking the couple and had been told by Milligan that he'd no idea where Charlie Perkins had gone off to and neither did he care. Joshua reckoned that this man knew *exactly* where Robin was. He'd admitted he was protecting the Waverleys as well as his own family and had moved him into hiding. With no way of catching up with his quarry, Joshua knew he couldn't do more. Without proof, any report that he made to the authorities would be thought fantastical.

In a lithe swoop, Lance retrieved the deeds, then placed them in an inside pocket of his coat. 'Here…fair exchange…' He approached to drop a piece of folded paper on to the desk.

Joshua could glean no emotion in the Earl's face, but aggression had been evident in every measured step that had brought him within punching distance. Joshua knew that being in his own home wouldn't save him. Having sidled out of immediate danger, he picked up the paper, curious to know why it seemed familiar.

He'd scanned just a few words when a furious glow spread upwards from beneath his collar. 'What else did Waverley give you? As though I couldn't guess!' The paper was screwed up and sent the same way as the deeds, but the Earl left that where it fell.

Bernard was trusting Houndsmere to get him and his son out of trouble in exchange for his daughter's virginity. Joshua was sure that was the deal they'd struck and it was making him seethe. He still couldn't accept letting Emma slip through his fingers. He had been obsessed with her for years and now railed at himself for missed opportunities. He'd been too lenient with the little vixen. He should have finished what he started when he'd tricked her to meet him at Vauxhall Gardens. But for the lack of a few more uninterrupted minutes he would have.

'Fortunately for you, I'm aware that letter was sent before you came to see me the other day. I'm prepared to believe it wouldn't have been written after we'd had our talk. You remember our talk, don't you?'

Joshua swiped up a dirty glass from his desk and downed the dregs of port in it before pouring another hefty measure. Had he not been so far in his cups, he might have proceeded with caution. As it was he slurred, 'I'll do as I damned well please. Now get out of my house.'

'Indeed I will when I've done what I came for.'

'I've given you the deeds.' The back of Joshua's hand was swiped over his wet lips.

'I didn't come for that. Or for the other documents pertaining to Waverley's debts. You haven't delivered them as stipulated so a court summons will shortly follow. I warned you I'd take this house.' Lance sounded quite uncon-

cerned. 'Not that you'll need it yourself. I antic-
ipate that very soon you will be residing at his
Majesty's pleasure. If you escape lightly, that
is. If not…' Lance grimaced. 'Let's discuss another matter that goes back many years. The
duel that supposedly was responsible for your
brother's death.'

Joshua had adopted an insolent expression,
but it vanished and the glass of port hovering by
his mouth found the desk with a crash. 'There's
no *supposedly* about it!' he bellowed. 'Waverley
shot him and killed him!'

'Ah…now there I believe you are wrong. I believe a court would come to the same conclusion
once presented with the facts.'

'What facts?' Joshua's glassy eyes became
fixed on the Earl's face.

'Facts given by the surgeon who attended that
day. After some persuasion Applegate eventually imparted some interesting news…not that
it's news to you. You already know that it was
you who killed your brother, don't you?'

Veronica had been just outside the door with
her ear pressed to the panels. Her complexion
had been steadily blanching and her stomach
curdling in anxiety as she'd listened to the hos-
tile conversation within. Now she gasped and
clamped her fingers over her mouth in dread.

From the moment she'd watched her husband

attempt to bolt from the Earl, she'd known something bad was about to happen. She'd guessed that Joshua hadn't taken a tumble when tipsy— his explanation for his injuries—but had been in a fight...possibly over a woman. Never would she have imagined her husband's enemy was a powerful man like Houndsmere. Neither would she have guessed that the Earl was in league with the Waverleys. She suspected that the common link in it all was Emma. Veronica twisted about on the spot in consternation, trying to make sense of it all. Soon she was concentrating on the most pressing aspects: how had the details of Simon's passing got out after all this time? Why would the Earl bother to track down Applegate and question him?

Now Applegate had blabbed Joshua could end up in gaol or on the gallows. And Houndsmere had said he'd take this house...*her* house. It had been part of her marriage settlement when Simon had been forced to wed her. When she became Joshua's wife, the property had transferred to him. But Veronica still considered it to be hers. Yet whatever mischief had recently gone on could rob her of it. She and her children would be homeless when they were the innocents in it all!

When Simon lay wounded she'd allowed his brother to take over his care, unable even to be in the same room as the man who had hurt and humiliated her in the worst possible way. From the start Joshua had told her the wound was mortal. Veronica had had her suspicions when Joshua banned the doctor's visits and dosed her husband with opium himself. But she'd believed she'd hated Simon on learning of his betrayal with Emma Waverley and had screamed at him that she'd wished Robin Waverley had finished him off. In the weeks that followed his death she came to realise she would have forgiven him in time. It was that little harlot who'd tried to steal her husband who was at fault. Veronica had gained nothing from Simon's death, other than a consolation prize of a reluctant second husband. But by forcing Joshua to marry her in return for keeping quiet about her suspicions over Simon's treatment, she had escaped widowhood and Yorkshire. And she had her sons.

Harsh male voices were again audible so Veronica ceased her jigging and again put an ear to the door, straining to hear every word that was said.

'You've no evidence, Houndsmere.' Joshua's voice squeaked with nerves. 'Neither has that sot Applegate. He can barely remember his own name.'

'A fistful of gold can be remarkably sobering, as can a threat of a prosecution. He remembers enough: your vows to ruin him when he discovered what you were about and wanted to report it.'

'I wanted to report it!' Veronica burst into the room. 'It was Applegate's idea at first to hush it up. He wanted to save his own skin after butchering Simon's arm when all the wound needed was a stitch or two and a dressing.'

'Keep quiet, you stupid bitch!' Joshua strode to his wife and shook her until her head wobbled on her neck. 'Can't you see he knows nothing? He's just fishing.'

'Well, if I was, I'm not now,' Lance said. 'So you might as well let her finish.'

'She'll say nothing to you and neither will I,' Joshua spat, glaring at his wife. 'Get out of the room. This isn't business for you.' He shoved her away from him, making her stumble.

Veronica seemed on the point of obeying until her eye landed on the paper bearing her husband's writing. She scooped it up from the floor and had read it before Joshua's intoxicated brain realised what she was doing. A moment later he lunged to tear it out of her hand.

'Leave this instant!' he roared.

'I knew it!' Veronica's eyes narrowed on him in despising. '*She's* the reason for all of this. You just couldn't leave her alone, could you? You fool! Why could you not stick to your cheap strumpets?' She turned to the Earl. 'I'll tell you what you want to know, my lord, if you promise to let me keep this house. It is mine, after all.' She sent Joshua a vicious look.

'You'll say nothing. You're my wife and will never bear witness against me.' Joshua grabbed at the glass of port with a palsied hand and emptied it into his mouth.

Lance pushed himself off the door jamb he'd been resting against while watching the warring couple. 'Well, no matter, you've both probably said quite enough for now.' He turned to leave. 'You can expect to soon be answering a magistrate's questions.'

Before Lance had got the door fully open, Veronica had flung herself at his feet. 'I beg you will listen to me, my lord. I had no part in Simon's treatment, I swear. I have children to care for...this is my home...'

Joshua dragged her up, spitting oaths into her face, then slapped her to the floor again.

Lance stepped back towards him in a menacing way. 'Leave her be. It's a shame you're not man enough to admit your guilt and finally take your punishment willingly. But it will come, I promise.'

'Waverley was the one who started it by calling Simon out,' Joshua roared.

'And you were the one who finished it because

your brother's injury wasn't serious enough to kill him. You took advantage of Applegate's negligence to rid yourself of the brother you hated. The brother who had won the woman you wanted.'

'And you want her, too, don't you?' Joshua screamed in hysterics. 'You might think to possess that ice maiden, but you will not,' Joshua hissed. 'Not up here...' He tapped his temple. 'My confounded brother ruined her for the rest of us after deceiving her.'

Veronica scrambled up, her expression a mixture of loathing and disbelief. 'You killed my husband just to have *her*? You said you would put Simon out of his misery with those drugs because he wouldn't want the life of a cripple.' She picked up the half-full decanter and hurled it at Joshua's head. He ducked and blood-red wine splattered the panelling and the carpet.

Lance stepped over the broken glass, went out into the hallway, then let himself out.

The Countess of Houndsmere had been expecting to receive a missive from her errant daughter at some time and it had now turned up. Sonia dismissed the maid with a finger-flick and put the letter on the table next to the breakfast tray.

Lance had told her that after finding Augusta he had despatched her out of town with her consort while matters were investigated further. He'd curtailed any questions, saying that the girl was safe and happy enough, and there was no point in rushing into a solution little better than the problem it was meant to solve.

At the time Sonia hadn't been inclined to pursue the matter. What she *was* inclined to do was find a way to seduce Lance. She knew he'd never marry her, but she'd heard that he'd lost interest in the opera singer and that his erstwhile mistress, Jenny, was now being squired by Lord Stevenson. Taken together, the gossip had encouraged her to think that there was a role in his life going begging. It had also encouraged her to think that as *she* had recently arrived in town he had cleared that space for her to fill.

Sonia began to read about what her daughter had been up to. Before she'd got to the end of the neatly scripted paragraphs her mouth had lost its pretty bow shape and slackened. A furious glint lit her eyes.

Lance had fallen for a woman called Emma Waverley, sister of her dear Robin, so wrote Augusta, and that was why he had helped them so kindly to travel to Yorkshire. If that were not bad enough, her daughter had gone on to sing the praises of the Earl's new fancy, saying she was very beautiful and nice and she could understand why Lance was smitten. Robin had said he wouldn't call the Earl out for chasing after Emma, even though being her brother he probably should.

Sonia dropped the paper to the table. For a moment she was too stunned to concentrate. Then pieces of a puzzle slotted into place. He'd given up his other women not for her sake, but because he was enamoured of Emma Waverley! Sonia jumped up and paced about. She snatched up the letter to reread it. There was little else in it to interest her. She had no wish to know her daughter was increasing and had been affected with biliousness! Sonia knew she was feeling jealous and annoyed…but most of all she realised she was intrigued. Who was this temptress who had done what no other woman had managed to do? Had he bedded her already? Or had he simply settled on a compatible chit with whom to set up a nursery and get heirs? He might improve his behaviour while he did his courting, but Sonia was sure he would revert to womanising once the honeymoon was over.

After some moments of intense thought, Sonia concluded that it didn't matter a jot if he got married. He'd still want a mistress and she still intended that role to be hers.

She'd never heard of the Waverleys. Before things had turned sour for her she had been exceedingly sought after as a guest by top hostesses. None of those people now had anything to do with her, and her stepdaughter wouldn't give her the time of day. Ruth had always hated her.

But Sonia had one friend in London. The woman was much like herself and had risen from nothing to gain a title and the heights before dropping back to somewhere in between the two on her husband's death. She was sure to have heard of the Waverleys and know where they lived.

Sonia sailed out of the room, calling for her maid to attend her because she was going out.

Chapter Eighteen

'Has the post arrived?' Bernard had heard voices in the hall and had come out of his study to investigate. His daughter was closing the front door and he approached, eager to see what she held in her hand.

'It was a fellow delivering leaflets, Papa.' Emma proffered it. 'The Horticultural Society of London is opening a new garden in Kensington.'

Bernard tutted disappointment. 'I hope Robin will write…but I must count my blessings. It is enough knowing my son is safe. I've been expecting Houndsmere to come, but I expect such an important chap has been busy. Now I feel better I should call on him. He deserves our humble thanks for all he has done. He is the finest of fellows.'

'I have thanked him, Papa. Why not send a note?' Emma speedily suggested.

'I will never commit to paper another word about Robin!' Bernard declared. 'I have deduced how that devil gained my friend's trust.' A gnarled forefinger assisted in making his point. 'Gresham was spying on my work on the last occasion he called. I suspect he remembered what he'd seen and tossed out words as bait. Alas, Roland bit. But I don't blame him and I wish I hadn't shouted at him. It was my fault for blabbing in the first place.'

'Don't upset yourself over what's done, Papa,' Emma soothed. 'We have survived to fight another day.'

When she let herself in after the Earl brought her home she had been relieved to find her father still slumbering. The powder he'd taken had done its work and had allowed her to immediately seek the sanctuary of her own chamber. A restless night had followed for her, but in the morning she had adopted a bright face. Her father had been overjoyed with the tidings she had given him at breakfast, listening intently as she related that Robin and Augusta had left town, courtesy of the Earl's generosity. Bernard had assumed Houndsmere had briefly called upon them and, finding him abed, had told Emma instead about developments. Thus, it had been easy enough to shield the true nature of the information's receipt during that bittersweet carriage ride.

She was more impatient than her father for his visit. The short while that had elapsed since they'd been together had seemed an age. Now she felt as though she were in limbo. Waiting... waiting...for something to happen. She'd advised her father not to go to see him, yet was tempted to do so herself and propriety could go hang. He must have read her letter by now. What had been his reaction? Perhaps he had thrown it away and gone to Haymarket...no, she knew him better than that. She was sure she might burst if she didn't discover his intentions and how they might affect all of them...her in particular. She had grown more selfish since falling in love. She had been selfish when infatuated with Simon, and underhand—just as she was now, sneaking about with Lance Harley. Had she been open with her father all those years ago...trusted *him* more than Simon, a man she had known just a few months...then the elopement and the tragedy that had followed would have been averted. The madness of passion made one do silly, shameful things—

'Ah...perhaps this is the post,' Bernard interrupted his daughter's pensiveness as another loud rap on the door was heard. 'I'm sure Robin will send me a note in code to put my mind at ease.' Bernard opened up and stared at the fan-

cily dressed lady stationed on his front step, a
maid hovering behind her.

'I would speak to Miss Emma Waverley, if
you please.'

Emma had been heading towards the parlour
when she heard that authoritative announcement.
She retraced her steps and joined her father at
the door. 'Might I ask your name?' Their visitor seemed more interested in boldly looking her
over than giving an answer.

'Are *you* Miss Waverley?'

'I am. And this is my father.' Emma didn't like
her attitude. The woman seemed slyly amused
because she had assumed the door had been
attended by a menial. From the way Emma's
plainly styled hair and dress was being studied it was obvious she was also deemed to be as
dowdy as a servant.

'I am here to discuss a delicate matter and
must come in.'

Curiosity overcame her pique and Emma
stepped aside, allowing the two women into
the hall. She'd have their caller's identity before
inviting her any deeper into the house. 'If you
would please introduce yourself?' The woman
was flamboyantly dressed and carried herself
haughtily; yet something about her wasn't quite
as regal as she would make out.

'I am the Countess of Houndsmere. Augusta

is my daughter. I believe we have a lot to talk about as your son, sir, has seduced her and carried her off out of town.'

Bernard's jaw dropped and he shot an aghast look at his daughter.

Emma had also been astonished to know who they were dealing with. But now apprised of the connection she could see a likeness between Augusta and her mother. She guessed that the Countess had been as pretty as her daughter in her day. Now she was rather too painted and plump.

'It is a matter for you to bring up with your stepson rather than with us,' Emma said coolly and took a step towards the door to see her out of the house. She knew now why the woman had scrutinised her from top to toe: the Countess had somehow found out she had a new rival for Lance's affections and had come to take a look at her.

'I will discuss this with you,' Sonia returned determinedly. 'Of course, the Earl is greatly concerned at this upset your family has caused me. But he has more pressing things to attend to.' She gave Emma a challenging stare. 'In future you will not bother his lordship with any of it, but will deal with me. Augusta is my daughter and I know what is best for her.'

So, there it was, Emma thought. The warning

signal to her to withdraw and leave his lordship alone. Well, she'd not solicited his help in the first place. And when he eventually showed up again she'd tell him so and to keep this vulgar woman at a distance from her!

'Let us sit in the parlour,' Bernard announced hastily, having recognised the combatant glint in his daughter's eye. He wasn't sure what was amiss, but sensed there was more to it than the ill-starred lovers who had bolted to Yorkshire.

Bernard ushered their visitor into the room. Having glanced distastefully at the shabby chairs, Sonia brushed the seat of one with a gloved hand before settling on it.

'Some tea?' Bernard suggested, darting an enquiring look his daughter's way.

'That won't be necessary, Papa. The Countess will not stay long as there is no benefit to be had in saying more than this: Augusta has not been abducted, she has left town of her own volition and with her stepbrother's help.'

'I know more of Houndsmere's ways than you do,' Sonia snapped. 'Although you're angling to know him very much better, aren't you?' She was worried. This was no nubile debutante. Emma Waverley was shabby genteel and past her prime. Her impoverished father doubtless intended shifting the expense of keeping his refined daughter to another man.

'I believe you do know him better than I, my lady.' Emma was unable to prevent a trace of sarcasm. 'Thus I can only repeat that you direct any questions about your daughter to him. So, if you will excuse us…'

'Ah…that surely must be the post now.' Bernard gratefully headed back into the hall as another knock was heard. He pattered towards the door, leaving his daughter with the dragon who could be his son's mother-in-law. He dredged from his memory what he'd heard of her. She had been a courtesan before snaring the old Earl, yet she had the cheek to come here, peer down her nose and accuse them of sucking up to his lordship! On passing, Bernard glanced at the mousy maid who was perched on a hall chair.

Almost before the door had closed Sonia was again on her feet and circling Emma.

'He favours blondes. His last fancy was blonde. She didn't last long.' Sonia fingered a piece of Emma's faded skirt with a scornful tut before its wearer snatched the material from her fingers. 'He likes a novelty, but you won't keep him beyond six months. He is as hard-hearted as he is handsome, my dear.'

'I've no idea what you're talking about,' Emma lied, subduing her wrath that the awful woman could speak to her like this. 'And I have nothing further to say other than you have outstayed your welcome, madam, so please leave immediately.'

'Don't get uppity with me,' Sonia scoffed. 'I tell you this for your own good. He has his doxies, but he always comes back to me in the end. I was his first love, you see.' She proudly tossed her head, setting flaxen ringlets dancing. 'I chose to marry the wrong man...the father rather than the son. But being Lance's lover has its compensations,' she ended on a bawdy chuckle.

'I've no idea why you think I would want or need to hear that.' *What I want or need...* The words circled her mind, bringing heat into her complexion as the memory of him uttering the phrase crowded in on her.

'My daughter has written to me from Yorkshire. She tells me you set out to gain the Earl's protection for yourself and for your coalman of a brother.'

'I will listen to no more of this!' Emma's temper flared out of control. 'You will leave this instant or I will throw you out of the house.'

'I'd do as she says. She can swing a good right hand. I can vouch for it.'

Emma twisted around to see her father just inside the door, fidgeting nervously. And behind him stood the man who'd spoken.

Sonia immediately swept towards the Earl

to clutch his arm, but he brushed her off his sleeve as though she were an irritating fly. 'You heard Miss Waverley. Go. Now.' He didn't bother glancing again in Sonia's direction. Neither did he look at Emma. He studied the shine on his Hessians, his cruelly thin mouth thrust aslant while he waited for his stepmother to obey him.

For a moment it seemed she might not. Being rejected had caused her eyes to resemble slits. She turned that hateful expression on Emma, then jerked up her chin and flounced to the door.

Bernard spluttered, 'I'll see you out, my lady.' He trotted after the Countess's rigid-backed figure, closing the parlour door behind him.

A silence ensued that throbbed with more intensity than the clock on the mantel.

'My apologies. I'd no idea she would resort to troubling you—'

'She hasn't troubled me,' Emma cut across him in a glacial tone. 'She's of no consequence. Neither are...' She pressed her lips together before agonising jealousy spurred her into being childish and foolhardy. Her father would be back soon and want to speak to him about vital matters. But humiliation and hurt had mingled into a potent force that raged in her chest like fire. The Countess might have been consumed with malice, but how much truth was in what she'd said? He was hard-hearted and wouldn't want her long. Emma had already pondered on that herself. He always returned to his first love when done with his doxies...was that wishful thinking on the Countess's part? Emma composed herself enough to unclench her fingers and raise her eyes. She'd guessed his expression would be ironic and so it was.

'Come...finish what you were about to say,' he invited with specious softness. 'Neither am I important.' A hollow laugh barely left his throat. 'A visit from a bitter scorned woman is all it takes to make you despise me.' He came a step closer to her. 'In which case I have to accept that it would be best if you were not important to me, Emma.'

'I have never fooled myself about that,' she returned. 'Oh, I know you will dance attendance while this squalid game we play is still underway. But what of when it is over? How important will I be then?'

'We won't know that until it is over. What did she say to you?'

'You should ask her that.'

'I'm asking you. You're more likely to tell the truth than a resentful harlot.'

'Was she always so, or is she what you made her?'

'She was always so and went to some trouble to hide her true nature from me.'

'But still you loved her?'

'I thought I loved her…when I was eighteen, as I told you. Now I am thirty-one and I have a clear idea of who she is. More importantly I know who I am…and what I want and need.'

Emma turned from his subtle smile as he deliberately chose words to remind her of the passion they'd shared in his carriage. 'I also now know who she is as she was at pains to impress on me her status. She is your father's widow and your mistress.'

'Indeed, she is my father's widow, but she hasn't been my mistress for over a decade. And never will she be again.'

'I've said before there is no need to explain yourself to me.'

Unable to dampen down the furnace bubbling within, Emma made to march past him and from the room. He caught her arm as she drew level and dragged her in front of him.

'I wish to explain myself and you will listen. And if after that you tell me to go, I will and I won't return, that I swear.'

Behind them, Bernard had entered and cleared his throat. 'Um…some tea for his lordship, Emma?' He imagined his daughter had confronted the Earl about his rude stepmother and that was why they stood so close together and the air was thick enough to slice with a knife. He had to admit that the Countess was unpleasant and he'd been glad to see the back of her. Nevertheless, his daughter's angry eyes were just visible over the Earl's shoulder and he sent her a most reproving look. The last thing they wanted when all was coming right was to upset the fellow working the miracle.

'The Earl can't stay, Papa…' Emma said, discreetly wresting her forearm free of five steely fingers.

'He can for a few minutes,' Lance drawled with a sardonic look for her. 'He has something to say. But no tea is required, thank you.'

'Sit down, sit down, my dear fellow.' Bernard wedged himself between them, ushering his esteemed guest towards an armchair. 'You have my greatest thanks for all you have done. Emma has told me how you have sent the couple to safety.'

'Are they safe?' Emma asked quietly, feeling calmer now there was space between them and talk had turned to business. 'Will the Countess be discreet about what she knows?'

'You needn't fret over anything she says or does.' Lance moved away from the chair he'd been corralled to and gazed out of the window, cursing Sonia Peak to hell beneath his breath. 'Your brother can return to London now if he wishes. He will no doubt be questioned by the authorities, but runs no risk of arrest.'

'How so?' Bernard had scuttled up behind him and was tempted to yank on his sleeve to gain his attention.

'Your son wasn't responsible for Simon Gresham's death. Others were. I've given a report of my investigation to the local court and it shouldn't take long to clear Robin's name.'

Emma frowned, wondering what to make of that riddle. Her father also appeared mystified, staring at the Earl's broad back as though he'd spoken in a foreign tongue. 'No…the duel did take place,' she blurted, having quickly regained her wits. 'Simon was hit in the arm.'

Lance turned about, gazing over the elderly man's head at his daughter. There could be no easy way of telling her what had happened to the man she'd hoped to marry. He desperately didn't want to hurt her, but the whole damnable affair had been mired in subterfuge for too long and it was time the truth was known. Perhaps hearing her brother was no killer would compensate in some small way for knowing that Simon Gresham would have survived but for lethal sibling rivalry.

'The injury your brother inflicted wasn't fatal,' Lance explained gently. 'The treatment Simon received afterwards was his downfall. I realise the information has come as a shock and it is a great pity that it has taken so long to be revealed.'

The momentous news started to filter into Emma's mind, causing her face to slowly drain of blood. She swished her hand to and fro behind to locate the chair for its support as she felt her legs weaken.

Lance strode to put an arm about her and urge her to sit down. Bernard continued quietly brooding, a finger at his mouth, as though he still struggled to make sense of it.

'But my boy fled abroad because his opponent died,' he insisted. 'I haven't seen or spoken to Robin in years.'

'Did you not check the veracity of what you were told about Simon Gresham's condition and his demise?' Lance found it astonishing that neither man would have made full and detailed enquiries of something so crucial.

'Indeed we did try!' Bernard snorted, having picked up on a note of criticism. 'My son wanted to visit Simon to apologise, but Joshua would have none of it. He threatened to have Robin arrested if he again showed his face. I approached Applegate, but he avoided me, too, and directed me to speak to the Greshams as they had banned him from further visits. I even bothered Simon's wife to beg news.' Bernard glanced at his chalky-faced daughter. 'In the circumstances I suppose it was no surprise Veronica would have nothing to do with us.' He clasped his hands behind him, fidgeting from foot to foot. 'When I discovered Simon's death was imminent my only thought was to save my son. Henceforth every second and every penny was spent getting him to France before he was arrested. But now you say my boy had no need to go?' Bernard fell quiet and his lips commenced trembling as the full force of the sacrifice made and the lost years settled on him.

Emma roused herself from her daze. Pushing herself from her chair, she comforted her weeping father. But as his mounting grief made him stagger, Lance took over, assisting Bernard to the small sofa.

'Have you any brandy?'

'No...but there is some port in the study.' Emma turned to fetch it, but Lance detained her, and produced a silver flask from an inner pocket. He unstoppered it then thrust it into Bernard's hand and commanded him to take a swig.

Bernard did, spluttered, then took another long swallow of cognac before falling, grey-faced, against the cushions.

Lance straightened up, then led Emma away so they could talk in private.

'He's in shock and should rest in bed. You, too, have suffered, Emma,' he said softly. 'It is bittersweet news and will take a while to sink in.'

'I still don't understand how this can be so,' Emma argued in a stifled tone. 'If the wound might have healed…why did Simon perish?' A small gesture conveyed her anguish and perplexity. 'Who has told you this, sir? A reliable source?'

Lance nodded. 'I have it from the people responsible for Simon's death. I tracked down Dr Applegate and after that I went to see Joshua Gresham. Neither wanted to speak to me, but both eventually confessed to their part in it. The tale that emerged from both parties is similar enough to be taken as truth.' He paused, scouring his mind for words to minimise the impact of the report. He found none and settled on brevity. 'Applegate made a mess of extracting the bullet when drunk. He wanted to amputate. At first Simon didn't consent, then before succumbing to fever changed his mind. His brother wouldn't allow the operation, saying Simon had agreed when delirious and not of sound mind.' Lance paused to ascertain how the tale so far was affecting Emma. Her limpid gaze was clinging to his face, indicating she was eager to hear him out. 'Joshua insisted nature be allowed to take its course and demanded the doctor supply opium as a sedative. When Joshua had the drug he banned the doctor from returning, threatening to sue for negligence if Applegate challenged him. The doctor complied, worried for his reputation and his livelihood…' Lance tailed off the moment he noticed the silent tears spilling from Emma's eyes on to her cheeks. 'I'm so sorry.' He tenderly cupped her wet face. 'I would have done anything to spare you from this hurt… I should have kept the truth from you.'

'No…' She gave him a watery smile, and her small hand covered the gentle fingers comforting her. She tilted her head to their clasped hands, closing her eyes. 'I owe you my thanks for uncovering who was responsible for what happened.' She shook her head. 'The cowards would sooner label my brother a killer than admit to their fault.'

As the anger drained out of her an odd apathy filled the space. She felt as though years of tension and sadness had flowed from her in seconds. 'It is a tragedy that Simon lost his life needlessly, but equally it is wonderful to learn that my brother, if not completely innocent, can at last come out of the shadows and be reunited with his father.' She sniffed, turning away to compose herself and to use a hanky on her wet cheeks. 'Did Joshua blame my brother from vengeance…to get him into trouble?'

'I think so, and to hide his culpability. Applegate warned him of the likely outcome of an opium overdose.'

'Joshua surely didn't administer too much on purpose?' she whispered, horrified.

'It's for a court to decide. My guess is that he'll plead it was an accident and that he had his brother's best interests at heart, not wanting him to suffer.'

'But...you don't believe that, do you?' A look of despair darkened Emma's eyes. 'They didn't like one another. Would Joshua have acted from jealousy...because of me? Am I partly to blame?'

Lance placed his hands on her shoulders, drawing her close. 'None of it is your fault, Emma.' He tilted up her anguished face so their eyes merged. 'You're guilty of no more than youthful indiscretion...as am I.' He smoothed a dusky tress off her pale forehead. 'We *are* alike. And not just in that we have family members driving us to distraction and reputations that don't bear scrutiny. We were both taken in by deceitful people when too young and inexperienced to spot their lies. But we can't let what we did then blight the rest of our lives. We deserve to be happy.'

'Did your family suffer because of your love for Sonia?'

He sighed and half-turned away as though ashamed of what he must tell her. 'Very much so. I adored my father and until Sonia Peak drove us apart we were extremely close. I begged him not to listen to her lies, or to let her beguile him with her tricks. He chose to ignore me and believe her instead. He died a bitter, broken man.' He paused. 'He discovered her cheating and separated from her eventually. I managed to repair bridges between us before he died. But we were never again the friends we had been.' He hung his head. 'I torment myself that his ill health was brought on by his association with her. He had always been a strong, healthy man and perhaps would have remained so for many more years had I not brought her into my life and thereby into my father's.'

'You cannot know that for certain, Lance. Illness can creep up on a person as they get older, as it has with my father.' Emma had instinctively used his name and soothed him as he had her, cupping his abrasive jaw.

He turned his face, pressing his lips to her palm. 'We have both made choices we regret and have paid the price for our past mistakes. Our relations have made their bad choices, too, even when we pleaded with them not to.' He removed her hands from his face and held them while a deep blue gaze caressed her features. 'You asked your brother not to get involved in a duel, didn't you?'

'I begged him not to meet Simon.'

'What more could you have done then?'

She gave him a grateful smile.

'Now we have the future to look forward to,' Lance said. 'So, will you allow that scheming woman to continue to spin her lies and cause trouble for me? Or will you listen to what I have to say?' As though to lure the right response from her he dipped his head, kissing her sweetly, and slipped the top button on her bodice from its hook to sweep a finger softly against her skin.

Chapter Nineteen

'Emma… I must go to my chamber, my dear, and see to myself. I have drunk rather too much. Help me up, please! I am sunk into the cushions. I must go…quickly…'

The couple, lost in their own world, had forgotten about Bernard until his rude interruption. He had been reclining on the sofa with his eyes closed while regularly upending the brandy flask.

Lance unsealed their mouths and Emma's lashes flicked up, merging with a warm sapphire gaze. Her cheeks became rosy. How easily he could make her forget where she was and every sense of decorum! She had actually let him kiss her with her father mere yards away. Wriggling free, she sped to Bernard as he continued his attempt to struggle upright.

'You are a good boy,' Mr Waverley slurred,

patting the Earl's sleeve as he came over to lift him to his feet.

Emma bit her lip, her amusement reflected in Lance's eyes. A thought passed between them that Bernard wouldn't praise his lordship did he but know what the fellow had had in mind for his daughter. The idea hadn't left his mind either, Emma realised, as two sultry blue eyes lowered to her gaping bodice. Hastily, she did up a button.

Bernard took a few steps towards the door, then wobbled.

'I'll help him upstairs.' Lance put an arm around the elderly man to support him.

'He struggles with his clothing,' Emma blurted, hurrying behind.

'I can assist him in that, too…' Lance said wryly. 'Pity my valet isn't here…' A muttered reference to Reeves's constant fussing emerged.

'I'll bring up a glass of cordial. It might help him sober up.' Emma realised she ought to feel embarrassed that her father had emptied the Earl's brandy flask and now needed his guest to help him to a chamber pot. But oddly she didn't. From the moment Lance Harley had entered her life he had dealt with her problems, her family, in a most pragmatic way…and she loved him the more for it, she realised wistfully.

By the time she entered her father's chamber

with the cordial, Lance had helped Bernard with his trouser buttons, settled him on the bed and was removing his shoes. Emma put the glass on the nightstand.

'Thank you, sir… I can see to him now, if you like,' she murmured.

'I don't mind. It's no hardship to remove a fellow's boots for him. I've done it for Jack Valance when he's fallen too far into his cups.'

'I imagine he has returned you the favour, my lord,' Emma said impishly.

'Indeed…on many occasions in my misspent youth…that's now behind me.' He gazed at her. 'I thought we'd done with "sir" and "my lord". You called me Lance before.'

Emma gave a bashful smile, peering round his broad torso to spy her father, open-mouthed, rumbling a snore. She gestured that they should leave him and closed the door quietly behind them. She would have immediately moved to the head of the stairs, but Lance stopped her, trapping her against the wall.

'Is that your room?' He tipped his head at a doorway, a wolfish glint in his eyes.

'It is, but I'm not inviting you in to it,' she said firmly and, slipping past him, lightly descended the stairs.

Her heart was thundering when she entered the parlour. There was very different business to attend to now…that concerned just the two of them. And no distraction from it. She was glad things had come to a head…the unremitting pull of magnetism between them was exhausting. She wanted to know what road lay ahead for her as well as for her brother. She heard the door click shut behind and slowly turned, watching him advance. 'You read my letter, then, and I imagine have no objection to my terms,' she started off quietly and clearly.

'What makes you think that?' he asked.

'You wanted just now to go to my bedroom… but I will never…beneath my father's roof…and you accepted that as it is one of my rules…as you would know having read the letter.' She was rambling, she realised, and fell silent before taking a breath and starting again more composedly. 'Of course, the house isn't Papa's now Joshua Gresham has the deeds. But you understand my meaning, I'm sure.'

'The house is mine, and, as I have no use for it, Mr Waverley is welcome to have it back. So… I am banned from your bedroom in your father's house. I understand and accept that rule.' He gave a slow, studied nod.

'You must be mistaken,' Emma burst out. 'Joshua Gresham owns the house. He said he would never give it up. I believe that to be true. He wanted a hold over us…over me, he said so.'

'He has no hold over you. And depending on how generous I'm feeling, he might lose his own house, too.'

Emma's frown deepened as she gazed up at him in disbelief. 'Are you joking?'

'No... I told you he lost to me in a card game. I stipulated certain things in payment of the debt or he would be sued. Your father owes him not a penny.'

When she eventually found her tongue she whispered, 'Why have you done all of this? For me?'

'Of course, for you. But also because I don't like bullies or liars...' His eyes trapped hers. 'Gresham boasted to me that he had you in his bed.'

'That's a lie!'

'I know...but something went on between you. What did he do?'

As Emma would have swung away, feeling embarrassed, he caught her shoulders, turning her back to him. 'Please tell me. What did he do, Emma?'

'He pretended to be our friend...that's what he did...at first...and like a fool I fell for it. After Simon's funeral he called to say he wanted no bad feeling between us. He appeared sympathetic and said he was sorry I'd been compromised and that both our families had suffered.

He proposed to me. Even when I turned him down he kept up the sham of being our friend.' She paused. 'My father took his loans. I'd never really liked him, but up until then I'd had no reason to suspect he might turn nasty. So when he invited me to meet him at Vauxhall to return an IOU my father had pledged at a card table I went. I guessed he might want to renew his proposal…and perhaps kiss me.'

'Did he rape you?' Lance's voice was hoarse and his eyes dark with pain.

'He was disturbed before he could.' Emma felt her lips tremble as she spoke of it. She'd not managed to banish from her mind one bit of the fury and fear she'd felt when the brute had tried to rip up her skirt and push her to the ground in that dark walkway. She put a hand to her face. 'I feel ashamed now…not only of being so gullible, but of acting like the whore he said I was. I guessed he might want to kiss me…and was prepared for that to try to keep my father from the Fleet.'

'Did he hurt you?' Lance asked, cupping her face as though it were as delicate as porcelain.

'He almost had me to the floor, but I kicked and hit him and a couple walking close by heard the commotion and came to investigate. I expect they thought no good of me either.' She tilted her chin. 'I don't care now anyway. I got away and it was just another lesson learned the hard way.' She gazed into his eyes. 'So will you take his house? He has a wife and children…'

'You are too soft-hearted, sweetheart,' Lance said gently. 'His wife would have seen you on the streets, as would he.' He swept a kiss on her brow. 'You decide his fate, as so often he has decided yours. If you say to me be lenient, then I will. I can deny you nothing. You know that.' He paused. 'If he hadn't been arrested, I would go and see him about this. He was never fit to touch the hem of your skirt. Neither was his brother.'

'You've no need to fight my battles. I can look after myself.'

'I know…' He realigned his jaw as he had after she'd slapped him, making her chuckle. 'But now you don't need to look after yourself any more.'

'Will you really return my father his house?'

'I really will.'

'Thank you.' Spontaneously, she went on to tiptoe and placed her soft lips to his hard cheek.

'You're welcome,' he said huskily. 'So where were we before we got side-tracked? Ah… I recall you were explaining your terms for consummating our love.'

Emma shyly averted her eyes, and occupied herself shifting to and fro the candlestick on the mantel. 'You already know my terms from reading my letter.' She paused. 'Of course, some of those requests aren't necessary now you have dealt with Robin's predicament.' She became quiet as a dark hand appeared in her line of vision and deposited her sealed letter on the mantel.

Emma stared at it, then slowly turned about. 'I don't understand…' And she didn't. He had made it plain just minutes ago how much he still desired her. He'd spoken of consummating their love.

'Do you believe what I have told you about Sonia Peak?'

'Yes.'

'Will you tell me what she said to you?'

After a moment's hesitation Emma reeled off, 'She said I was a novelty and you would soon tire of me and preferred blondes…especially her as she was your first love. I knew she had come to cause trouble and be spiteful. But I felt jealous and angry and that's why I was cross with you.'

'I don't blame you for being cross. She would have been pleased to know she'd succeeded in hurting you and had come between us. None of what she said is true. And you'll never have cause to be jealous. I swear it.'

'Is she spiteful to all your mistresses?'

'No…just to you because she's guessed how deep are my feelings for you.'

Lance came closer until just inches separated them. He braced an arm on the mantel. 'I've been feeling jealous, too, Emma.'

'You had no need to be. I told you from the start I hated Joshua.'

'He's never bothered me. I worried you might be unable to give your heart again because you were still in love with a dead man.'

'Well, I'm not,' Emma said firmly. 'I'm not sure I ever was in love with Simon. Infatuated, perhaps.' A nostalgic smile touched her lips. 'That year we met, my debut passed in a whirl, so much excitement…balls and parties…new friends. I thought it was the best time of my life…' She tailed off.

'And a few months later all the happiness was gone.'

'Yes…' She ached with the poignancy of it. Then blinked the memories away and gave him a smile. 'But enough of that. You have no need to be jealous, sir… Lance,' she corrected herself with a tiny apologetic nod. 'I will not forget Simon…how could I? And neither, I imagine, will you forget Sonia Peak.'

'I won't if you keep mentioning her,' he said ironically.

Emma tutted and rolled her eyes, feeling glad that they could tease one another. Just a short while ago it would have seemed impossible for them to be friends. Now she felt she might be able to tell him anything…ask him anything…confide in him her troubles. 'Will you now open my letter? My rules are not stringent…discretion to protect my father, of course, because I don't want him to know…although spiteful people have a way of finding things out—'

'I don't want your letter, Emma,' he interrupted her gently. He moved his hand from the mantel and slid it beneath a fall of silky raven hair to straddle her nape and urge her closer. 'I have decided I don't want any more mistresses…although I have been in sore need of one for a while,' he added ruefully.

'What does that mean?'

'It means that I have always been faithful to you during my courting.'

She gazed up at him with huge unblinking eyes, gleaming with disbelief.

'It's true!' he protested. 'I know it's hard to believe. But I swear I haven't been with another woman since I met you,' he said solemnly.

'Why don't you want my letter, then?' she whispered. 'Do you fear I will cling or plead to stay when it is my time to go? I promise to try not to, or to be a disappointment.'

'You would be if you'd give me up so easily. I'd fight to the death for you.'

His blazing blue gaze roved every inch of her

face in a leisurely caress. 'I love you, Emma Waverley, and what I want and need is you as my wife.' He dipped his head, touching her face with his lips. 'And I want a daughter with black hair and brandy eyes who will wrap me round her finger in the way her mother does. Those are my rules.'

Emma searched for a hint of playfulness in his face, but there was none. Adoration and desire were there and she wondered why she'd never interpreted that intense look as love before.

'Do you want me on my knees? I will grovel if you wish it. I know I deserve to... Don't cry...' he said softly as the gathering dew on her lashes spilled to her cheeks. 'Do you love me? Just a little bit would do,' he groaned before capturing her sweet soft lips in a persuasive kiss.

'Aha! I knew it!' Bernard ambled into the room, waving his gun. 'You thought to get me out of the way to seduce my daughter, you rogue. Well, I can hold my drink better than you think. You might have done us all a great service, but you'll not have my Emma in payment. She is too precious to me.'

Lance dropped his forehead to rest on Emma's shoulder and groaned an oath. 'Perhaps I should now drop to my knees.'

'You can come away from him now, my dear. Your papa is here to save you. I found a bullet in the drawer and put it in my gun.' Bernard shuffled over on stockinged feet, jabbing the pistol.

'Put the gun down, Papa.' Emma turned around and approached her father, pulling Lance by the hand. 'He hasn't seduced me, I promise, he has asked me to be his wife.'

Bernard lowered the gun a fraction, squinting suspiciously. 'Are you sure that's what he meant? You know what these rakes are like.'

'Yes… I'm sure. He loves me. Lance wants to ask you for my hand in marriage, Papa.'

'Oh…so will you have him, my dear?'

'Yes… I will.' Her eyes glowed with serenity as she turned to look at Lance and, father present or not, pressed her lips lightly to his. 'Because I love him.'

'Capital!' Bernard boomed. 'I'll get the port to celebrate.'

Emma flung her arms about Lance, resting her cheek on his chest. 'You can't get out of it now. If you try to, he'll shoot you.' She started to laugh as he lifted her off the ground and spun them both about.

'I haven't yet an engagement ring to give you, but I have a gift…something I think you'll like.' He used the back of a finger to stroke her face, then withdrew from his pocket her gold locket and held it out to her.

'How on earth did you get it?' she exclaimed.

'Gresham had it. He claimed you left it in his bed.'

Emma's eyes widened in shock. 'I left it at Solomon Pope's pawnbroker's shop and the villain promised me he would keep it safe for me to redeem it.' She took the precious gold. 'You didn't believe such a stupid tale from him?'

'Of course not… I knew he was lying,' Lance said gently. 'Gresham was in Cheapside the same day you were. I saw him enter his solicitor's office. He must have watched you go into the pawnbroker's and gone in afterwards and bought it. Besides, you had been wearing it after he said he had it from you. I felt it against your breast the first time I kissed you, in my sister's garden.'

As she blushed, he took the locket, fastening it about her neck, then placed his lips to her nape before dusky curls swayed back into place.

Bernard came into the room with the decanter and glasses. He poured them all a drink. After a single gulp of his he put down his glass. 'Now I must stay sober and go out and see Roland. I hope he will still be my friend. I was mean to him, but there's no time for pussy-footing. This news won't wait.' He kissed his daughter's cheek, then patted his future son-in law on the arm before hurrying towards the door. 'You may speak to me, my lord, about your worthiness to have my Emma on another occasion. I believe you are in luck and I shall give my consent.'

'He is the happiest he has been in an age and it is all because of you,' Emma said huskily.

'I'm glad,' Lance said. 'Are you happy now, Emma?'

'More than I thought it was possible to be,' she answered, her eyes aglitter with blissful tears. 'And you, Lance?'

'I feel blessed and overjoyed, but I'll be happier when you're my wife.' He groaned and kissed her hungrily.

Emma heard her father call out his goodbyes, then the door banged shut. She went to the window and watched him set off along the road in a sprightly, if meandering, manner, barely relying on his stick. Her thoughts turned to Dawn.

'My friend has not seen Jack Valance for a while.' She turned to give him an arch look.

'Acquit me of scheming in that.' Lance gestured surrender. 'My only hand in it was to loan him my landau. The rest was all his own doing.'

'She likes him.'

'He likes her.'

'But he cannot afford a wife,' Emma said on a sigh.

'I haven't seen him myself for a week. He's gone out of town. I believe his aim is to improve his prospects before he returns.'

Emma gazed out into the sunny afternoon, thinking the azure sky seemed bluer than ever she remembered it to be, the verdant buds on the lime trees greener than they had been yesterday.

'I've offered to help him financially, but he turned me down. When it comes to something as serious as taking a wife there are some things that a man must do for himself if he is to keep his pride.' Lance slipped his arm about her waist, drawing her back against him and kissing her neck.

Emma leaned into him, revelling in his touch. 'I agree and so would Dawn, I'm sure.' She turned about and looked up at him with shy directness. 'Alone at last…so what would you like to do, my lord?'

'Is that a trick question?'

'No, it isn't.' Taking his hand, she led him to the door and across the hall to the stairs. She started up them, tugging him behind.

'What about your rules?'

'There are no rules Lance, other than that you love me…'

* * * * *

MILLS & BOON

Coming next month

HIS CONVENIENT HIGHLAND BRIDE
Janice Preston

Lachlan McNeill couldn't quite believe his good fortune when he first saw his bride, Lady Flora McCrieff, walking up the aisle towards him on her father's arm. Her posture was upright and correct and her figure was... delectable. The tight bodice and sleeves of her wedding gown—her figure tightly laced in accordance with fashion—accentuated her full breasts, slender arms and tiny waist above the wide bell of her skirt. She was tiny, dwarfed by her father's solid, powerful frame, and she barely reached Lachlan's shoulder when they stood side by side in front of the minister. True, he had not yet seen his new bride's face—her figure might be all he could wish for, but was there a nasty surprise lurking yet? Maybe her features were somehow disfigured? Or maybe she was a shrew? Why else had her father refused to let them meet before their wedding day? He'd instead insisted on riding over to Lochmore Castle, Lachlan's new home, to agree the marriage settlements.

Their vows exchanged, Lachlan raised Flora's veil, bracing himself for some kind of abomination. His chest loosened with relief as she stared up at him, her green eyes huge and wary under auburn brows, the freckles that speckled her nose and cheeks stark against the pallor of her skin. His finger caught a loose, silken tendril of coppery-red hair and her face flooded pink, her lower lip trembling, drawing his gaze as the scent of orange blossom wreathed his senses.

She is gorgeous.

Heat sizzled through him, sending blood surging to his loins as he found himself drawn into the green depths of her eyes, his senses in disarray. Then he took her hand to place it on his arm and its delicacy, its softness, its fragility sent waves of doubt crashing through him, sluicing him clean of lustful thoughts as he sucked air into his lungs.

He had never imagined he'd be faced with one so young…so dainty…so captivating…and her beauty and her purity brought into sharp focus his own dirty, sordid past. Next to her he felt a clumsy, uncultured oaf.

What could he and this pampered young lady ever have in common? She might accept his fortune, but could she ever truly accept the man behind the façade? He'd faced rejection over his past before and he'd already decided that the less his wife ever learned about that past, the better.

Continue reading
HIS CONVENIENT HIGHLAND BRIDE
Janice Preston

Available next month
www.millsandboon.co.uk

LET'S TALK
Romance

For exclusive extracts, competitions
and special offers, find us online:

- **f** facebook.com/millsandboon
- 🐦 @MillsandBoon
- 📷 @MillsandBoonUK

Get in touch on 01413 063232

For all the latest titles coming soon, visit
millsandboon.co.uk/nextmonth

COMING SOON!

We really hope you enjoyed reading this book. If you're looking for more romance, be sure to head to the shops when new books are available on

Thursday 21st March

To see which titles are coming soon, please visit

millsandboon.co.uk/nextmonth